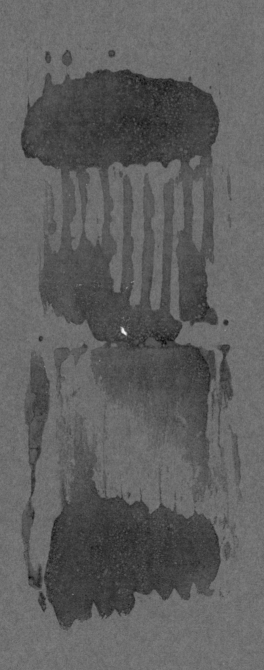

Sins
of the
Mother

Sins
of the
Mother

by Cheryl Saban

DOVE
BOOKS

ISBN 0-7871-1268-2

Printed in the United States of America

DOVE BOOKS
8955 Beverly Boulevard
Los Angeles, CA 90048
(310) 786-1600

Distributed by Penguin USA

Text design by Carolyn Wendt

First Printing: May 1997

10 9 8 7 6 5 4 3 2 1

"Regard each day as an unblemished page in the book of life. Treat each day as the untarnished future and handle it as carefully as if it were already a published record of your past."

—Ruth Montgomery
Companions Along the Way

This book is lovingly dedicated to
my husband, Haim,
and our children,
Tifany, Heidi, Ness, and Tanya.

They are my past, present, and future.

Prologue

Country's bearded face contorts as he reads the newspaper article. The muscles in his neck grow taut. He cracks his neck quickly, wills his body to relax. Within seconds, the blue veins bulging through the coiling serpent tattoo on his forearm retreat. The girl from the beach, the one who screwed him over years ago, has done it again. His face resumes its normal, cold, unreadable mask. Once again, he is in control.

COUNTRY SHOOK HIS LONG HAIR OUT OF HIS EYES AND LIT A cigarette. He looked around the cell in Folsom Prison, which had been his home for eighteen long years. Ten by ten, gray cement floor, gray painted walls. He'd covered the walls completely with intricate illustrations: morbid netherworld scenes, starkly cruel and highly graphic. His legacy to the joint. Most of the drawings mirrored his own gaunt appearance: sunken eyes, sallow skin color, rotting teeth.

A slight redirection of his eyes revealed a metal bed with a mangy, stained mattress, and a foul-smelling, stainless steel piss pot in the corner. This was it. Home sweet fucking home.

But no more. He'd served his time. Make that double time due to bad behavior. Those asshole cops should have known better than to lock him up with another inmate. He couldn't tolerate being in close quarters with the last whiny wimp they'd assigned to his cell. A week hadn't gone by before the man *accidentally* fell out of his bunk and broke his neck.

That wasn't the only time one of his roommates ate it. Eventually the pigs wised up and gave him a cell to himself. The prison officials couldn't prove the deaths weren't accidents, but the parole board kept slapping extra time on his sentence anyway. He was a troublemaker, they said.

Country had even opted to do an extra year to keep the parole officers off his butt. But that was all behind him now. Today he was getting out.

His eyes darted around the cubicle, coming to rest on the newspaper spread out on the bare mattress in front of him, and his breathing quickened. A large photo of a woman and her teenage daughter smiled up at him.

It was her. The horny little bitch from the beach, right there in black and white, smiling at him, teasing him. The memory flooded back, causing a hot sensation in his groin. What she'd put him through. Lotta nerve, the bitch.

Normally he didn't give a shit about the news, but today's was an omen. He'd grabbed the *San Francisco Chronicle* from some little faggot out in the exercise yard who had just received it from some relative.

How convenient that all the information he needed was right here in print: what city she lived in, where she worked.

Alison Young. The little liar was a woman now, and fate was serving her up on a platter. He touched the photo with a dirty finger. She looked the same.

And the girl. The daughter.

Young, uncontaminated. She looked *real* good. Just like Sara. Sweet, dead Sara. His eyes quickly moved to the poems scrawled on the walls next to his drawings. His gift to her.

As Country reread the caption under the picture, the veins in his temple pulsed. *The daughter made her singing debut to the cheers of the crowd. Watch for her. Destiny Young could one day be a household name.*

But she had the wrong name. Alison was taking all the credit.

He folded up the paper carefully and tucked it into his duffel bag. He would deal with that. As he stood in the corner to take a leak, he thought about her. He could still remember her legs—long, tanned, trembling at his touch. Her eyes, dark and defiant. Her tits, small and smooth.

But the best part was her ass. He had loved her ass.

So now she was in San Francisco. He had friends there, though when he thought about it he realized that *friends* was too broad a term. *Soldiers* was more appropriate. Guys he had ridden with, men who had followed him without question and took care of his affairs while he was locked up. They invested his share of the cash from all their deals.

Eighteen years hadn't dimmed the other bikers' memory of him. His reach was long and brutal. He'd proved many times over that he was still their leader, inside the joint or out. The guys respected that and did his bidding.

Before today he hadn't given much thought to where he'd live after he got out. He had plenty of options. But that was before he learned where his bitch was. Country's eyes narrowed as he remembered the feel of Alison's body.

Jangling keys jolted him from his reverie. A prison guard opened the cell door. "Let's go, buddy," the guard barked. "We need the cell . . . unless you'd like to stay around and keep sticking it to these other ass-wipes for a few more years."

Country calmed his breathing, but his heart pounded with hate. He didn't want to overreact. Not today. Instead, he spat on the wall and watched the thick, mucousy globule make its way down to the concrete floor. He zipped up, then slowly turned an icy gaze toward the guard. The man's grin instantly disappeared. Inhaling quickly, he touched his gun and stepped back. Country's sheer strength emanated from him like a force field. Invisible but obvious. Though Country hadn't made a move toward the guard, his nostrils were flaring, his muscles pumped up, filled with angry blood.

The guard began to perspire. He coughed and glanced at his shoes. He slid the cell door open wide so Country could pass, keeping a hand ready on his gun all the way down the corridor.

Country tossed his hair back behind his shoulders and walked out, his head straight, his eyes level.

He didn't look back.

Some of the men along the corridor mumbled their good-byes through the bars, but Country didn't respond. His mind was miles away, focused on the picture in the paper. Focused on getting to San Francisco.

Chapter 1

WHEN NOTHING ELSE WORKED, ALISON YOUNG SOLVED HER problems by seeking refuge in the past. She'd used that technique this morning after yet another spat with Destiny. Pulling out her collection of journals and photo albums, she'd pored over each page, remembering days gone by, looking for clues. Clues that might help her resolve the tension that had been brewing between her and her teenage daughter.

Alison's diaries were a ragtag collection of notebooks she'd begun compiling from the first day she could write. She had recorded *her* version of history in these journals. In them she captured moments of her life, if they were happy. If they weren't so pleasant, she edited them to suit her fancy. Looking back, she remembered events the way she wanted to remember them.

But this morning she wasn't looking for fantasy. She wanted to recall how it *really* felt to be close to her daughter, for that longed-for sensation was proving to be painfully elusive these days.

As Alison's black Audi idled at a stoplight, she munched on a granola bar, worrying that the crumbly, organic substitute for a real breakfast would get all over her outfit. Of course it wouldn't, for she would be careful. She was nearly obsessive about her appearance and her belongings, a characteristic that had developed from childhood. Her parents didn't care about dressing nice or fixing up the house, not that they could really afford to. But Alison had learned how to make a dime look like a dollar. In her early teens she worked as a babysitter so that she could buy her own clothing and special items for her room. She learned to maximize an outfit by complementing one or two good pieces with well-selected bargain items. Appearance was important to her, but so was financial security.

Even now that she could afford it, her clothing was not necessarily designer. But no matter what she wore, it was always tasteful and classic. She kept her nails manicured and her skin soft, and she used a natural-looking application of makeup to enhance, rather than hide, her flawless skin.

Her inward musings were interrupted by the sight of a young mother and her child as they crossed the street with a shiny bicycle. The little girl was smiling up at her mother, radiating unqualified adoration, and the scene tugged at Alison's heart. Destiny used to look at her that way, too.

When her daughter was a child, they were inseparable. A private club of two. Girl-to-girl talks, inside jokes, and a special, three-squeeze handshake that was theirs alone. Alison had entered motherhood very young, and though she'd had to work long hours to support them, she, unlike older mothers she'd met, had boundless energy left over to devote to Destiny. And Destiny had turned out exactly as Alison had prayed she would: a spirited, happy, completely normal child.

It had been easy to protect her, to teach her, to mold her into the kind of strong, self-reliant young woman she herself had struggled hard to become. Easy, that is, until recently. Now she hardly recognized her daughter. Destiny had become so independent, she barely listened to anything Alison said anymore. It was her worst fear come true. The adage "Be careful what you wish for; you might get it," came to mind.

The fog had lifted. Alison switched off her lights and drove the few remaining blocks to Union Square and her monthly parking space in an underground garage. Summer was coming. *Perhaps a family vacation will help*, she thought. After Destiny's graduation, maybe they could finally take time off and relax. They could go to a resort and learn to play tennis together, something they had often talked about.

Alison sighed and filed that thought away. She suspected a family vacation would be the last thing Destiny would want.

She got out of the car, carefully brushed granola crumbs off her tweed blazer, and headed for the stairs. She and Destiny had locked horns too much lately. But the troubles weren't confined to their home life. Her daughter had become a problem at work as well, and Alison knew she'd have to do something about it.

Rushing to her office and past the tempting smell of freshly baked bread from the nearby bakery, she put her anxious feelings aside, delegating them to another corner of her brain, as she'd learned to do with predicaments she couldn't conquer on the spot. She'd deal with Destiny when the right moment presented itself. As co-founder and editor-in-chief of *Hers Magazine,* Alison knew enough to wait for opportunity.

A cutting-edge compendium of women's issues, *Hers Magazine* was emerging in the publishing business as a force to be reckoned with. Much more than a fashion magazine, the publication had acquired a reputation for spearheading dialogues on current women's issues, often playing devil's advocate to ensure that both sides of a debate were heard, dissected, and ultimately clearly represented. Though Alison and her partners hadn't tried to attain high visibility as individuals, their faces and names were becoming well known in connection with the magazine, and by default they were on their way to becoming celebrities in their own right.

The *Hers* offices were housed on the third floor of the famous Circle Gallery building on Maiden Lane, a quaint, cobblestoned walking street between Stockton and Kearny, within sight of Union Square. Based on Union Square's colorful history, this was an appropriate part of the city for the magazine's headquarters.

The square was dubbed "Union" because of pro-union rallies

held there in the 1860s on the cusp of the Civil War. Over the years, the spot witnessed the staging of a multitude of civic protests. One of the most titillating of these occurred in August 1958 and perfectly illustrated the diversity of interests embraced by San Francisco. In the late 1950s, North Beach's beatniks—the predecessors of the sixties and seventies hippies—had grown weary of being gawked at by tourists. They staged a protest of sorts, which they called "The Squaresville Tour." A hundred bearded beats, wearing black slacks and sandals, paraded through town. Accompanied by a bongo player, they marched from North Beach across Union Square and through major department stores and hotels, carrying banners that read: HI, SQUARES! THE CITIZENS OF NORTH BEACH ARE ON TOUR!

Since then, San Francisco's population had evolved into anything but square. The city had been the trailblazer for everything from gay rights to equal opportunities for women. Union Square and its environs became expensive real estate, sharing the neighborhood with Gumps and Neiman-Marcus, two modern, exclusive department stores that had replaced the oldest of San Francisco's specialty emporiums, I. Magnin.

The area was also home to several graphic design firms, art dealers, and one-of-a-kind boutiques. Many well-known advertising and modeling agencies were within walking distance. Alison loved coming to work each day in such an upbeat, vibrant part of the city.

Press time turned the usual buzz of activity at *Hers* up a notch from routine chaos to hectic agitation. As editor-in-chief, Alison kept a close eye on every facet of every issue, a practice that was at once rewarding and frustrating but always fulfilling. She was good at what she did and proud that she had forged a successful career for herself. The hope for this kind of success had been the driving force behind getting her hard-earned college degree.

The first item on her agenda today was the cover shot for the issue that was being shipped. As Alison stared at it, her face screwed up into a frown. It wasn't right, and today was too late for this to be happening.

She leaned over her desk, studying the retouched photo. A stubborn lock of wavy brown hair fell in front of her eyes, and she flicked it back impatiently, thinking it was time for a trim. She usually kept her hair in a blunt cut at the jawline, but she'd been so busy lately, she'd canceled her regular hair appointment. Now she admonished herself silently.

Her forehead creased into a deeper frown. Glancing at her partner and lifelong friend, Kelly McAllister, co-founder of *Hers,* Alison shook her head. "What a power play," she said. "I can't believe Marlene's agent got the photographer to set up the session this way. And on top of that, to give her first look at the contact sheets. This isn't a cover, it's a makeup ad. It's awful."

"I'm surprised he pulled this," Kelly replied, grabbing a butterscotch candy from a dish in Alison's open drawer. Kelly placed a schedule of cover alternatives on her desk, then popped the candy into her mouth. "Take a look at these."

Physically, Kelly was the exact opposite of Alison. Kelly was short; Alison was tall. Kelly wore glasses; Alison had perfect vision. Kelly couldn't go outside without getting freckles; Alison worshiped the sun. Kelly's long white-blond hair was so frizzy it formed a halo around her face if she let it hang loose. But most often, like today, she used a #2 pencil to tether it into a knot at the nape of her neck. Alison's hair was dark and wavy but professionally groomed, almost glamorous. These differences had earned them the nicknames "Mutt and Jeff" and "Frick and Frack."

Alison and Kelly were on the same wavelength emotionally, however, and had been so nearly all their lives. Growing up next door to each other in a lower-middle-class neighborhood of East San Diego, the two girls endured similar chaotic, dysfunctional, and sometimes violent childhoods.

A shadow crossed Alison's face as she recalled her exodus from that lifestyle, but she brightened when she thought of her cohort. Kelly's way out had been to marry her high-school sweetheart and have kids right away. Despite the odds against them, Kelly and her husband had stayed married and in love for nineteen years, and Alison had always admired her for that.

Alison didn't know what she'd do without her friend and sidekick. Her move to San Francisco had been bitter in many ways, not the least of which was the pain of leaving her best friend behind. She'd thought their friendship would fade away. But life was full of surprises. Six years after Alison left, Kelly's husband, Kurt, took a graphic design position in San Francisco, and she and her soul mate were reunited. They picked up their friendship where it had left off— close as ever.

Kelly had assumed the position of art director at the inception of the magazine, but it hadn't been given to her capriciously. Though Kelly, Alison, and Sally Murphy, fashion director and the third cofounder of *Hers,* were the best of friends, friendship alone didn't provide Kelly with the tools necessary to help *Hers* make its stellar climb.

As a young wife and mother, Kelly had juggled household and child-rearing duties to study part-time at a San Diego junior college, later transferring to UC San Diego to obtain a degree in graphic art. Her focus had always been fashion, though no one, including her artist husband, thought she'd ultimately work in publishing. Oddly, she had always assumed she'd be a teacher.

But from the moment she entered the workforce, Kelly fell in love with the hectic, pressure-ridden publishing business. Her first job, assisting a project director at a design firm in San Diego, involved proofreading promotional material for the firm's main client, Taco Bell. Though paid to correct copy, nothing more, Kelly couldn't resist offering comments on the design and layout of the ads. Her suggestions proved to be clever and innovative.

She didn't get much credit for it at the time, but after a tenure of four years at the design firm, she was offered a position at the *San Diego Tribune* Sunday magazine, editing the fashion insert.

Kelly's experience helped kick-start *Hers Magazine,* and her creative talent and educational background made her perfect for the art director job. She didn't rest on her laurels, either. Though she had a staff of ten, Kelly had been the one to come up with the cover look that was so popular with the *Hers* readership.

Now, studying the failed cover concept, Kelly pushed her signature granny glasses up on her nose. Her disgruntled expression mirrored Alison's. "Dakota Johnson's been trying to work for us for years," she said, referring to the photographer.

"Too bad he didn't research his market a little better," Alison countered, throwing her hands up in the air. "He won't get another chance. Damn! Don't you hate being torpedoed like this?" Softening, she added, "I bet the poor guy got a lot of pressure from Burkette's public relations firm."

"I'd say so," Kelly agreed. "What do you want to do?"

Alison glanced at the schedule and pushed it aside. "Even if we had time to switch to another interview, I don't want to. This one's too important. I've decided to do it myself, as a matter of fact. But we can't put this issue out without a killer cover. There's got to be another solution. We're ninety percent printed. Didn't Dakota what's-his-name take at least one shot we can use?"

Alison searched through the alternatives Kelly had given her. "We should talk to Marlene herself. This wasn't her fault, after all. It's her PR agent."

Kelly pulled out the pencil and reknotted her hair thoughtfully. Her mind was already envisioning the cover that should have been shot.

"Let me check something in my office," she said after a few moments. "I think I have a solution."

"God, I hope so," Alison said.

Last-minute changes were not new to Alison, but finding herself coerced into using a cover that didn't live up to their standards was aggravating. The entire staff planned their year around the covers. Covers sold the magazine.

They had back-ups, of course. A magazine had to be ready to handle such emergencies. But Alison didn't want to use a back-up, and neither did Kelly. Sally would certainly concur, because this cover girl was *the* star of the season. Marlene Burkette was a hit with the American Film Institute, which was holding its annual conference at the Embarcadero Center next month. At present Marlene was a media darling, and her face on the cover of *Hers* meant instant purchase. Her popularity notwithstanding, Marlene was also a prominent spokesperson on women's issues, and Alison admired her—more than anyone could possibly know.

Alison rubbed her neck and nibbled the inside of her cheek. *As if I needed more complications today,* she thought. Between this and fielding a rumor that they'd lost their funding, her patience was wearing thin.

The room suddenly felt warm. She took off her blazer and hung it on the back of her chair, bending momentarily to inhale the sweet smell of the peach-colored roses in the vase on her desk. Kicking off her penny loafers, Alison wiggled her toes and walked across her office to crank open a window. She looked down at the people strolling along Maiden Lane, three floors below.

It was a lovely street. Red and white geraniums spilled over the sides of the tree boxes bordering the street. Colorful umbrellas and tiny tables had been set up in front of the Del Arte Bistro, where people sat sipping frothy cappuccinos in the morning sun.

Alison caught the yeasty, home-baked aroma of fresh bread floating up from the small bakery below and sighed. She should have stopped and bought a cinnamon bun. The soft, warm dough drenched in creamy, sugary frosting would be a great comfort right now. But she didn't want to push her luck. Collin, her husband, liked her youthful figure as it was, and she planned to keep it that way.

She returned her focus to the pleasant street scene below. When she and her partners had relocated here two years ago, they'd been thrilled at the prospect of working in such an inviting environment of whimsical shops, elegant restaurants, and outdoor cafes. Time to browse, time to eat, time to talk to friends.

Alison smiled at the naive notion that they'd have time to partake in such leisurely activities. Rarely did she and her fellow workers actually enjoy the bustle of the street below after hours. She had Destiny and Collin to think about, Kelly had Kurt and her sons, and Sally was on the road all the time. Still, none of them regretted it. They'd worked hard to get where they were, and they had every intention of continuing on the same track.

Alison scrutinized her office, one of four niches on the entire floor equipped with doors. The remainder was organized into cubicles, the most efficient way of optimizing the floor space they'd rented.

She liked her little corner and had decorated it herself in a tan monochromatic color scheme. Though she loved the country look at home, there was little room for so-called charm in her office. It was chic without being overdone, and impressive-looking without being excessively expensive—adjectives that described Alison as well. She now had financial security, but spending money frivolously went against her grain.

Her bookshelves were filled with neat stacks of back issues of *Hers,* as well as a wide selection of competitors' magazines, which she devoured as soon as they hit the newsstands, then saved for research and comparison. Underneath the piles of page layouts, editorial notes, and ads, her desk sported a tan leather blotter, pencil holder, appointment book, and computer.

Alison's gaze settled on the few personal items in her office: silver-framed photos of her daughter, Destiny, and her husband of eight years, Collin. The sight of him made her feel a tug of guilt. He'd phoned twice this morning, but she'd been away from her desk both times. Thank goodness he understood her schedule. His days were generally the same.

Collin Archer was one of the most dedicated, hardworking individuals she'd ever known. Even though he owned his own advertising firm, he didn't take the slow road. He was a self-made man, tirelessly trying to better his company. Everything he had, he achieved on his own, a feature they shared.

Collin was usually the first one to get to the office in the morning and the last to leave. Although he was a sports enthusiast, he rarely indulged his passion unless he could include a potential client. To that end, he often played racquetball either before or after hours. It always pleased him to be able to accomplish two things at once. Collin worked harder than any of his staff and loved every minute of it. Alison had modeled much of her own business behavior after his.

But her daughter was something else. Destiny never seemed to understand her motives. They couldn't agree about schools, schedules, work, money, boyfriends, time. Lately, they bickered about everything.

Alison pushed thoughts of Destiny from her mind and refocused on the problem at hand: the dubious cover. The covers of *Hers* were not glamour shots. They were real. The beauty in the photos was more than skin deep. A profound understanding of the person could be gleaned from viewing them. Thanks to Kelly's foresight years ago, *Hers* had become famous for its provocative, soul-baring portraits of the personalities interviewed for each issue, and Alison wasn't about to jeopardize that claim to fame now.

She slipped her feet back into her shoes as Kelly swept back into her office. "I hope you've got an alternative," Alison said. "Because the more I look at this one, the more I hate it. Marlene's not a pin-up girl, and we can't portray her that way." Alison took out a pen and scrawled a large red X on the offensive photo.

"I think I have the answer," Kelly said. "It's a bit underhanded, but then again, her agency did the same to us. Turnabout is fair play, isn't it?"

Alison was interested. "Tell me."

"One of our associate editors did an interview with Marlene a couple of years ago, but we didn't use it. It was Manny Bowman. He was covering the political beat then. Remember?"

Alison nodded. "I remember Manny, but not the interview."

"It was early in her career. Marlene had appeared in only a couple of movies. Even though the article on her was really good, the local elections happened at the same time. At the last minute, Manny had gotten a coveted interview with Dianne Feinstein, and naturally we ran that piece instead."

"What was the article on Marlene about?"

Kelly pointed to the log line in the file folder she'd brought in with her. "Violence against women. We know she's a card-carrying women's rights activist now, but back then she had just become involved with women's issues. She'd been hauled off to jail for participating in a sit-in in front of the federal building. It had to do with them not granting funding for special programs for spousal abuse. The article was powerful because she had firsthand knowledge about spousal abuse. She'd lived it."

Alison flashed her a knowing look. "I remember that sit-in and being so appalled by the unfairness of the system. I can't wait to do this interview with her. What a courageous thing to do . . ." Her sentence trailed off in a whisper.

Kelly touched her shoulder gently. "We do what we can, right, Ali?"

Alison nodded. Kelly knew her so well. Every hurt, every secret.

"But the point is," Kelly continued, "Marlene authorized photos for that interview, and they were more in keeping with our style. I'm sure we still have them on file."

"I know we want to give our readers what they like, but we don't want to make an enemy of someone who had the guts to get herself thrown in jail for something she believed in."

"Our covers aren't unflattering, Alison. Just realistic."

"She authorized the photos?"

"Yes."

Alison thought for a moment. "Maybe we should run a retrospective of that first article along with this interview, and stir up the issue again."

"Good idea," Kelly said. "Marlene will probably be thrilled. It'll show the world who she really is."

Alison sighed. "Let's just hope she's one of those people who wants the world to know that." She felt her neck tense up and took a deep, cleansing breath, yoga style. "Okay. We have to go forward. We're almost out of time."

"Don't worry, Ali. I'm sure Marlene will like it. Besides," Kelly said, holding up the crossed-out photo and grinning, "the touched-up cover art was inadvertently ruined, and there was no time to make a dupe."

Alison shook her head in mock chagrin. "What a sneaky bunch we are." Kelly smirked at her and rushed out.

Alison took a butterscotch candy from her drawer and popped it in her mouth. She needed a sugar boost. Two cups of coffee and a granola bar didn't cut it. Though she was concerned about her figure, she really had no reason to be. She was in great shape. Although she was in her late thirties, Alison looked, acted, and dressed like a woman several years younger. She wasn't Cover Girl beautiful, but she had learned how to optimize her features. Next to her long, shapely legs, her complexion was her strongest physical asset.

Suddenly her mother's face popped into her mind, and Alison felt a twinge of sadness. If Rita Young had lived a different kind of life, *she* would have been considered beautiful. Her skin had been soft and youthful, too. But the scars from endless domestic battles had taken their toll on Alison's mother. She had looked forty when she was twenty-six.

Alison shook away the memories. Her mother had been dead for eighteen years.

Glancing at her schedule, Alison realized that she had a staff meeting in twenty minutes. A voice crackled over her intercom, startling her. "You have a call on line one, Ms. Young."

Being called *Mizz* made her feel strange. Everyone usually called her Alison.

"Who is it?"

"Oh, I'm sorry," the temp answered, flustered. "I didn't ask. Want me to check?"

Alison sighed. "Never mind." Wishing her secretary would hurry back from her doctor's appointment, Alison picked up the phone.

"Alison speaking."

"Hi, Ali." It was Sally. The oldest of the three friends, she was the most free-spirited and was perfectly suited to her job. Sally was a trend-setter, ahead of all the fashion fads, and it often seemed as if she'd invented some of them herself. She counted as friends some of the top designers in the country, and in the world, for that matter.

"I convinced Dick Cantor at Kinsey Advertising that the rumors weren't true, and they promised they wouldn't pull their ads," Sally continued.

"Thank God," responded Alison. "Did they say how it got started?"

"Yeah. When we laid off that last bunch of interns, one of them groused to an ad exec at Kinsey just as they were making a nine-page buy for their Revlon account. He wouldn't tell me who it was, but apparently this person made an offhand remark that our Malaysian partner was pulling out, and the rumor made it through the mill all the way to Dick."

"Damn." Alison pressed a hand to her forehead, rubbing away the headache blossoming behind her eyes. "Interns aren't privy to our financial information. Most of them don't have a clue we have a Malaysian partner, and they certainly can't have known about the cash-flow problems we had a couple of months ago. Besides, it was all resolved."

Sally was silent for a moment. "I know that, and you know that. But apparently one of them did overhear something, Ali, because the details are just too close for it to have been a coincidence."

Alison closed her eyes. Was it possible Destiny had overheard her talking to Collin about it? "Do you think Destiny could have said something?" she offered. "Why would she do that?"

"Kids talk," Sally said, quickly adding, "but if she was the one, I'm sure she thought she was being helpful. Don't go blaming it on her now."

"Thanks, Sally," Alison said softly. "I'm glad you managed to patch things up in time."

Putting down the phone, Alison looked at the silver-framed photo of her daughter. This was turning out to be a hell of a day.

Hers Magazine was doing well. In eleven years, Alison had watched their readership grow from zero to two hundred thousand strong, and they now had long-term contracts with several substantial advertisers from Revlon to Mercedes-Benz. Rumors like the one Sally had just dismantled could rock their foundation to the ground. All it took was one big advertiser to pull out, and things could swiftly snowball into disaster.

The magazine hired interns on a regular basis, especially when they were in a crunch, then trimmed down when fewer people were needed. Alison thought of herself as a good boss, tough but fair. She expected everyone who worked for the magazine to be conscientious, devoted, and responsible. Most of them were.

When she gave her own daughter a job, Alison assumed Destiny would perform like the other employees. That hadn't always been the case.

She pulled a newspaper article out of her drawer and smoothed it flat. *Hers* had hosted a Career Day during which Destiny's boy-friend's band had performed. Destiny had sung onstage and received rave reviews. She deserved them. She was good. The newspaper crew had taken a picture of Alison and Destiny as an example of a mother and daughter working together. A pretty picture, but unfortunately, it didn't exactly reflect the truth.

Though Alison desperately wanted Destiny to work with her, that wasn't on Destiny's long-term agenda. Music was her passion. But Alison wasn't happy about it. The music business frightened her. It reminded her of the modeling business in some ways, a rough indus-try, full of rejection, overindulgence, late nights, and strange people. She didn't want Destiny to fall in with a bad crowd. She didn't want anything unpleasant to happen to her daughter, ever.

Alison was obsessively protective of Destiny, but at the same time she also wanted her to be self-reliant. That mixed message she'd been sending over the years had finally caught up with her, and she didn't know how to cope with it.

Wanting to show her daughter she meant well, Alison had tried to set her up with music business professionals she knew, people with integrity who wouldn't lead her daughter down some dark, danger-ous road. Destiny rejected her efforts. She hated being told what to do, hated being contradicted, hated submitting to anyone else's authority—particularly her mother's.

A recurrent fear engulfed Alison, causing her to catch her breath. Though she'd buried her worries deep within herself, the recent arguments and constant power struggles caused her to wonder. Who was her daughter? What was going on inside her? Who was she really?

Alison quickly admonished herself for her grim thoughts. Her daughter was going through a typical, independent teenage phase. Nothing abnormal for a girl her age. It was difficult to handle right now but surely would become easier in time. The conflict was a com-bination of age, peer pressure, and environment. It had nothing to do with genetics at all. She hoped.

Alison put the newspaper article away. In truth, she was deeply proud of Destiny, proud that her daughter had bona fide talent. But Destiny had other things on her mind besides *Hers Magazine.* She was often late to work, though in fairness, Alison knew she made up the time after hours.

Nevertheless, Alison had noticed that her daughter spent a good deal of her on-the-job time writing lyrics or cruising the Internet and sending notes via E-mail. It was becoming increasingly difficult for Alison to justify Destiny's lackadaisical attitude.

She'd have to talk to her. Interns couldn't go around spreading dangerous rumors, especially if the intern in question was the boss's daughter.

Alison straightened up her desk, then headed past her confused temporary secretary toward the art cubicles, where Destiny worked.

Destiny munched on a handful of trail mix as she realigned the border around the copy she was editing for next month's Music News section. Her young face, devoid of makeup save for the bright red lipstick she wore, was fixed in a thoughtful expression as she studied her handiwork. She leaned back in her chair and carefully read the article again. Satisfied, Destiny hit the Save button. She dug into her backpack and pulled out an apple before rolling her chair away from the large Quadra over to a smaller Macintosh that she used for word processing, E-mail, and the Internet.

Destiny perched on the edge of her chair, her black patent-leather combat boots planted firmly on the floor, her tight leather skirt inched up to the middle of her thighs. She tapped furiously on the keyboard between bites of apple, entering codes into the program to access the company on-line system, and finally the World Wide Web.

She had received a fax from Harvey Anderson this morning: "The dates you've given me don't concur with the research I've done so far. Would you please check them?"

Destiny was frustrated. What did he mean? She knew her own birthday, for chrissakes. The dates were exactly those her mother had told her. Was this guy a moron or what?

She E-mailed Harvey, assuring him that the dates she had given him were correct, and asking him to E-mail her next time instead of faxing. This was a personal matter, and she didn't want anybody in the office to know about it.

She wondered again if the private detective she'd hired in San Diego was a complete bozo. But Harvey had been recommended by her boyfriend's father, a former police officer. He had to be good.

Destiny was impatient. She would turn eighteen soon, and she wanted to know about her real father, *now*. Her mother wouldn't tell her much. It wasn't a subject that came easy for either of them and always made her mom act weird.

Collin had been the only father she'd ever known, but he wasn't the talkative type either. He was nice enough and she loved him. Still, she'd always felt there was something missing, as though he were keeping her at arm's length, afraid to get involved.

Her mother had told her that her *real* father, William Statler, had been listed as MIA in Vietnam before she was born. They'd been high-school lovers and probably would have gotten married if he hadn't been shipped out.

But that slight piece of information didn't cut it. Destiny wanted to know more. Perhaps she was like him. Maybe he liked to sing or paint. Maybe he was artistic, as she was. *It would just be nice to know,* she thought.

Destiny was sure there had to be more information on him. Orphan or no, surely there was some record of a family somewhere, and if so, she was determined to claim it. Using money she'd earned by working part-time at the magazine and other jobs she'd held throughout high school, she'd hired Harvey Anderson. She figured she could always save up again for college, if she actually ended up going. What could be more meaningful than finding out about her lost family?

Destiny glanced back at the layout on the Quadra and shrugged. Her article was almost finished. Just one more polish, but it would have to wait. Right now her life was more important than this deadline. She knew she'd get it out on time anyway.

One of the art department interns poked her head over Destiny's cubicle wall and jerked a thumb in the direction of the hallway. "Heads up, Desi. The boss is coming."

Destiny acknowledged the girl's warning with a dispassionate nod and kept working on her E-mail message. "I'll be done in a minute," she said distractedly. "This is important."

The intern raised her eyebrows and retreated.

Alison reached the doorway and immediately noticed that Destiny had logged on to America Online. "I thought you were supposed to finish that page layout for Music News," she said as she glanced over at the screen-saver image of Captain Kirk on the Quadra. Destiny quickly logged off.

"This is no time to be answering E-mail, Destiny," continued Alison, an air of irritation in her voice. "We're on deadline, in case you hadn't noticed!"

Destiny glared at her mother. "This is important, Mom."

"Your *job* is important," Alison snapped.

Destiny was fuming. Her mother had turned into such a tyrant. Every day she felt their connection slipping further away. Had she bothered to ask if the layout was done? No. Destiny slid her chair back over to the Quadra and moved the mouse, bringing the layout back on screen. "Don't get so snippy, Mom. It's done already. I just have to do one more polish."

"Then you should be doing it."

Staff members hurried past the doorway of the cubicle, heads down, pretending not to listen.

"You make it seem like I'm so darned necessary around here, but this is just a part-time job. Anybody could do it. It's not what I want to do. This was *your* dream, remember?"

Indignant, Destiny turned her back to her mother. She tossed her apple core into the wastebasket and flipped her long hair behind her shoulders. Destiny's honey-brown hair was lighter than Alison's but similar in texture. Light from the ceiling fixture above played on it, showcasing natural highlights in each wave.

Destiny's heart-shaped face, usually optimistic, was pinched into a frown as she put a booted foot up on the edge of the chair to retie the lace, revealing her long, slender, very sexy legs.

Alison whirled the chair around so that her daughter faced her. Cognizant of workers nearby, she lowered her voice. "Destiny, I know you want to be a singer. And I've told you I'd set you up with the right people, but you refused my help."

"I don't want to be set up with your contacts, Mom! I can get gigs on my own. It's my life. I can handle it."

Destiny took her well-worn denim jacket off the chair and stuffed her arms into it. "Besides, I was just working on something important and personal."

"This isn't the time for that!" Alison insisted. "You're doing a terrible job of compartmentalizing. Deal with it on your break or at home. We're running a business here. You'd be surprised how many people would be happy to intern for a magazine, who wouldn't compromise the rest of the staff by shirking their responsibilities. Get your priorities straight, Destiny. This is work, not a hobby. You need it to survive. You have to focus on that."

"Right, Mom, you're focused all right. Ms. Compartmentalized personified! Everything you do is focused, except your time with me. You and Collin have assigned time for everything except what I want to talk about. I have personal needs, Mom. Feelings. I guess I must take after my real father!"

Alison looked away. "That's not fair. Every time we get into a fight, you bring that up."

"I'm almost eighteen. I have a right to know about him. I've been trying to get you to talk about it for a long time."

"We've been through this," Alison said, gripping the chair tightly. "I've told you all there is to know."

"Which is basically nothing," Destiny blurted, her blue eyes blazing with anger. Defiantly she grabbed her backpack and stuffed her notebook into it. "I'm leaving. I was only scheduled to work in the morning, and I have studying to do. I have one more final before graduation, then you won't have to bother with me anymore."

She pulled on a hat and glanced back up at Alison. "Don't pay me for the last fifteen minutes if you don't want to. That's all the time I spent on my personal stuff. But believe me, *that's* what's important as far as I'm concerned."

Mother and daughter faced off. Alison hated this feeling. She had always vowed it wouldn't happen to them, but she was swept away by her frustration. She knew she should count to ten or suggest that they pick this up later, but she couldn't.

"That's just fine, Destiny, because I came down here to tell you that you needn't come back. You're fired. Loyalty is important to me. And by the way, someone leaked some highly confidential information that could have cost us a bundle."

Destiny's eyes narrowed. "Oh. So now, not only am I irresponsible at this shitty job, but I'm also disloyal, right?"

Alison felt the bite of Destiny's remark and immediately regretted having been so accusatory. She softened slightly. "Well, since you hate this job so much, it probably would be better for both of us if you didn't work here anymore."

"Perfect. See if I care!" Destiny stormed out of the cubicle, then stopped abruptly. "For your information, I wasn't the one who blabbed. It was one of your other so-called loyal interns that you let go last month!"

Alison watched Destiny disappear down the hallway and heard the door to the reception area slam.

Defeated, she walked slowly back to her office. "Shit," she muttered under her breath. Every staff member she passed along the way tried to act busy and unaware, but Alison knew she and her daughter had just treated the rest of the staff to a slice of domestic pie.

She entered her office and slammed the door.

"Shit, shit, shit." Alison sat down heavily and kicked her shoes across the room.

Kelly entered and gave her a consoling look. Alison propped her elbows on her desk and opened her hands in a gesture of defeat. "Did you hear that?"

"Who didn't? But you really can't blame her. You did coerce her into this job."

"I didn't coerce her. I asked."

Kelly shook her head.

"All right," Alison admitted. "So I asked her a hundred times till she gave in. I just want to make sure she's okay, Kelly. I hate the thought of her working nights singing in some cafe, out on the streets . . . you know."

Kelly opened the file in her hand. "It'll be good for her to do her own thing for a while. You can't manage her life forever. She's growing up. Look at my boys. I hardly have any impact on them at all anymore."

Alison peered up at her friend. "I just hate it when you're right all the time. I'm really not trying to manage her life, you know. Just trying to protect her, that's all."

"You can't, Ali."

Alison closed her eyes, wishing she could block out the way she felt. She tried to focus her attention back on her job, but she couldn't help thinking that Destiny was right. She did compartmentalize everything. She'd been doing it for a lifetime. Years ago, it was the only way she could face waking up to another day.

As a little girl, Alison would pretend that her father hadn't really hit her and her mother the night before, that the dishes hadn't been smashed all over the house. She'd file that information into a separate part of her brain. Alison learned to hide things. Certain parts of her *had* to be put away.

She bent her neck left and right, stretching it, allowing her hair to fall gracefully from side to side. Another yoga tactic. "So much for my personal problems, Kelly. Let me see the famous photo."

Kelly put her arm around her as they studied the black-and-white eight-by-ten photo of Marlene Burkette. Alison's face slowly broke into a grin. "This is wonderful. At least one thing went right today."

"Don't let it get to you, Ali. I hear the survival rate of mothers of teenage daughters is pretty high." Kelly's face softened into a look of compassion. She walked out of the office, closing the door behind her.

Alison sank into her chair. Now she could think about her daughter. In isolation, she could dwell on it if she wanted to. She had to allow herself this luxury once in a while.

Destiny. Her only child. Her precious daughter. Everything about her was different, including her name. Alison had chosen to call her Destiny because it had a special meaning. *Destiny: that which is to happen in the future. Whatever is destined or inevitably decreed for one.*

Alison couldn't think of a better word to describe her emotions at Destiny's birth. She looked upon that angelic face and was filled with an overpowering sense of love and acceptance. Fate. Destiny. One and the same. Someday she'd have to tell Destiny why she'd given her that name, but disclosure wasn't going to be anytime soon. Not with the level of animosity that existed between the two of them now.

Kelly had been warning her for months that she was too protective, that she'd have to cut her daughter some slack. Let go. Apparently that time had come, but she wasn't adequately prepared for it. On the contrary, she didn't want to let her daughter out of her sight.

Several lines lit up on Alison's phone at once. (Where was that temp?) Alison snatched up the receiver and punched one of the lines. "Hello!"

"Whoa, back down, honey. Did I catch you at a bad time?"

Alison restrained her voice. "I'm sorry, Collin. A bad time is an understatement. Try a rotten time."

"You sound like hell."

Alison rubbed her eyes wearily. Collin didn't deserve to hear her grouse. He probably had troubles of his own, but he rarely revealed them. He was a wonderful husband. Handsome, muscular, attentive. She loved him, but more important, she was *in love* with him. They were both deeply committed to their careers and had purposely avoided dragging each other on the emotional roller-coaster rides inherent in their respective businesses.

"I didn't mean to take it out on you," Alison said with a cheeriness she didn't feel. "How's the water account going?"

"It's Votre Santé, and we landed it. Between that and the Green's Coffee Stop account, we've just about locked up every available liquid in town."

"I'm glad for you, honey."

"I did pitch a new account today, but this time I've ventured into recreational beverages. It's the Napa Valley Wine Train, up in Calistoga. I have ulterior motives for this one. It's a great excuse to take you on a vacation. From the tone of your voice, I'd say you could use one."

Alison tried explaining. "It's been a bitch of a morning. Our cover shot had to be changed at the last minute, and one of our biggest advertisers nearly pulled out because of a groundless rumor."

"That doesn't sound like you, Ali. Those are all situations you've tackled before. You can eat them for breakfast. What's really bothering you?"

Alison paused. "I had another blow-out with Destiny."

"That's becoming a regular event between you two, isn't it?"

"I fired her."

"Must have been some fight."

"She hasn't had her mind on her work here for too long. I couldn't close my eyes to it anymore. Then, of course, she brought up the subject of her real father again. Same old story."

"Maybe it's time to open up to her, honey. It'll do her good to hear the truth," Collin said softly.

Alison didn't want to hear that from Collin, especially since he didn't know what he was suggesting. "There's nothing for her to find, Collin. He was MIA nineteen years ago. He's most certainly dead, poor guy. What possible good could come from Destiny dredging it all up now? There was no family. He was an orphan. I've told her that."

Her stomach tightened. This was the part of the conversation she hated.

"We have to talk to her," Collin said finally. "Or maybe I should talk to her. The only reason she's searching for her real father is because she doesn't feel close enough to me. I should have adopted her years ago. Now that we've told her we want to have a baby—"

"That we're *thinking* of having a baby, Collin," Alison corrected.

"Are you changing your mind?"

"No. Well, maybe. I'm not getting any younger, you know. Oh, hell, that's not it. I'm not that old. I'm just worried about Destiny."

Her phone line lit up again. Alison watched it blink, agitated. "I have to go, honey. Mariah's at the doctor and my temp seems to have disappeared. This magazine has to go to press whether I have a baby or not. Can we talk about this when I get home?"

She glanced down at the phone, saw that the line had been picked up, and relaxed.

"Okay," agreed Collin. "I did have a reason for calling, though. I'm sorry to have to do it under the circumstances, but I have to go to Napa in the morning. Want to come along?"

Alison sighed a little too audibly. Even though this trip was totally coincidental, Collin seemed to have a habit of leaving town whenever there was any kind of a crisis, and she had a hard time not taking it personally. "It would be great to get away," she said, "but I can't leave right now."

Collin was quiet. Alison felt a familiar longing. She would love to go with him. To be carefree and relaxed, to have room service, to dine in a fabulous restaurant. She longed to enjoy his company as a wife and lover, with no time constraints and obligations other than to kiss him to sleep. Somewhere along the way in the last few years, they had forgotten to make time for the simpler things in life.

But right now she just couldn't do it. She had an upset daughter who at this moment probably hated her with a passion. Alison couldn't leave her at a time like this.

Collin broke the silence, trying not to sound disappointed. "Maybe next time. I'll plan a trip on that Wine Train one of these days."

"I'd like that."

"Don't worry too much about Destiny. I'm sure she'll be fine by the time she gets home tonight."

"*If* she comes home tonight," Alison said, a mixture of ire and reproach in her voice.

She hung up, uncomfortable and edgy. Their family was changing. She wasn't sure they all wanted the same things anymore, and that left her with a disturbing sense of loss.

When she and Collin had first met, they talked about everything: politics, the environment, Vietnam, nuclear power. Everything, that is, but past relationships. Both had been reluctant to venture very far into that area. Now they'd have to learn how to change that. Destiny had her reasons for wanting to find out about her real father, and Collin's assessment was right on the money. As wonderful as Collin was as a stepfather, there was a reserve in him that Destiny detected. Add that to Destiny's frustrated attempts to get information out of Alison, and it was easy to see why their family life had become strained.

They both had work to do.

Chapter 2

PRIVATE DETECTIVE HARVEY ANDERSON RAISED THE LOUVERED blinds in his office, squinting as the sunlight assaulted his eyes. He wiped a thick layer of dust off one of the old, once-white metal strips and gazed outside, surveying the beginning signs of after-work traffic.

Rubbing his tanned but balding head, a constant reminder of his own aging process, he paced around his office, thinking about his current case. He was confused, as he usually was, whenever information he'd gathered took him down several thought-trails at once.

A police officer for twenty years, he'd learned that those apprehensive thoughts were usually warning signs. Warning him about what, he didn't know. He'd gotten caught up in his current investigation, but that was normal behavior for Harvey. He didn't like to do anything halfway.

He picked up a file folder off his desk, weighing it in his hands. Hearing his stomach growl, he realized it was time to pack it in for the day. Dinnertime. Patting his hard-earned beer belly, he knew his rotund frame carried enough extra fat to keep him going until breakfast. He could stay a while longer to ponder this case.

Two weeks ago he'd been hired by a girl from San Francisco who wanted to find out about her real father. Harvey usually didn't take clients from out of town—travel expenses were above and beyond what most folks wanted to pay. But she said she'd been referred by his old buddy Mac McCauly.

Harvey and Mac met when they were just starting out on the force. Mac was in San Diego on vacation. Harvey was a rookie motorcycle cop. Harvey's enthusiasm and his desire to do a good job made him a bit overzealous. He couldn't wait to give his first ticket and pulled Mac off the road for going five miles over the speed limit. When he found out Mac was a fellow cop and a fellow rookie at that, he'd let him off with a warning. They kept in touch for years but, like many long-distance friendships, eventually drifted apart. Years ago Harvey had heard through the grapevine that Mac had left the force because his wife couldn't stand the pressure. Now, his name had come up, and for old time's sake, Harvey accepted the case.

He probably would have taken it even if the girl hadn't been referred by Mac. The last ten years or so, he'd developed a soft spot for ladies in distress, a far cry from the way he was when he was first on the force. Back then, he'd been the poster boy for male chauvinism. He thought women had a place, and that place was under him. He certainly had learned a thing or two since then, thank God.

Harvey sat down at his desk, his wood-and-leather chair creaking in contempt. *This job shouldn't be difficult,* he thought. He'd helped several adopted kids investigate their real parents. The girl who had hired him wasn't adopted, but the research on it amounted to the same thing.

Destiny Young had informed him that her father's name was William Statler, and that he'd been listed as MIA before she was born. According to Miss Young, the man never knew he had a child. Harvey had been hired to unearth information on any living relatives of Statler. The girl hinted that Statler might still be alive. Harvey suspected she had her hopes set on that.

But once he started checking, what should have been a quick research project turned into a confusing mess. The dates the girl had given him were out of sync with the facts. According to available records, Statler hadn't been in San Diego for two years prior to the girl's birth. He was stationed on an aircraft carrier, the USS *Independence*. Harvey unearthed no record of a San Diego shore leave during which Statler could have fathered this child. That didn't mean the girl's mother didn't go somewhere else to meet Statler for his R & R; it just meant Harvey would have to dig a little deeper. He didn't mind. For some reason, the case intrigued him.

He'd been mulling over the girl's mother's name. Harvey had a vague recollection of meeting someone named Alison Young. As a cop, one of his strong suits was remembering names of people he'd met, even if he saw them only once. The downside was that he couldn't always remember why they'd met. A person could just as easily be his nephew's seventh-grade teacher as he could be a convicted felon. Go figure.

Reaching into his desk, Harvey took out a piece of Juicy Fruit gum to stave off his hunger. He still missed his cigarettes, but not the hacking cough. Though he had gained weight after he quit smoking, he didn't drink as much.

He had been a reflex drinker. He would drink, for instance, upon learning that after hours of hard work to convict a sleazy cocaine pusher, a judge let the guy walk on a stupid technicality. Now he drank just enough to have a good time around friends and to avoid being called names by his bowling buddies.

Harvey looked around his office. Fresh white paint covered the walls, making them acceptable. If the painter had also painted the ceiling, nobody would have guessed how dingy the place really was. The faded venetian blinds had seen one too many sunny days.

Still, despite the stained bindings that held the metal strips together, the blinds served their purpose, and Harvey didn't have the disposable income to squander on excess interior decorating. The gray linoleum floor was easy to clean, and though his chair squeaked, it was comfortable. The office was nothing special, but for five hundred bucks a month, you couldn't beat it.

He could have picked a place in a more picturesque area of the city, like Point Loma, near the now defunct Naval Training Center, or Balboa Park, surrounded by eucalyptus trees. But he rented this space because the building was adjacent to the San Diego Police Department, Harbor Division, and he wanted to stay close to home. After twenty years on the force, he wasn't ready to cut the umbilical cord just yet.

Besides, Harvey liked being near the harbor, where he could still pop into El Indio's on India Street and get a bag of taquitos and an orange soda whenever he liked. Or, he could hang out at Chewie's place in the old bunker on Market Street, eating enchiladas, drinking Dos Equis, and playing pool with the Mexican cops from Chula Vista.

Harvey glanced at the laminated wood-and-brass plaque he'd mounted on the wall the first thing this morning. It had been given to him at the retirement dinner last night—a year late, but just as welcome.

The plaque suddenly brought him back to the file in his hand. At last night's dinner, he'd overheard a couple of officers discussing the most recent Adult Authority Prisoner Release schedule for a man they'd helped put in Folsom Prison. They were angry the guy was getting out and had offhandedly expressed sorrow that someone hadn't popped him in the joint. When they mentioned the name Country Davis, Harvey paid closer attention. The unusual name struck a chord in him. He knew he'd heard it before, but he couldn't recall the particulars.

What was even more disconcerting was his certainty that the run-in had involved Alison Young, his new client's mother.

His secretary, Gerri Reiner, breezed in to set the last cup of coffee of the day in front of him as he was accessing his on-line system. He navigated to the research center and typed in his request. An hourglass icon appeared on the screen, alerting him that it would take time to download the information he wanted.

He crinkled his nose. He had known Gerri for fifteen years, and he still wasn't used to her habit of using cheap, dime-store perfume. One for every day of the week. She never seemed to notice that her musk wafted around her like a cloud.

Harvey tugged at his collar, grumbled something about the heat, and vigorously fanned himself. She was oblivious. Gerri was good at what she did and loyal to him, so he tried to ignore it. He gazed at his computer screen.

He was proud of the fact that he'd become computer literate, and he rarely made handwritten notes anymore. He enjoyed traversing the Information Superhighway. He used E-mail to send messages to friends, participated in chatrooms, posted opinions about everything from the weather to basketball scores on local bulletin boards, and even got a vicarious kick out of eavesdropping in the singles room.

He wasn't supposed to access the police computer system, but he'd discovered a roundabout way in, so he couldn't resist. It was too easy. And if it helped him crack a case, what was so wrong if he bent the rules just a little? When he couldn't access something on his own, he'd ask his friend Dave Sanchez, a younger cop on the force, to help him out.

Harvey took the refill from Gerri gratefully just as the desired file finished downloading. When the text appeared on the screen, he scrolled through the roster of the Adult Authority Prisoner Release Schedule and spotted the name. He guided the mouse to the printer icon and clicked it, then got up to stretch as the printer kicked in.

The detective turned to his secretary. "Do me a favor before you go, Gerri. Call the Parole Index and speak to someone in the Parole and Community Services Division. I want to find out about a man named Charles Davis. He's on today's release schedule. See if all the info is correct."

"Is he someone from your past?" Gerri asked.

"I think so, but I'm not sure."

"I'm surprised you don't remember," Gerri said, dialing the number. "You're starting to depend on a machine."

"Don't remind me." Harvey chucked his gum and dug through his pencil drawer for a bag of corn nuts. "I didn't put this guy away," he continued, chomping on the nuts, thinking only briefly about what the snack might be doing to his bridgework. "Just find out which jurisdiction he was released to and whether he was put on parole."

While he waited, Harvey returned his attention to the open file on his desk. He flipped through the two-page printout. What was bothering him?

Gerri put down the phone and handed him a piece of paper with Country's full name and the other information he'd asked for written neatly across the top. He held his breath when she stepped closer to him.

"He was definitely released this afternoon," she confirmed, clipping a large fake pearl-and-rhinestone earring back on her earlobe. "But he's not on parole. Apparently he opted to do the extra year."

"Do they know where he was going?" Even as he asked it, Harvey knew it was a stupid question.

"The clerk I spoke to thought he was going to stay with a friend in Sausalito. That's what was written on his release papers, but he couldn't be sure, of course."

Harvey tapped the file and threw another handful of nuts into his mouth. "The new case I'm working on came in from San Francisco. The girl's mother's name is Alison Young."

"Someone else you know?"

"I think I might have met her years ago, when I was still on the force. The weird thing is, I keep thinking she had something to do with Davis. Strange. To be working on a case for this woman's daughter, and suddenly hear the name Country pop up."

"What makes you think they are connected?"

"Just something tugging at me. Country isn't a common name."

"And your client's mother?"

Harvey massaged his bald head, then caught himself and stopped. Bea always said his habit was probably why he'd gone bald in the first place.

"It must have been an investigation I took part in," he said, as much to himself as to Gerri. "Hell, she would have been nothing more than a kid. It had to be eighteen, nineteen years ago or more. According to the prison report, Davis has been locked up for almost eighteen years." Harvey took a sip of cold coffee, then pushed it away.

"Probably just a crazy coincidence."

"I doubt it."

Gerri took her white plastic purse out of the closet and straightened her desk. "Are you staying?"

Harvey didn't lift his eyes from the papers in front of him.

"Don't forget to lock up," she said, a warning tone in her voice. She walked out and closed the door behind her.

Harvey nodded, not hearing her. *She's right,* he thought. Must be a coincidence. He had other cases that demanded his attention: the woman whose husband had ditched her, ignoring a court order to pay child support; the abused wife who wanted pictures of her husband fooling around so she could embarrass him into divorcing her; and the old man dying of cancer who wanted to find his long-lost son and leave him the deed to his ranch in Lakeside, California.

But his mind wouldn't let go. Why had the girl felt the need to hire a private detective? Why hadn't her mother told her everything she wanted to know?

The whys and wherefores about Alison Young's choices were not his business. She and her family must have had their reasons for withholding information. But the daughter was almost eighteen now and had a legal right to know about her father.

He had a job to do.

First thing in the morning, he'd get in touch with his client to recheck the facts. His note-taking skills were rusty. He must have written something down incorrectly. Harvey's stomach started rumbling again, and he automatically checked his watch. It was seven. No wonder. He'd been planning to treat himself to a prime rib dinner tonight, and his body knew it.

Bea was going out. She'd planned to have dinner at Horton

Plaza, do a little shopping, then play pinochle with some friends, which gave him the perfect opportunity to indulge himself.

But as he was getting ready to shut down his computer, he glanced again at the note Gerri had placed on his desk. The names. Country Davis. Alison Young.

Screw it. He'd go for the red meat some other night. Call down the block and order in a pizza instead. Tomorrow, he would ask his buddy Dave to do a background check on Davis. Tonight he could run a check on Alison himself. He scrolled down the main menu to the on-line network and double-clicked back on.

Two pizzas, a six-pack of diet cola, and several hours later, Harvey flicked off his computer. He stared at the printout on his desk, stretching his neck. He'd been sitting for hours.

He crinkled his nose again, this time at the smell of his own gamey body odor. Natural for a man who hadn't showered in twenty hours. It was 3 A.M. He'd been so engrossed in his research, he'd lost track of time.

The spoils of his investigation gave him a fairly good idea of what kind of person he was dealing with, and he had found nothing out of line. Certainly nothing that would have provoked a visit to the police station. But he still couldn't figure out why he knew Alison's name.

He didn't have access to his old police files, and those were the ones he needed. If there was anything explaining the connection between Alison Young and Country Davis, it would be there. Records that old were on a warehouse shelf in the police archives. Though they were his files, technically they were police property. And technically, he was retired. He'd have to ask another favor of Dave. He'd owe his buddy one hell of an expensive meal by the time he was finished with all his requests.

From what information Harvey could gather, Alison Young was
something of a success story. She'd flourished without much help
from anybody. Apparently, that included her father and mother,
because the first piece of data he'd found revealed that her parents
had been killed in an automobile accident in 1971. She would have
been only nineteen years old. Tough break for anyone, especially a
girl with a baby.

He'd tracked the course of Alison's life through Department of
Motor Vehicles reports. She was a good driver. No tickets. He traced
her move from San Diego to the San Francisco area in 1970, based
on a California driver's license renewal in Marin County.

He searched for the registration of the birth of a baby girl, and
found it at Marin General Hospital in Kentwood. No father was listed
on the birth certificate.

Harvey accessed records from Marin Junior College and San
Francisco State University. Alison had maintained a 3.0 grade-point
average. Not bad, considering she had a baby to take care of. She'd
been so young and must have been so vulnerable, yet he found no
record that she'd received subsidies from the government.

Alison married in 1981. According to the caption in the newspaper announcement, she wed a successful San Francisco advertising
executive. She was twenty-nine years old at the time.

Harvey recalled what he was doing at age twenty-nine. Still in
blues, riding shotgun in a patrol car in Mission Valley. His paycheck
had barely allowed for an annual vacation, and if it hadn't been for
the bank's Christmas club, his wife would have put him in hock,
charging too many gifts on their credit cards.

Snooping into the woman's past, Harvey began to develop a feeling of protectiveness for her. Alison Young had been determined. She
never quit working, never went on welfare, and paid her taxes every
year. A stand-up member of the community.

He found a newspaper article announcing Alison's entrance into
the world of publishing. She and two other women had launched a

sophisticated pop culture magazine with funding they'd solicited from a wealthy Malaysian publisher. It had been one of the first publications in California to be produced almost entirely on desktop computers. News of its inception was heralded in several pieces in the local and regional press.

Harvey stuck the last piece of gum into his mouth, grinning at the idea that he was part of the PC phenomenon, and that he and Alison Young had something in common.

It was late. He stuffed the file into his briefcase and, remembering Gerri's admonition, locked up the office. No wonder Alison's daughter had taken it upon herself to hire a private detective. She had her mother's drive. The apple hadn't fallen far from the tree.

Harvey pulled up his collar against the cool, predawn San Diego breeze and walked around the block to his car. He could smell the ocean salt in the air.

Then he saw the pink ticket stuck to the windshield of his '85 Chevy. He yanked it off, cursing, but chuckled when he saw that it had been left in jest by one of his buddies on the force. On the back a scribbled note had asked him to meet the guys at Chewie's for a nightcap. He'd catch up with them another time.

Heading east on the deserted freeway toward Fletcher Parkway, Harvey continued to wrestle with his thoughts. What did an ambitious, intelligent woman like Alison Young have in common with a loser like Country Davis?

The lumbering bus bumped over the metal grids on the Golden Gate Bridge. Alcatraz Island loomed in the distance. Country squinted at the deserted fortress as they passed, feeling an odd appreciation for the place. His lips moved the toothpick he was chewing on from one side to the other. He cracked his knuckles several times, then his neck. The sound caused people near him to stare.

Fuck them. Country's hollow-eyed gaze was forbidding even through the dark sunglasses he wore. Heads immediately turned away, repulsed by a malevolence they felt rather than saw.

A road sign announced that Sausalito was up ahead. Country read through a brochure he found on the bus seat. "Sausalito!" the brochure trumpeted. "A posh jewel of a town just north of the Golden Gate Bridge, this coastal cliff-hanging village is nestled on a hill that overlooks the San Francisco Bay. The local ferries bump and toss in their moorings at the dock at El Portal. Those waiting to cross the bay to Fisherman's Wharf can enjoy magnificent views of the city as they stroll along scenic Bridgeway, a charming street at the water's edge near the famous Sausalito Inn.

"Sausalito's Caledonia Street is filled with shops, restaurants, and inviting little pubs serving the local residents. Adjacent to the bus stop is Vina del Mar Plaza, a green stretch of parklike grass with benches for the weary and a lovely fountain. From this spot, one can see the area of the harbor that boomed during the Second World War.

"Formerly the Kaiser shipyards, just outside Gate 5 is a ragtag assortment of houseboats constructed of salvage material. Although Marin County has waged a continuing war with the bohemian enclave, the houseboat colony remains one of the most colorful points of interest for Sausalito visitors."

This visitor included, Country thought as he spat out his toothpick onto the floor. He ran his tongue along the rough edges of his teeth. They had rotted to blackened stubs when he was in his teens. In Folsom, rotten teeth were an advantage. Not so here. To carry out his plan for the future, he'd need to make a couple of subtle physical changes.

The bus pulled up at El Portal. Country slung his duffel bag over his shoulder and scanned the crowd. A man in biker colors and a long ponytail approached him and took his bag.

"Welcome back, Country. You ain't changed a bit."

Country grunted a hello and gave him the bikers' handshake. The tattooed, bearded man led the way to a dusty blue pickup truck.

"I need a beer, Jake. And a broad."

"I got plenty of Coors on the boat and anything else you want, man. A chick's comin' over for ya in an hour."

Country nodded and lit a cigarette while Jake drove the short distance to Gate 5. He led Country to a ramshackle houseboat at the end of the dock. Inside the houseboat, Jake screwed the top off a cold brew and thrust it at Country. He also took out a box of marijuana and started rolling a couple of joints.

Taking the newspaper out of his duffel bag, Country opened it to the page with the picture of Alison and her daughter and studied the accompanying article. He took the fired-up joint from Jake and inhaled deeply. Then he put his booted feet up on the coffee table.

"You get the information I called about?" Country asked.

"Yeah, most of it." Jake dropped a large manila envelope and a bottle of black capsules in Country's lap. "We got the address of the magazine, some pictures out of the library, and the name of the kid's school."

"You get the home address?"

"Not yet." Jake watched Country's eyes turn flinty gray as his forehead furrowed into a frown. "But I'm working on it. Don't sweat it."

Country didn't change his steely gaze. "Get me the name of a dentist who can do some work on me after hours."

"Okay, man."

They heard a car door slam outside.

"Your afternoon delight is here," Jake said. He wrote down a number on a piece of paper and handed it to Country. "I'll be at this bar if you need anything."

Jake departed just as a cute blonde in tight leather shorts appeared in the doorway. Country eyed her, taking in all the details of her body. Her pale skin was exposed from the hip-hugger shorts all the way up to the white knit crop-top that barely contained her large breasts. Her belly button was pierced with a small silver hoop earring from which a tiny bell dangled.

His lips curled into a smile, but his eyes remained cold and hard. He patted the sofa, shaking his long hair behind his broad shoulders.

"C'mere, Tinkerbell. I been waitin' a long time for real pussy like you."

The girl swallowed hard and walked toward him. She'd been in this business for years and thought she was tough enough to handle it. She'd done two women at a time, three men and a woman, and a man who liked to spank, but none of those people had given her the creeps.

This guy was different. The hairs on the nape of her neck were standing on end. Something about the look on his face warned her that he liked to play rough. When he put his hand on her thigh and squeezed it till she winced, she knew she was right.

He grabbed her hair, yanking her onto her knees, pulling her head toward him. She obeyed, beginning a set of movements she knew by heart. He tugged her hair again and groped at her clothes. She picked up speed and prayed he would get it over with quickly.

An hour later, bruised, frightened, with a bloody lip and a black eye, the girl hastened from the stuffy houseboat, scrambling in her high heels over the rough planks of the dock toward her car. She swore under her breath and looked back once, panicked that the man with the Southern drawl might change his mind and want more. Then she pulled off her heels and broke into a run, grateful that when he'd finished his game, he'd left her alive.

Alison dialed Marlene Burkette's number, content to focus on work-related issues for now. "May I speak with Marlene, please?"

"Speaking."

"This is Alison Young of *Hers Magazine*."

"Hi. I've been waiting for someone to call, but I didn't expect it to be you." Marlene's voice had genuine enthusiasm in it, which instantly appealed to Alison.

"I'd like to set up a time for our interview. In our article on you, I was also thinking of reintroducing the contents of an interview you gave one of our reporters a couple of years ago. That okay with you?"

"Are you kidding? I'm honored."

"When can we get together?"

"I don't start shooting the movie until the end of next week, so my schedule is open until then."

Alison checked her appointment book. "Would Friday work? About ten-thirty?"

"Perfect. I'll have brunch set up for us here, where we won't be disturbed."

"Sounds good. Kelly McAllister is going to call you about the cover shot. We had a problem with it, but I think it's been resolved. She'll fill you in."

"Fine. I'm sure whatever you decide will be perfect. Your covers are incredible."

"Well, we think you're incredible, Marlene, and so do our readers. I'm really looking forward to this interview. I respect what you've done and continue to do for women's rights."

"I don't do much, Alison," Marlene said, clearly uncomfortable with the compliment. "I just open my mouth once in a while and hold up protest signs."

Alison chuckled. "I can't wait to meet you face-to-face. We have plans for a very interesting article."

"God, I'd better hurry up and do something worth writing about, then," Marlene joked.

Alison liked the sound of Marlene's voice. She had an endearing, self-deprecating style. She didn't wear her star status like a queen's robe, and Alison found that refreshing.

She had begun organizing her notes for the staff meeting when the temp buzzed her and announced another call. The temp didn't know who it was, of course. Annoyed, Alison wished Mariah would hurry up and get back to the office. Resigned, she punched the button on her phone and sat down. "This is Alison," she said evenly.

There was silence, followed by a deep, mirthless laugh. "Well, hello there, Ali. Been a long time."

Alison froze. A hot flash swept over her body. Her palms became instantly moist.

"Looks like life's been treatin' you pretty good these past eighteen years, eh, doll?"

She gripped the phone tightly, adjusting it to her ear, hoping she hadn't heard what she'd heard.

"Who is this?"

"Don't play coy with me, babe. You know who it is."

Alison's face went taut and her body broke into a cold sweat. He was right, of course. That voice was the one she knew she'd never forget.

"What do you want," she whispered, unable to regain her equilibrium.

"You got something that belongs to me, Ali, and I've come to claim it."

Alison felt the room twist sideways. She should hang up. It was a wrong number. It couldn't be him. But even as she tried to fool herself, she found she was glued to the phone. She had to respond.

"How did you find me?"

"You can never hide from me, doll. Remember what I told ya? But that's all water under the bridge, ain't it? Now you're famous. Saw it in the paper. I'm real proud of you. You done a mighty fine job of bringing up that pretty little girl. It's just the way I'd expect my woman to be."

"I'm nothing to you, Country," Alison said, her voice rising an octave. "And keep my daughter out of this!"

"Don't take that tone with me, darlin'. I was disappointed when

I saw the kid's not using my name, but I'm gonna change all that. We're family, Ali. She's my kid."

"You stay out of my life, do you hear me? I'll call the police!"

Country laughed, a low, sinister, guttural cackle. "Go ahead. They can't stop me. I'm back, and I'll get what I want."

"Never!" Alison yelped, as if she'd been slapped. She slammed down the handset and stared at it in horror, not wanting to touch it. Quickly realizing he might call back, she punched in a code to activate her private voice-mail system. Then she recoiled once again from the phone, as if it, instead of the incoming call, was the intruder.

Events from the past came rushing toward her, bringing on a feeling of claustrophobia. The room suddenly felt hot and tight. Had she screamed? Could the temp have heard? Alison held on to the sides of her chair for balance as her eyes darted to the picture of Destiny.

Panic gripped her and set her in motion. She needed to figure out what to do. She didn't want anyone picking up that phone again, didn't want anyone to see her in this state.

Sprinting to the cubicle where the temp sat, she tried to sound unruffled, yet she had trouble pushing the sound from her vocal chords.

"You can leave now, Miss," she said in a voice barely above a whisper. "My answering system is on, and I'll be unreachable for the rest of the day."

The temp looked at her curiously, then shrugged. "Can you sign my hour report, or is there someone else I should talk to?"

Alison felt her cheeks burning. Her heart pounded so hard she thought the girl would hear it. She signed the report impatiently in an illegible scrawl. Attempting a polite smile that she was sure looked more like a spectral glower, she retreated into her office, shutting the door behind her.

Staring at the phone, Alison tried to calm her breathing. *Maybe he won't call again,* she thought. Then she watched in horror as the incoming call light came on again. It blinked twice, then stopped, indicating that her voice-mail had picked it up. She pushed the button that allowed her to monitor the call. As she listened, tears welled up in her eyes. It was him again. Threatening, demanding to see her. To see Destiny.

Alison didn't know how to react. She didn't want to talk to him or see him again, ever. She didn't want to believe that he had found her, that he could invade her life again. But as she sat there, dazed, she knew that hanging up on him hadn't sent him back into the hole he'd crawled out of. Alison grew cold. A single tear rolled down her cheek and onto her crisp white blouse. She gazed at the photos of Destiny and Collin on her desk. Another tear trickled down her cheek.

She'd tried the best she could to build a life that would protect her from any intrusion from her past.

But he was back.

Chapter 3

THE MORNING FOG THAT HAD KEPT THE TEMPERATURE IN THE LOW fifties had finally lifted. It was replaced by a blistering heat that baked the already weathered wood siding of the two-story Spanish houses lining Clipper Street.

Clipper was a nondescript street on the edge of a worn-out, low-rent neighborhood in the historic Mission District. Located on the southwestern side of the city, the district was named for the presence of Mission Dolores, built originally at Albion and Camp Streets in 1776. Franciscan friars who migrated north from Mexico City to bring Christianity to the so-called savages built twenty-one missions in Spanish Alta California. Mission Dolores was the sixth and had the distinction of being one of the two oldest Spanish foundations in San Francisco.

The Mission District, or the "Mish," as it was sometimes called, looked almost as old. The area had been home to a wide variety of American peoples over the course of two hundred years, from Native Americans to English and Scottish settlers. Now it was primarily a barrio, a colorful mix of mostly Latin Americans. It had come full circle.

The district bordered Noe Valley and the unorthodox Castro area, where writers, artists, and gay activists were known to reside. The section that included Clipper Street was still under the auspices of rent control, which made it affordable for a struggling musician.

That had been Marco McCauly's main concern when he took the apartment. That, and the fact that it was close to the Castro and the Haight, where he had most of his gigs.

Marco pulled the rubber band off his long ponytail and shook his black hair loose, stretching his neck back and forth to rid it of tension. He'd just spent three hours in back-to-back classes at San Francisco State, and the course material in both physics and philosophy had been dry and heavy.

He opened a bottle of spring water, his one real luxury, from a six-pack on his kitchen counter and chugged down half of it on the way to his small living room. He looked around for a flat surface on which to put it and decided that the floor was the best option.

To say Marco's apartment was sparse was an understatement. His possessions were a ragtag collection of hand-me-downs and garage sale finds, and only the bare essentials at that. He owned a bed, a large chair, and a couple of lamps. Fortunately the apartment kitchen had come equipped with a small refrigerator and stove. This was a man's domicile. No attempt had been made to make the place cozy or homelike, aside from a few large India print pillows from Cost Plus tossed about for comfort.

Marco didn't need fancy furnishings and didn't miss them. Raised on a cop's salary, he and his parents had lived modestly until his mom and dad divorced. By then, he was seventeen and almost out of high school. His mom died of a heart attack shortly after the divorce, and Marco moved into a place of his own as soon as he could. He'd had his fill of family turmoil. He barely had any communication with his father; the call he'd made on his girlfriend Destiny's behalf had been the first time they'd spoken in over a year. Grief had driven father and son apart, and neither one of them had made a serious attempt at reconciling.

Now he concentrated on work, finishing college, and getting his band, Chain, signed to a record label. He'd worry about material possessions later.

Marco owned nothing of value except his music equipment, but it was the best available. The money he made working in restaurants was funneled directly into his music and toward booking studio time to work on the band's demos. They were close to being signed by a well-known record label.

He slipped a cassette into his Aiwa system and pushed Play. He pulled his overstuffed chair to a spot equidistant between his two huge Tanoy speakers, peeled off his well-worn flannel shirt, and kicked off his black motorcycle boots. Then he sat down to check out the first mix of Chain's latest demo.

Marco listened dispassionately, wanting to be objective. He closed his eyes and crossed his muscular arms over his chest, each tanned, bulging bicep sporting tastefully applied tattoos of medieval crosses.

The song, a collaboration between him and Destiny was good. He was pleased. Opening his eyes, he reached for his guitar. Holding his unplugged Fender Stratocaster, he hunkered down, eyes closed again. His long black hair hung over the strings of the guitar as he listened to each of the chord changes. Marco fingered the strings, marking the chords along with the recording while planning an alternate riff for the next time they played the song.

Destiny sang the lead vocal, and her voice came off clear and strong.

Powerful.

It was the first time she'd been in a recording studio, but she'd performed well. He knew she was ready for a regular gig singing with the band in public.

A knock at the door interrupted Marco's thoughts. "It's open," he called out.

Destiny entered, breathless, and dropped her backpack on the hardwood floor. She stood in the middle of the room, pouting.

Marco pushed Stop and walked over to her. "What's up, baby? I thought you were working today."

Destiny moved into Marco's arms and buried her head in his chest. "I've had it," she said in a strained voice. "She has no compassion for my feelings at all!"

Marco pulled her face up to meet his, brushed her brown curls out of the way, and kissed her. "Fight with your mom?"

Destiny nodded. "It's always the same. She watches me like a hawk, but when it comes to my doing something I like, she's not interested. Or she has a better way to do it, or she knows someone who should do it with me, or for me. She doesn't think I can tie my shoes by myself."

Marco picked up his guitar again and began plucking gently at the strings, watching her. A shadow crossed briefly over his face, and he turned his focus to his guitar.

"I want to get on with my life," Destiny continued. "I'm almost eighteen, for God's sake. I have things I want to do. Can't she understand that?"

She went to the window and looked out at the shabby-looking structures squeezed in side by side. Marco's apartment was on the top floor of an old Spanish-style building on a street where the front yards were nothing more than dried-out lawns and tired-looking trees. Very different from the houses on the next block, which looked like they had been transplanted from tony Pacific Heights.

Destiny peered over at those glittering gingerbread houses and cool green lawns. Some ambitious young architects had purchased and restored four aging Victorians. That part of the neighborhood now had perfectly trimmed lawns, climbing roses, and clean windows, and looked like a page right out of *House and Garden* magazine.

She knew she'd buy a house like that one day. But that was in the future. Probably the far-off future. Thinking about what might lie ahead frustrated her, and she sighed heavily, arms crossed.

Marco interrupted her thoughts. "What started it? She find out you hired that detective?"

"Did she ever. I was sending him an E-mail when she walked in.

She busted me for doing my own thing on company time. Then she fired me."

Marco looked at her for a moment, then switched to random chords. Destiny watched, fascinated, as he plucked the guitar strings. The rings he wore on all of his fingers had become his signature trait. One of them had been a gift from her, and the fact that he wore it made her feel good.

"Mom would like it if she could make all my decisions," she said. "Get me to have the same career she has. When I talk about music, she thinks only her contacts are the right ones. Doesn't think I'm capable of achieving anything without her."

Marco smiled.

"It's not funny, Marco," she snapped.

He shrugged. "Lighten up. Did you come here to pick a fight with me, too?"

"Sorry," Destiny said, the edge gone from her voice. "I'm just pissed off. I didn't mean to bitch at you."

She grabbed a large pillow, plopped it on the floor next to him, and sat down. "So what do you think?"

"It's your life. It's a call you have to make, I guess."

Marco tucked his hair behind his ear and leaned into the Fender, caressing it as he played. Destiny waited patiently for him to finish the riff. He was centered on his music. It was all-important to him. He didn't let anything get in the way. It was one of the things that had attracted her to him from the start.

Destiny and Marco had met a year ago at a college band fest. She'd been drawn to him right away. His long hair was tied back into a loose ponytail with a piece of red yarn. The raven black of his hair was a vivid contrast to his pale skin, which she had discovered later was due to his mother being Latino and his father Scotch-Irish. Marco was wearing a sleeveless T-shirt, and she admired his lean, muscular arms.

But when she watched him play, listened to the way he interpreted his songs, she was mesmerized not only by his looks, but also by his talent. She thought he was brilliant. Afterward, she pushed her way through the crowd to meet him. Luckily, he had liked her, too. They began dating that week.

Marco was a second-year music major at San Francisco State. She was only a high-school junior then, but he hadn't been put off by her age, especially after he watched her perform at a local coffeehouse. He encouraged her to pursue her musical talents, had even told her he'd use some of her lyrics in his songs.

She knew he would live up to his promise.

Destiny stared at him until he finally looked up. Marco shrugged, put his guitar down, and strolled into the kitchen.

"I don't want to get in the middle of your family fights, Destiny," he said, pulling an apple out of the fridge. "I had enough of my own and I'm over it. Life's too short. But you're almost eighteen—legally an adult. If you want to find out about your real dad, go ahead and do it. No one's stopping you. But you should try to remember that your mom is just doing the best she can."

Destiny chewed on the inside of her cheek, a habit she shared with her mother. Her blue eyes squinted in thought. "She's not supportive of me," she repeated.

Marco pushed Rewind on the tape deck. "You two are really on a collision course, aren't you?"

Destiny pouted, chagrined. "It's not like I'm planning it, you know."

He came over and wrapped his arms around her. "She probably doesn't want you to get hurt. Most moms are like that."

"Right. Well, people get hurt sometimes. She can't walk me across *every* street."

"Don't be so tough on her, Des. You might not be able to take any of it back. I couldn't. My mom died before we could sort things out between us."

Destiny nodded, her expression changing from anger to remorse in a flash.

Marco pushed Play and went to his small closet to get dressed for his job at the Castro Street Cafe.

"Listen to this," he called out. "Derek and I mixed it last night. It's our first pass for the demo. Not too bad. It still needs a little work, but check out your vocal. It's fine."

Destiny listened, thrilled. She couldn't believe her ears. It *was* good.

Marco smiled at her reaction. He unzipped his blue 501s, shimmied out of them, and pulled on a clean pair of black jeans for work. He brushed his hair back into a ponytail as Destiny watched, captivated. His small gold stud earring sparkled in the sunlight pouring in through the bedroom window. Destiny's eyes traced Marco's body. His bare chest was lean and muscular, and his arms, even without flexing, had great definition. She was proud to be his girlfriend.

"Prove you're serious about a singing career and quit bitching," he said, pulling a clean white shirt off a hanger. "You graduate next week. Register for classes at State. Get a job you like and start taking care of yourself. You can't expect your folks to give in to all your whims when they're footing the bill."

"You're right. My parents need to see that I'm capable of getting what I want on my own."

Destiny's eyes swept the small apartment, absorbing the surroundings, considering it in a different light. An idea had hit her. She mulled it over for a moment, then smiled. "And I think I know the best way to get the message across to them."

She moved closer to Marco and slipped her arms under his shirt, caressing his bare back. "Can I move in with you for a while?"

He turned to face her, surprised. "Are you sure you're ready for that?"

"I'm ready for all of it. Are you?"

Marco's dark eyes narrowed. He cocked his head sideways, scrutinizing her. Then he looked around his small apartment as if he were surveying it for space.

Destiny became nervous. She couldn't read Marco's thoughts. She was half afraid he was going to say no when he smiled and put his arms around her. He kissed her.

"I wasn't thinking about living with anybody yet, especially here," he said. "But if you want to, I guess it's okay."

They embraced again, the kiss lasting longer this time. Marco's face broke into a wide grin, showing off his perfectly straight, ultra-white teeth. "I still have some time before I have to go to work," he hinted, pulling her into his small bedroom. He kissed her again, tumbling with her onto the bed.

They'd never made love in the daytime before, and Destiny was self-conscious. Marco wasn't. He looked right into her face, gazing into her eyes, even when he kissed her. She couldn't maintain the eye contact. It was still too new. She closed her eyes and imagined him instead.

Marco found the place on the side of her neck that made her tremble when he kissed it, then began to disrobe her. He knew exactly where every button was and how to unclasp every clasp. Once her blouse had been casually tossed aside, his hands moved over her body with ease, quickly dismantling her sexy white bra. Self-confidently caressing her soft, small breasts, he pulled her body close, possessing her.

His kisses became fervent, powerful, and soon Destiny was warm and breathless. She finally had the nerve to look into his dark eyes and saw there was nothing to be afraid of. Suddenly, she wasn't self-conscious anymore.

She helped him pull off her black combat boots, then lay still while he pushed down her skirt and panties. After she fumbled with the zipper on his jeans, she sat on the edge of the bed, waiting, while he kicked his pants onto the floor.

Marco moved next to her and pressed his naked body close, staring deep into her eyes. The mixture of his cologne and the sweet smell of sexual arousal made Destiny's heart race. He gently kissed his way down her neck, causing shivers to crawl across her body. He caressed her breasts, flicking her nipples with his tongue until they stood at attention like tiny pink marshmallows. Finally, he moved back up to seek out her waiting lips, kissing her deeply as he covered her body with his own, rhythmically grinding, pushing, and pulsing until she was ready. With tenderness and passion, he guided himself inside her.

They moaned softly together, their breathing erratic. He pulled her legs up higher on the sides of his body as their yearning mounted.

Destiny thought she was on fire. A flutter from deep within the core of her body escalated into a whirlwind that rushed through her with unstoppable force. She clutched at his back, letting out a shrill yell as she wrapped her legs tightly around his body.

Marco's moan became a roar, shocking Destiny back into the present. Suddenly she was afraid the neighbors would hear them. Then, just when she thought she would scream again, it was over. A cloudburst of energy, then calm.

They lay still together, sweaty and content. Destiny smiled dreamily and put her hand on Marco's chest, feeling the rapid beating of his heart. The fierce rhythm of her own heart matched his, not only because of their passionate lovemaking, but also because of her anticipation of the step she was about to take. Moving in with Marco meant her whole world would be changed forever. At this moment in time, that was all Destiny could think of.

The receptionist at Archer Advertising looked up when the scruffy-looking man in jeans entered the lobby. *Must have gotten off on the wrong floor,* she mused. The man gazed briefly at her, then turned his attention to the poster-size prints of the company's latest advertisements, which adorned the lobby walls.

Before the receptionist could question the visitor, Collin breezed into the lobby. Straightening in her seat, she smiled at her handsome boss, her eyes darting about her desk in a last-minute check to make sure the pencils and message pads were organized into neat rows. She hoped to move into a better position within the company soon and was always careful to make a good impression.

"Anything come in for me, Leigh?" Collin asked, as he picked up the latest issue of *Advertising Age* off the counter next to her desk.

"Nothing new, Mr. Archer. I put all your calls through to Kristin. Are you expecting something in particular I should be on the look-out for?"

Collin picked up a few other trade magazines. Suddenly he frowned. The heavy, stale odor of cigarette smoke hung in the air. He looked at the young receptionist. "I didn't know you smoked, Leigh."

The girl's eyes went round with horror. "I don't smoke, Mr. Archer! I never have!"

"Sorry," Collin quickly said, using his most disarming smile. "Must have been someone else."

Leigh glanced at the scruffy-looking man, who was now on the other side of the lobby, near the elevator. Collin followed her gaze, catching a glimpse of the man just as several office workers entered the lobby, blocking his view.

Collin jerked his head toward the man. "Who's that fellow waiting for?" he asked the receptionist.

"I don't know. He didn't ask for directions or anything. He just started looking at the ads."

Collin shrugged. "Let my secretary know I've got my cell phone on if anyone needs to reach me," he said as he made his way across the lobby. The elevator doors opened and the strange man stepped inside, followed by the gaggle of chattering workers. Collin stepped into the elevator just as the door timer began to buzz.

Conversation dwindled to whispers as the car made its descent. The rancid smell of smoke permeated the small space, and Collin felt the air in the elevator become dense and oppressive. He began to perspire and felt inexplicably edgy. Standing within kissing distance of the silver elevator doors, Collin watched the buttons register the passing of each floor.

When the car finally reached the main lobby of the office building, most of the workers filed out. The unidentified man glanced at Collin before exiting the elevator and disappeared into the sunlight streaming in through the large front doors.

As the elevator continued down to the garage, Collin spied a smoldering cigarette butt on the floor in the corner. Cursing the fool who had so flagrantly disobeyed the law, he ground the butt into the already scorched carpeting, feeling his chest tighten from the lack of clean air. He loosened his tie and burst out of the elevator when it reached P-1.

Alison left her office feeling chilled to the bone, despite the warm temperature outside. She'd left a message for Kelly, saying that something had come up and she'd have to miss the staff meeting. She couldn't face anyone right now.

The phone call had jolted her back in time. Alison was forced to feel the pain of old wounds and old mistakes. As she dashed, unseeing, down Maiden Lane toward the garage, she tried to think of what to do. She couldn't have this craziness in her life. He couldn't do this to her. Not again.

Being in the fresh air and moving among the daily crush of people going about their business helped shore up Alison's shaken inner strength. She wouldn't let him scare her. She was a businesswoman, not a child. Not like before. It was different now. Things had changed. The police would surely do something about it—this time.

Alison drove straight to the police station at the embarcadero and strolled through the doors, bold and self-confident. But with each step she took down the busy entry hall, she felt her strength ebb. The place was depressing and impersonal and had that institutional smell. The pale green walls were too familiar. The sounds were too loud, the people moving around were either disinterested or looked threatened themselves. In the space of a minute's time, Alison was intimidated and felt like a victim. Again.

Alison approached the two police officers standing behind the main counter with bored expressions. One was questioning a trio of young men in bandannas; the other was listening to a middle-aged couple's story. Doors opened, more officers passed through the corridor, file folders in hand, guns in holsters. There was no privacy here.

A group of men in dark slacks, white shirts, and ties, walked by her, stopping at a water cooler on the opposite side of the room. The stale odor of cigarette smoke remained in their wake. Alison watched them drink water and laugh. Her eyesight went blurry. Déjà vu. She'd been here before.

By the time it was her turn to speak to an officer, Alison felt like nothing more than a frightened, timid little girl. The officer at the main counter stamped a piece of paper and directed the middle-aged couple to a bench at the far side of the room. "Next," he said without looking up.

Alison opened her mouth to speak but found she'd lost her voice. She bit the inside of her cheek hard enough to taste blood, then cleared her throat. "I need police protection," she croaked.

"What happened, ma'am?" the officer said flatly.

"A man called me at my office today. He . . . uh, he attacked me nineteen years ago, and, uh, now he wants to see me."

"Is this man an ex-boyfriend? Ex-husband?"

"No, nothing!" Alison could feel her composure slipping away. "He just called me out of the blue! I feel harassed and I want you to do something about it!"

The police officer sighed and glanced at the clock. "We can't go around locking people up for talking, ma'am. What's your name?"

Alison began to perspire. If she told him, there was a chance he'd recognize it. Though she didn't think of herself as famous, she *was* the publisher of a popular magazine, and if she used her married name, the officer would surely be aware of Archer Advertising. The company was nearly a San Francisco legend.

As she looked into the officer's face, Alison felt she was at a loss. She couldn't explain her whole story to him. He seemed as detached and dispassionate as the police had been nineteen years ago. Why should this cop understand? He couldn't help her, but he'd have her name and be able to spread rumors that might reach the ears of people she was trying to protect.

The phone rang, and the officer put down his pencil to answer it. He shoved a complaint form in front of her, gesturing for her to fill it out. Alison stared at the page, weighing her choices. The noise in the station seemed louder than normal, and there was no air. She felt a trickle of sweat drip down between her breasts. If she didn't get out of that room, she feared she'd suffocate.

The police officer busied himself with the phone call, flipping through the pages of a file folder. Alison pushed the paper away, mumbled, "Never mind," and made a dash for the exit.

The drive to her home near the marina was a blur. Her strength, her resolve, her power had vanished. Alison tried to focus on her work agenda in order to conquer her panic. There were seven regular feature articles in each issue of *Hers,* and only four had been scheduled so far for the holiday issue, the one they were comping at the moment. But her brain refused to comply. It was all Alison could do to keep from hyperventilating.

At the front door, she fumbled with her keys. Collin yanked the door open, making her jump. "Sorry, babe," he said quickly. "A little nervous tonight, aren't we?" He affectionately planted a kiss on her cheek.

Alison walked past him into the house, avoiding his eyes, focusing instead on some lost item at the bottom of her purse. "Is Destiny here?" she asked.

"Not yet."

Alison threw her purse on the sofa and bolted for the bathroom.

"Hold on a minute," Collin said. He reached for her arm and missed.

Alison hurried through the living room and into the bathroom, closing the door behind her. She wanted to fix her makeup before her husband got a good look at her. "I'll be right out, honey. I've been holding it for twenty minutes!"

She peered at her face in the mirror. It was pale, and suddenly she looked twenty years older. Amazing what a sudden dose of fear could do.

Country's reappearance changed everything. Tears welled up in her eyes, and she squeezed them shut, refusing to give in to them. She had to stop this. He had merely called her. That was all. He couldn't possibly know where she lived. He had only her work number, and no one at the office would ever divulge her home address. He was harassing her. She could deal with that.

Alison took a deep breath and tried to focus on more positive thoughts. She spilled the contents out of her purse, found her blusher, and applied it. She dabbed on lipstick and studied the results. The makeup brought some color back to her face, but her eyes were another story. There was nothing she could do to camouflage the strain reflected in them.

If she were smart, she'd sit down and tell Collin the whole sordid story right here and now. Maybe he'd understand. Maybe he'd know how to help her.

But she couldn't do it. Tonight, she didn't feel in touch with an ounce of her intelligence or business savvy. At this moment she was being pushed through space by fear alone.

Alison flushed the toilet for effect, then opened the door and joined Collin in the living room. He held out a glass of wine, studying her. "That fight really threw you, didn't it, babe?" he surmised.

Alison gratefully took the wine and nodded. She gazed at her husband of almost eight years, suddenly fearful of losing him. Collin Archer was of medium height, about five feet eleven inches, but he carried himself in a manner that made him appear much taller. He was trim and handsome in a tanned, outdoorsy way. His sandy-blond hair reminded her of Robert Redford's. When he smiled, the dimples in his cheeks made the resemblance even stronger.

As he grew older, Collin had become even more attractive. Every time he came up with a new marketing idea, he always got a childlike gleam in his eye that was absolutely contagious. She knew he could charm the pants off any young woman if he were so inclined, but thankfully he didn't go that route. He seemed devoted to her, and for her part, Alison was as attracted to him now as she'd ever been. Perhaps more.

She fell in love with Collin the first moment she laid eyes on him. It was a day she would never forget. Alison had been renting Collin's old apartment over the garage attached to his mother's house. She'd been pregnant with Destiny at the time, and he'd been dating someone else, but when Alison saw him in his leather motorcycle jacket and jeans, she realized Cupid's arrow had hit its mark. Collin had a scruffy week-old beard then and had just started up Archer Advertising. Although he was kind and flirtatious with her, he was clearly not interested in her romantically. It took ten years for their love to bloom into a life partnership.

The idea of having more children crossed Alison's mind early in their relationship. Having known the loneliness of being an only child, she wanted Destiny to have a brother or sister. But for some reason, Collin continuously resisted the idea, and she left it at that.

Deep inside, she knew Collin loved Destiny. He always made sure her needs were met, and tried, in his own way, to show her that he cared. At the same time, though, he kept her at a calculated distance.

Alison never wanted to push him. She always wondered if it was because Destiny wasn't his natural daughter.

A few months ago, Collin had felt a sudden parental tug. Alison thought it was because he'd reached his mid-forties and felt his own biological clock ticking. Or perhaps it was because several of their friends had decided to have children. Whatever the reason, he began to talk about having a baby. Alison thought it odd because this new-found desire was happening at a point when she and Collin rarely had private time together. His frequent business trips left him little time to be a parent to Destiny, much less anyone else. It seemed to Alison that his idea of expanding the family was less than realistic, all things considered. Being a parent meant responsibility and required total dedication and presence. Alison also thought that the subject should have been discussed with Destiny in a gentler fashion than it had been.

"I've been thinking about what happened today," Collin said, leading Alison over to the sofa. "The friction between you two is par-tially my fault, but she's taking it out on you."

"I probably overreacted by firing her," Alison replied as she sat down. "The heat of the moment, I guess. Her blasé attitude was putting me in an embarrassing situation at work."

"Still, work isn't the only issue, Ali. I'm the one who started talking about having a baby. I haven't adopted Destiny, and she's resentful. That's the real issue."

Alison threw him a quick glance. *At least he realizes it,* she thought. She gulped down the rest of her wine. "Do you really think adoption would change anything? You're the only father she has—the only one she's ever known."

Even as she spoke, she was cringing inside. She thought about Destiny's curiosity, knowing that unresolved feelings and unanswered questions about her real father had probably instigated her daughter's search. Alison's feelings of dread became more intense as she consid-ered the honest answers to Destiny's questions. She'd spent a lifetime convincing herself that those answers would never have to be revealed. Now she wasn't so sure that was possible anymore.

Collin got up and refilled their glasses. "I don't know if adoption is the answer or not, but I called my lawyer this afternoon and told him to look into it."

Alison raised her eyebrows. "She'll be eighteen in a couple of weeks. She's practically an adult. It won't matter anymore."

"Who knows? Maybe it's the gesture that's important," Collin said, rolling up his shirt sleeves. "Clearly the issue's been bugging her for a long time."

Collin headed down the hall toward their bedroom.

As Alison stared after him, she thought about her own wake-up call. An image of Country appeared in her mind. How could she maintain any sense of normalcy right now? She felt hot again. She got up, cranked open one of the living room windows, and took a deep breath. The night air was filled with the salty mist of the sea, a scent she usually enjoyed. But now the scent conjured up vivid memories of a night many years ago.

Alison cursed under her breath. The man behind the surprise phone call could reach out and destroy her happiness, even from a distance.

Nineteen years hadn't erased the memory. His long, unkempt wavy brown hair, his shabby navy peacoat. His naked, brawny chest. The frightening tattoo, his worn-out bell-bottom jeans. Those mesmerizing, ice-blue eyes. The habit he had of cracking his knuckles.

Alison forced the image out of her mind. She downed the wine and considered pouring herself another glass but decided against it. She'd already had more than usual, and it hadn't done anything to soothe her raw nerves. The conversation with Collin wasn't helping, either. Too much was happening at once.

The front door flew open, startling her. Destiny stood in the doorway, her face flushed.

Alison rushed over to her. "Oh, Desi, I'm glad you're home. I'm so sorry about today, honey."

Destiny pulled her backpack off her shoulder. Dragging it behind her, she strolled past her mother toward her bedroom. Alison followed. "Forget it," Destiny said curtly. "I don't want to discuss it, okay?"

Collin emerged from the master bedroom. "Come on, Destiny, let's talk about it," he insisted.

Destiny walked into her bedroom, stopped, and turned to face them both. "Why should we? It'll just turn into another fight. I only came home to get my stuff. I'm leaving."

"What do you mean, leaving?" Alison asked, her voice rising several octaves. "Are you going to Caroline's?"

"I'm not talking about a sleepover. I'm moving out, Mom. Permanently. I'm going to live with Marco."

Destiny began rummaging around her room, throwing bare necessities into a duffel bag. Alison hovered near the door. "You can't move out. You don't know what it's like out there! I won't allow it, Destiny. It's too dangerous!"

"Oh, give me a break, Mom. Why is everything I want to do too dangerous? What about you? You moved out! You had me when you were only eighteen. Did your parents allow that? Well, *I'm* not going to run off and have a kid, you know. I just want to get on with my life!"

Alison's shoulders slumped. She felt nauseous and tired. Hearing her daughter speak to her with such defiance was crippling. "What do you mean, get on with your life?" Alison said in barely more than a whisper. "I haven't been standing in your way, for God's sake."

Destiny rolled her eyes and went back to her packing. Collin gave Alison a placating look and gently moved her aside. "You're mad, Destiny, and you have a right to be. I have a feeling this whole baby issue has gotten to you. I should have realized it would be hard on you, and I'm sorry. I'm going to try to set things straight. I'd like to adopt you, Destiny."

Destiny dropped her stuffed duffel bag on the floor and stared at both her parents. "You can't be serious. You think that's what this is all about? Wanting to be adopted?"

Rattled, Collin looked at Destiny, then at Alison. "Isn't it?" he said, seeking reassurance.

Destiny's eyes flashed. "I did want that to happen years ago, but now it doesn't matter."

Alison saw Collin stiffen. His handsome face pulled into a frown, and he looked away, wounded. She turned back to her daughter. "Dammit, Destiny, don't talk that way to Collin. Your fight is with me. He's not involved in this."

"Exactly!" Destiny snapped. "It's always feast or famine around here. You're either all over me and suffocating me, or you're not there at all." Destiny looked straight at Collin and shook her head. "You're a nice guy, Collin, but our relationship has been a little impersonal, you know? Just like the gifts you have your secretary send me when you're away on a business trip. It's always the same perfume, and I've told you over and over again that I'm allergic to it. You'd think eight years would be long enough to get to know someone."

Collin listened to her tirade in silence, understanding reflected in his face. Alison looked from her daughter to her husband. "Destiny. That's enough!" she commanded.

Destiny stopped and shrugged. "I agree. So I'm outta here." She picked up a teddy bear from her bed. Then she locked eyes again with Collin. "Look, Collin, I didn't mean to hurt your feelings. But it seems that either you don't hear me or you don't care, 'cause you really don't know me. So why would you want to adopt me?"

As Destiny put the stuffed animal inside her bag and zipped it shut, tears filled her eyes. Her demeanor changed. "I'm sorry if I'm not what you wanted, and I'm sorry I didn't live up to your expectations. But I have to be true to myself. I have dreams of my own, and I'm going to prove to you that I can achieve them!"

Destiny stormed out and marched down the hallway, duffel bag in hand. Alison ran after her. "Please don't go, Destiny! This isn't the way it's supposed to be."

"Oh, come on, Mom! Don't tell me you have a set of rules for how a teenager leaves the house, too?" her daughter retorted without looking back.

"Destiny," Collin said, "we just want to help."

"If you really want to help," Destiny continued, "tell me more about my real father and save me the trouble of all this searching."

Alison clenched her teeth until the muscles in her jaw burned. She glanced at Collin, who nodded in agreement. Destiny pulled a piece of paper out of the pocket of her leather jacket and placed it on the coffee table. "Here's Marco's number." She wiped her eyes and flipped her hair out of her face. "You probably don't believe this, but I *do* love you both."

Slinging her duffel bag onto her shoulder, she gave them a last look, then walked out.

Alison stood frozen in the hallway, tears running down her cheeks. "How did this happen?" she said, her voice choking.

Collin wrapped his arm around her. "She's just angry, Ali. Give her some time to cool off. At least we know where she's going."

"What if she doesn't cool off? I never wanted it to come to this. After my own rotten childhood, this is the last thing I wanted for my daughter."

Collin's expression darkened. "People fight, Alison. It's not the end of the world. You can't compare Destiny's childhood with yours. You've been a wonderful mother to her. And though I haven't been a great father, at least I haven't been a mean old toad."

Alison looked away, hiding her face. Her dad had been far worse than a mean old toad. She had shared some of her childhood traumas with Collin, but not all of them. The most sordid details of her life she kept to herself.

"I just didn't want her to leave home angry, Collin. I know what that feels like, and I didn't want it for her, okay?"

Collin looked at her, seeing that she'd thrown up a barrier. "I didn't mean to be flip, honey. Destiny's just searching for herself, like any kid her age. We all went through it."

Alison stared at him numbly. *Not everybody went through this,* she thought. Destiny was desperately seeking answers, and there was one man out there ready to give them to her. If he got the chance to do that, her daughter would never be like any kid her age again.

Chapter 4

DESTINY AND MARCO WALKED ARM IN ARM ALONG HAIGHT Street. The boulevard was alive, vibrant. Although it was late, most shops were still open; the nightlife was in full swing.

During the day, Haight-Ashbury was full of tourists. A handful of head shops had cropped up in recent years, reminiscent of the kind that flourished during the tumultuous sixties, an era that had permanently altered the consciousness of the district.

Pictures of the famous marijuana leaf were plastered on the shop doors, alerting tourists that hippie paraphernalia could be had inside, a piece of the past that was still popular today. The Haight represented an epoch, and lava lamps, charm candles, incense, Indian pillows, water pipes, and coke vials were all part of it.

At night the Haight teemed with local inhabitants, a heterogeneous group that made a broad spectrum of cultural, spiritual, ethnic, and sexual statements. There were bikers, punks, skinheads, stoners, guys with arms around each other, girls with arms around each other. A heavily tattooed, heavily body-pierced populace. It was a creative, artistic crowd, many of them college students from nearby campuses. The night scene was a circus, but it was one in which Marco and Destiny felt at home.

The music blaring from most shops was courtesy of KUSF, a radio station broadcasting from the nearby University of San Francisco. The music was far from mainstream, but it was what the locals preferred, Marco and Destiny included.

The two lovers stopped in front of Reckless Records to peer into the window at the latest releases. They knew most of them by heart. Reckless was well known for showcasing offbeat groups, most of them deriving a good part of their popularity from the airplay they received on KUSF. A couple of CDs being sold had been recorded by good friends of Marco, and he and Destiny stared at them for several moments, paying homage. Both Marco and Destiny were anxious for the day when they would see their *own* CD in this very window.

They had coffee at a late-night coffeehouse that smelled of sandalwood incense and chicory, then wandered through Uma's Occult Shop and bought each other crystals. It took Marco a long time to wind down after a set. His skin still glistened from the sweat caused by the heat of the stage lights. They were both still wired as they continued their journey toward Rockin' Robins, a dance club at the end of Haight Street.

Tonight Marco's band had played at Nightbreak, a club that specialized in contemporary underground rock, and Destiny sang the last set with them. It was her first live performance, other than local coffeehouses and the Career Day event she'd done for her mom, and the experience had been earth-moving for her. Destiny's heart had soared. There was nothing like knowing your audience approved of a song, its style, its voice. To sing and hear their applause—nothing could be better, as far as Destiny was concerned. Her decision to pursue a singing career was reaffirmed.

This is where she belonged, and she planned to follow Marco's advice and get serious about her singing. Maybe then her parents would understand and be supportive. She wanted to make her own mark, have her own accomplishments. Her mother had done so against all odds. Destiny wanted to do it, too.

When she'd rushed out of her parents' house, she'd been more hurt and unhappy about what had transpired than she'd let on.

Moving away from home was a big deal, and she hadn't arrived at that decision entirely realistically. After she left the house, she drove around for an hour or so, brooding over the words she'd exchanged with them. A tiny voice inside her kept whispering that she was being irrational, hard-headed, spoiled. Why was she behaving this way?

Destiny knew part of the reason. Her mother had been infuriatingly close-mouthed about her real father all her life, and Destiny couldn't understand why. She could only imagine that her mother didn't think her strong or smart or competent enough to handle the information. Whenever she started asking questions, her mother withdrew even further. A friction had developed between them that just didn't seem fixable.

Destiny had finally stopped her car at the lookout station on the city side of the Golden Gate Bridge. She sat there wondering about her real dad and what kind of information Harvey Anderson would dig up. What if she had relatives alive somewhere? What if he found William Statler? Would he want to see her? Would his family care about her?

Destiny knew it was possible the guy wouldn't want to have anything to do with her. She was a stranger to him. That must have been why her mother had shielded her from any specific knowledge of him.

The young woman wrestled with her conflicting emotions. Collin was a good father to her. She should be satisfied. Some kids didn't even have that. Marco had a father, a real father, but they rarely spoke, and years of bitterness kept them worlds apart. At least Collin was civil. He was distant and not exactly expressive, but he cared about her. She should have left well enough alone.

But Destiny couldn't. She was too curious. She just hoped she hadn't started something she'd be sorry about later.

Her thoughts came back to the present, and Marco, as they walked down the street. She wondered what living with him would be like. She loved Marco, but the whole thing had happened very fast. She wasn't sure how much he loved her. He wasn't talkative about those things.

Marco was sometimes introspective and moody. He didn't always want her around, but he was getting better about that. His reaction when she'd asked to move in with him today had proved it. And he'd taken it a step further by letting her sing with his band again tonight. That had meant a lot to her. She had to work hard to fit into his group, but she was in it now, and Marco seemed to like having her there.

But even as he pulled her closer to him, Destiny felt scared. She shivered, as much from the cold as from her apprehension. Her battles with her mom were familiar ground. Now she was venturing into uncharted territory.

As if he had read her mind, Marco planted a kiss on her neck. Destiny breathed in his musky odor, remembering what he'd said earlier about being ready, and shook off her worries. She wanted to be with him, and she'd make it work.

Mom must have been in love with my real father when she was this young, Destiny thought. After all, she'd gotten pregnant, hadn't she? And despite her age, her mom had managed to make a good life for herself.

Well, she would do it, too. She'd show them all.

Alison and Collin made salads together, then ate them almost entirely in silence. The harshness of what had transpired had Alison's mind in a whirl, and she'd spent a good part of the evening staring at the lettuce on her fork.

Collin had had the good sense to leave her to her thoughts, and he took the opportunity to read the paper and catch up on the trades. But when the mantel clock chimed ten o'clock, he couldn't keep silent any longer and reached for her hand. "You've got to snap out of it, Ali. I've never seen you act like this before. You've been staring at the wall for hours. Why don't we go out for a cappuccino or at least a walk around the block?"

Alison saw the concern in his eyes but shook her head. "I know I'm not very good company tonight, and I'm sorry," she said, drawing on all her inner reserves to bring the sudden chaos of her life back into some semblance of order. "And you've got an important meeting tomorrow. You didn't need this to worry about tonight."

"We can't arrange for our family problems to happen at our convenience, Ali. And don't worry about my meeting, because that's not what's upsetting you. I think you're taking this fight with Destiny too much to heart. She's a teenager. This kind of thing happens all the time."

Alison's tired eyes burned. She felt her ire rise. "I know that, Collin. It's common as hell, and I shouldn't get upset about it. But this time it's happening to me, to my life, to my daughter, and I don't like it."

Collin's eyebrows shot up in surprise at the harsh tone of Alison's voice. "Hey, I'm not the enemy," he said, pulling back. "Don't get so hot about it. I'm trying to help, that's all."

He got up, threw the paper on the coffee table, and walked away, grumbling under his breath. "Women. I swear to God, I'll never understand them."

Alison winced and rushed after him. "I'm sorry," she repeated. "I didn't mean to be such a witch. You're right, of course. I'm taking all this too hard."

Collin eyed her quizzically, his angry stance relaxing. He wrapped his arm around her and guided her toward the bedroom. "I guess it's a mother's prerogative to get emotional, but it's not healthy to go overboard. I'm here for you, Ali. And like I told you earlier, even though Destiny says it doesn't matter anymore, I'm setting the paperwork in motion for her adoption. When she cools off, she might come to realize she wants it after all."

His hand slid down Alison's back to her bottom, and he caressed it gently, pulling her closer to him. "Don't think a little family friction is going to put me off, Ali," he reassured her. "I'm still serious about having a child."

Alison could only respond with a faint smile. She didn't have the heart to argue with him, or tell him that it was out of the question. Sex—not to mention another baby—was the farthest thing from her mind. All she could think about was holding on to the baby she already had. Still, Collin seemed intent on getting her aroused. He adjusted a night light so that it cast a golden glow over the bedroom.

"I love you, babe," he whispered. He kissed her neck gently, then rolled her over onto her stomach and began to massage her tight shoulders.

"Darling, I love you, too," Alison said softly, "but I don't think I'd be a very good partner tonight."

But Collin ignored her and nibbled her earlobe. "Oh, yes you can, Ali. Just close your eyes and let me take care of you."

Collin slowly peeled off her white nightgown. His lips followed the line of her spine as he caressed her buttocks. He rolled her over slowly, his eyes grazing over her body. Alison met his gaze, her own face a mixture of longing and denial. She started to shake her head no, but he would have none of it.

Grasping her slender waist, he buried his face in her soft belly, his hands reaching up to surround her breasts. Alison moaned her reservations again, but Collin didn't stop. He knew how to please her and continued to massage and rub until her breathing came faster, and the moans that escaped her mouth were now of pleasure rather than protest.

As his lips kissed her abdomen, searching slowly downward, Alison's body relaxed into him. She needed him now more than ever, and she forced the tumult of conflicting thoughts from her mind. Relinquishing all resistance, she grasped his head in her hands and pulled him closer. For the moment, at least, they were one.

Despite their tender lovemaking, Alison slept fitfully. She'd been awakened several times in the night by her recurrent nightmare, the lingering specter so real it made her nauseous again. She'd always feared that someone was watching her, following her. In her night-mares, Country appeared round every corner, menacing her.

By the time Alison rolled out of bed and into the kitchen the next morning, Collin was showered, shaved, and in his suit. She noticed his overnight bag and attaché case by the door, ready to go.

Yawning, she padded up to him. "Leaving already?"

Collin kissed her and handed her a cup of coffee. "I have an early flight. I would have canceled it, but this one's too big an account. The CEO would be offended if I didn't show."

"Of course you can't cancel. You've never missed the launch of a big account in your life, and I wouldn't expect you to!"

A frown crossed Collin's face. "Wait a minute. Is that reverse psy-chology, or are you actually trying to get rid of me?"

Alison laughed as she rooted around in the kitchen cabinet for an antacid. "You can say that with a straight face after last night?"

Collin shrugged, childlike.

Alison dropped the Alka-Seltzer tablet into a glass of water and watched it fizz. She gulped it down, hating the taste, hoping it would calm her stomach. She glanced at Collin standing there, so handsome in his suit.

A part of her regretted not being able to join him on this trip, but for the most part, she was glad he was leaving. She had to get a grip on the situation and figure out what to do. How would her loving husband react to all her secrets? Alison wondered if she would ever be able to tell Collin the truth.

This wasn't a nightmare she could wake up from. She was wide awake, and living it. Country was back. And she knew that by not confiding in Collin now, she was lying to him again.

She sipped her coffee.

Collin touched her cheek, a look of concern on his face. "He's not that bad, honey."

"Huh?" Alison bolted upright, confused.

"Destiny could've done worse, you know. Marco's a good guy."

"Oh, him." She felt her face flush. She wasn't thinking about Marco. Bile rose in her throat. Covering her mouth, she ran for the bathroom and vomited.

Collin followed her. "Are you going to be okay?"

Alison wiped her mouth with a towel and mopped the perspiration from her forehead. She was furious that she'd let her fear get the best of her and quickly turned on the shower.

"I think I caught a twenty-four-hour bug. Don't worry. I'll be fine."

"Are you sure?

"I took an Alka-Seltzer, remember? It didn't mix well with the coffee, that's all. Stop worrying and go. You'll be late." Alison dropped her robe down on her shoulders and forced her lips into a smile. "I'll be waiting right here when you get back."

Collin winked and Alison held her smile until he left the room. When she heard the front door close, her smile disappeared, and she rushed back to the toilet.

Harvey Anderson sat at his desk in the corner of the cozy living room of his house on Montezuma Road and dialed Destiny's number. The answering machine referred him to a different number, which he dialed. *Modern conveniences,* he thought, listening to the phone ring. You almost don't have to speak to a human being anymore if you don't want to.

A sleepy male voice answered, prompting Harvey to look at his watch. It was eight o'clock. Not too early, he decided.

"May I speak to Destiny Young, please?"

The male voice grunted something. Harvey heard static and muffled sounds as the phone was passed to someone.

"This is Destiny."

"Sorry to bother you so early, Miss Young. This is Harvey Anderson."

"Oh, hi, Mr. Anderson. I'm glad you called. Did you check your E-mail yesterday?"

"Yes, I did. But are you *sure* those are the exact dates? I'm going to do some more research today, and I wanted to verify them one more time."

"I know my birth date, Mr. Anderson. And my mom's."

Harvey rubbed his head. The girl thought he was insulting her intelligence. It was clear she didn't have anything new to add. But he pressed on, thinking she might remember some tidbit she'd left out.

"And what you've already told me about William Statler is all you know, correct?"

The girl let out a perturbed sigh. "Actually, you know everything I do, Mr. Anderson. Are you going to be able to find anything?"

"I'll give it my best shot, young lady. I'll let you know as soon as I do."

"Thanks. I'd really appreciate it."

"By the way, say hello to Mac McCauly for me," Harvey said as an afterthought. "Tell him thanks for the referral. I lost track of his address and phone."

There was a pause. Then Destiny said, "Well, I haven't actually met the man, but I'm living with his son. They don't talk very often."

That explained the male voice. Harvey assumed that the number she'd left on her answering machine was Marco McCauly's, and wondered when she had moved in with him. The last time he spoke to her, she was still living at home.

Harvey guessed there was friction between Destiny and her parents. Based on the surreptitious way Destiny had hired him, he wasn't surprised. He thanked her again and hung up the phone. Time to do a little scouting. Harvey would get his breakfast on the road.

Montezuma Road used to be a quiet, convenient street on which to live, but now it had become noisy and nearly always full of traffic. It was the gateway to San Diego State University, and because of the parking problems on campus, many students hauled bicycles on the backs of their cars, parked along this road, and pedaled to the campus. That kept the streets clogged with parked cars all day long. God forbid he and Bea ever wanted to throw a party. Zoning regulations also had been altered, and now the neighborhood included low-rent apartment complexes in which turnover was high and upkeep low.

Fortunately Harvey and Bea lived farther east, near the junction with El Cajon Boulevard, three blocks from Pep Boys and Uncle John's Pancake House. On Sundays, they sometimes walked the short distance to Uncle John's, stopping at the College Lutheran Church for a moment of spirituality on their way home.

Their simple two-bedroom house with a concrete patio and a small patch of grass in the backyard hadn't changed much, other than the family room add-on Bea had insisted on several years back. Bea was a formidable woman, and he tried not to cross her. She held an odd combination of political beliefs, having been raised a Republican as he was, but she preferred to be considered nonpartisan. She was vehemently pro-choice, which was unusual for her age group, and she was also supportive of affirmative action. Because she was not able to have children, Bea gave generously of her time to charitable institutions that benefited underprivileged kids, and was on the auxiliary at Sharp Hospital. Her curly brown hair had turned completely white over the last ten years, but her body was still toned and vital. Harvey adored her.

He said good-bye to Bea, who was watering the fuchsias and azaleas on their trellised patio, and headed down Montezuma toward College Avenue, continuing on to Interstate 8, heading west.

Harvey made a pit stop in Mission Valley. Across the freeway from the Sports Arena and one of San Diego's largest shopping centers was his favorite breakfast joint, Adam's. Harvey loved coming

here on a weekday when the lines weren't as long. He ate steak and
eggs at the counter and savored two of Adam's famous corn fritters.
Bea had offered to make him a protein shake and some oatmeal, but
he couldn't cope with that kind of punishment today.

As he sipped his last cup of coffee, he thought about the places
he wanted to check out. First he'd go to Naval Hospital to see if
Statler had ever had his appendix out or anything. Then he'd go on
to North Island, and after that to the Veterans Building. If he had
time, he would check out the library to see if he could get a hold of
the senior yearbooks from Patrick Henry, Grossmont, and Crawford
high schools.

But by three-thirty, after a long, tiring day mostly spent in his hot
car, Harvey had come up with precious little. Statler had never checked
into the Naval Regional Medical Center for any illness or surgery.

When he spoke with the records officer at the U.S. Naval Air Station on North Island, he was told he had to file a special request to
access information about soldiers who were reported missing in
action. To obtain it, he would need a notarized statement from a
family member.

He'd have to call Destiny.

By this time Harvey was bushed and decided to skip the Veterans
Building in La Jolla. Not only would it take him an hour to get there
in afternoon traffic, it was completely out of his way. Instead, he
headed back downtown and treated himself to a fish burger at the
McDonald's near Horton Plaza.

Later, at San Diego's main library on E Street, he found something tangible: all but one of the high school yearbooks. He scanned
through Crawford, Grossmont, University, even San Diego High,
and almost laughed when he discovered the picture he was searching
for wasn't in any of them.

I'm 0 for 0 today, Harvey thought. He deduced that William
Statler had attended Patrick Henry High, the one book the library
didn't have on hand.

The archivist on duty was a gentle lady in her seventies who seemed to know everything there was to know about the books in her library. She told Harvey that the Patrick Henry yearbooks for the years 1967 through 1970 had been checked out but were due back the next day, if he'd like to request them.

Harvey scribbled out a request form and told her he'd have them picked up. He flipped through the yearbooks again, this time looking for Alison Young's picture. He found it in the Grossmont High yearbook, graduating class of 1968.

She was a beautiful girl, yet the smile on Alison's face wasn't a happy one. That familiar face had a story to tell, and now, after such a fruitless day, Harvey was determined to find out what it was.

Collin checked the time as he crawled along in typical morning traffic on Gough Street. His plane took off in an hour, but he'd make it. He knew how long the drive would take; he'd traveled it a thousand times. Soon, he'd jump on the freeway heading through South San Francisco and on to the airport. He'd be there in twenty minutes if traffic wasn't backed up any more than it already was.

It was a good thing he was familiar with the road, because Collin wasn't paying attention to it. Something nagged at him, but he couldn't put his finger on it. Alison was acting very strange, and he wasn't convinced her behavior stemmed from the latest fight with Destiny. She certainly had a right to be upset about it, but he knew Alison. She handled problems in her life with much more control than she'd exhibited last night. Destiny was almost an adult, and both he and Alison would have to learn to deal with her on those terms.

Collin knew this latest episode had hurt Alison deeply. Maybe she was being so introspective because she thought she'd made some awful mistakes in the way she'd raised her daughter.

But she hadn't. He would have liked to say that he'd helped in the parenting of Destiny, but the truth was, by the time they'd gotten married, Alison had been a single mother for so long that she had difficulty sharing the job. Alison shouldered her responsibilities without compunction. Her determination and attention to detail were inspiring. That courageous nature was one of the characteristics Collin admired most about his wife. But it was also unsettling.

When they'd first met, she was living at his mother's house, in the garage apartment where he'd once lived. He thought Alison was charming, but not much more than a girl. A pregnant teenager, another sad casualty of the Vietnam War.

As he got to know her, however, he became intrigued. She was incredibly sage for her years, and in time he discovered that much of her wisdom had been earned the hard way. She had left home young and had been taking care of herself for a long time.

Though she had never divulged the extent of her parents' shortcomings, he surmised from her sketchy accounts that her father was an abusive alcoholic who, during his explosive, drunken rages, had physically abused Alison and her mother.

Alison had been reluctant to talk about her childhood at first. She had protected herself, kept parts hidden. Collin eventually understood that since her parents were both dead, she didn't want to sully their memory by dwelling on the bad times. That protectiveness, or possibly pride, had for a long time prevented her from revealing how she felt about him. They had a lot in common, because he behaved the same way.

He was drawn to her over the years and watched her blossom into a formidable woman. But her strength was intimidating. He'd been burned in love by a strong woman before, and that had left deep scars.

Collin thought back to his first real love, Laura Mason. Control and manipulation were her main attributes. When he met Alison, the self-assertiveness he saw in her reminded him of Laura, and he'd instinctively kept his distance. But the two women were worlds apart.

Alison was pure, kind, honest, and innocent. Laura was a liar, totally dishonest and self-serving.

Collin's jaw tightened. He guessed he hadn't completely gotten over the humiliation of his experience with her.

He didn't begrudge Laura her use of personal contacts to advance herself. That was business. But Laura had been manipulative in a cruel way. She used affection to lure him, and he took the bait. She'd succeeded in making him believe she loved him, when all along that was the furthest thing from her mind.

Collin had designed a brilliant advertising campaign for her line of cotton clothing. He'd named it Everywear, designed the packaging, set up the media-buying protocol, handled the entire program. The advertising community dubbed it spectacular.

But just as exciting to Collin was the fact that they were in love. In the middle of the design phase of the campaign, Laura got pregnant. She acted delighted and decided this was the perfect time for Collin to buy her a beautiful engagement ring, which he did. But she wanted to keep the pregnancy a secret from their friends. They would get married after the campaign had been fully launched, she told him.

The Everywear advertising campaign won every award and put Laura's company on the map. To add a personal touch, Collin had cleverly incorporated Laura's image into many of the ads. Her smiling face appeared in magazine after magazine, and the clothing line was beautiful. Laura's company wrote half a million dollars in orders at its first sales show in New York, and everyone attributed her initial success to her advertising firm. Collin was proud.

The airport was near. He pushed his foot down on the accelerator, picking up speed as he recalled what had happened next. While his career took off in a big way, his personal life began falling apart. As soon as Laura got what she wanted from him, she became a different woman. She started canceling dinners, not answering his phone calls, not being home. She began to avoid him completely. She was suddenly too busy.

Then she called him and announced she'd gotten an abortion. First he was shocked, then angry, then saddened. She hadn't consulted him. She told him it wasn't any of his business, that it was her body after all.

Collin had anticipated fatherhood with joy. To have that wrenched from him was more devastating than he'd ever imagined. He believed in a woman's right to choose, but he was in love with Laura. She was supposed to have been in love with him. How could she do this to him?

While he was still reeling from the news of the abortion, Laura abruptly broke off their engagement. Then she disappeared. Moved out of her apartment. Her office was awkwardly tight-lipped as to her whereabouts.

The next communication Collin received from Laura was in the form of a telegram from Switzerland. She had married a wealthy financier. Although Collin was bitterly hurt, he was no longer surprised. She'd left him for an older man who could give her the capital she needed to take her fledgling company to the next level. Apparently, that was all that mattered to her.

Collin shook his head vigorously. The memory still haunted him. He arrived at the airport and took his seat on the plane without paying attention to the bustle of activity around him. *Interesting that this memory should pop up now,* he thought. This was one loud and clear wake-up call. He'd never told Alison the whole story about Laura and how deeply she had wounded him.

All these years, Collin suddenly realized, *he* had been the one who was reluctant to have a child, not Alison. She had wanted to have a baby right after they were married, but his personal demons had moved him to put her off. Both his mother and Alison had broached the subject of adoption many times, but he had never taken it to heart.

As his plane headed for Napa, he resolved to make things right with his family, and that meant sharing more truths about himself. Gazing at the cottonlike cloud cover below him, Collin hoped he hadn't waited too long.

Chapter 5

COUNTRY FLICKED HIS CIGARETTE INTO THE MURKY BLACK water and polished off the rest of his beer. The morning had been productive so far. He had caught a glimpse of Destiny as she entered one of the school buildings for class. Her eyes were as blue as his. She was fine. A rare beauty, like Sara had been.

As the heat of the sun sent the rest of the fog scurrying out over the bay, Country began formulating his plan. He chucked his empty Coors can into the water to join the rest of the garbage and went inside. Ignoring the sleeping lump on the sofa, he pulled the phone into the bedroom and punched in Alison's number.

At home, Alison lay on the bed, waiting for her upset stomach to subside. She had dozed off when the phone rang, jerking her awake. Shaking the cobwebs from her brain, she rolled across the bed to answer it. "Hello?"

"Rise and shine, doll."

Alison breathed in sharply, now fully awake. "How'd you get this fucking number, Country?"

Country's voice was a thin, dry hiss. "I know everything about you, girl."

"What do you want?"

"It's time for us to get together, doll."

Alison's voice took on an animalistic growl. "Go to hell."

"I came by this morning, you know."

Alison sat up abruptly. She peered out the window and into the street, as if she could still see traces of the man's aura.

"Saw the man you're shacking up with," Country went on. "Saw him at his office, too. You'll have to get rid of him, you know."

Alison shivered involuntarily at his remark. "You're out of your mind, Country."

Country didn't respond at first. Alison heard him breathing hard over the phone. The hairs on her forearms stood up on end.

"I always get what I want," he finally said in a guttural whisper. "Don't try to fight me."

"Leave us alone, dammit!" Alison barked, her heart pounding. Country knew how to make her squirm. He listened to the silence on the phone line, then let out a deep, evil-sounding chuckle. "By the way, Destiny looks fine. A regular woman almost. I knew I'd be proud."

Alison's stomach lurched as she felt a new wave of nausea rising up in her. Fighting it, she leaped from the bed, dragging the phone with her. "You can't have seen her. It's not possible."

"Anything's possible. If you don't meet with me, I'll show you just what I mean. Think about it." The line went dead. Alison slumped into a chair, staring at the phone.

The Stinson Beach Bar was a popular place. The pseudo country-western haunt had been a local biker hangout for years because it was out of the way, served up a good beer, and for the most part was left alone by the local authorities.

Country took in the surroundings as he walked toward the entrance to the bar. A cluster of shiny road hogs parked over to one side made him feel right at home. The raw smell of oak trees, sage, and other underbrush reminded him of the unkempt, wooded areas in McKeesport, the small town near Pittsburgh where he grew up.

Not that he wanted to be reminded of those days. He was a different man now, ready to partake of a different kind of life. A life that should have already been his.

A frown creased his brow as he thought about Alison. But he soon relaxed. She would come around. Meanwhile, Destiny would be easy. He had her number. Music. That was her thing. Destiny wanted to make a career of singing with the leader of that band, Marco McCauly. He closed his eyes, picturing the boy behind the name. That punk had better not be laying his hands all over her. He envisioned the backseat of the dusty old Chevrolet down by the river all those years ago, and Sara. Sweet, innocent Sara. Country cracked his knuckles sharply and went inside the bar.

Slick Jackson was waiting behind the counter. Anyone seeing Slick for the first time would think twice before approaching him. He was a frightening man. Both arms were heavily tattooed, though it was hard to distinguish the designs through the furry tufts of hair that covered them. Hair covered most of his body. His head, however, was kept as bald as a billiard ball.

Large and muscular, Slick had been the drug jockey of Country's private entourage in San Diego. He either possessed or had instant access to a host of mind-altering drugs. When Country got busted, Slick became the guardian of Country's money and moved to Marin County, along with several other bikers from the group. Though many years had passed, there was never a doubt that Country would show up one day to collect what was his. No one would cross him. His strength and his penchant for extreme behavior were legend and respected.

Slick let out a low whistle when Country entered. "Hot damn! You're looking good, man."

A movement near a door behind the bar caught Country's eye. "Who's back there?"

"Last night's squeeze. I was breakin' her in for ya," Slick said, chuckling and scratching his crotch. "That's the office, but it's got a bed in it. It's yours."

Country walked around the bar and pushed the door open. A young redheaded woman stood near the small bed, trying awkwardly to cover herself with a sheet. Her voluptuous body was sticking out all over. Country stared at her red-painted toes and worked his way up her body, stopping briefly at the center, where a dark auburn patch showed through the thin white veil of sheeting. His clear blue eyes grabbed her line of vision and held it.

She cleared her throat, embarrassed, and tried to rearrange the sheet, but it slipped down, revealing her left breast. Country moved toward her, snatched the sheet away, and examined her body.

The woman shrank back, shivering as she shifted from foot to foot. Country watched her fidget. She didn't know what to do with her hands. She tried covering her breasts, then moved them over her pubic area, then back to her breasts. Finally, as her face turned as red as her hair, she put her hands behind her back and just stood there, looking at him. Without taking his eyes off her, he wrapped the sheet around her, his hands purposely touching her nipples.

"Better get back in that bed, little gal, or you'll catch somethin'."

She nodded mutely. Country left the room, a smirk on his face.

Slick handed him a beer. "Cute, ain't she? Name's Charlene."

"You always did know how to bring home the bacon."

"I aim to please, man," Slick said.

Country sat down at the bar and tossed back his brew. Glancing around at the stage and dance floor, he tapped out a cigarette and lit it. "I have a singer I want you to hire."

Slick grinned. "You fucking a country singer now? Christ! Didn't take you long to get back in the saddle."

Country flashed a steely look at Slick that immediately wiped the smile from his ugly face. Flustered, Slick raised his hands. "Okay. Fuck, man, relax."

Country pulled hard on his smoke. "I want her to audition alone."

Slick shrugged. "Is her pussy worth all the trouble?"

This time Country didn't turn his head toward Slick, just his eyes. He narrowed them into snakelike slits and stared at him, speaking quietly. "Don't fuckin' question me, man. I got too many fucking people questioning me." The muscles in his face tensed. Slick coughed and spat on the floor, edgy.

Suddenly a bird flew into the bar through the open double doors and fluttered helplessly in the space above the pool table, trapped.

Country looked at it, grabbed a pool cue off the wall, and swung it through the air a few times, trying to chase the bird back out the door. Confused, the bird dipped down from the rafters, flapping its wings frantically.

"Fuck it," Country muttered. "You had your chance."

With extraordinary dexterity, he whipped the pool cue through the air once, whacking the bird like a baseball and killing it instantly. It landed on the counter in front of Slick, its head crushed.

Slick recoiled. Country put the cue away and calmly lit a cigarette. "Which day you closed?"

"We're always open for the regulars, man. These bikers'd kill me if I locked 'em out."

"I need you to close the place down for a night."

"That's gonna be a bitch, but I guess I can say I'm taking inventory or some other bullshit."

"Set up a meeting with a chick named Destiny Young."

"'Scuse me?"

"Get one of your 'music' guys to call her. Somebody who can put on a good act. He can say he's with Stinson Records or whatever bullshit he can cough up, but he's got to get her to come to the bar alone. Then I'll take over. It'll be a *private* audition. Understand?"

Slick nodded. Country reached into his pocket, took out a piece of paper with Destiny's number scribbled on it, and shoved it toward him. "Now bring me a joint," he rasped, heading for the back room. "I'm gonna get to know Charlene."

Harvey entered the Adobe Restaurant and spotted the man he'd come to meet. Dave Sanchez was seated at a table in the corner, digging into a bowl of tortilla chips.

Harvey greeted his old buddy. "How's it going, Dave? Did you order?"

"Yeah. Cheese-and-chicken enchilada combos for both of us. Okay with you?"

"Why not? I love that greasy stuff. Bea never lets me order cheese enchiladas without giving me nasty looks and warning me about how it's gonna kill me one day."

Harvey let his body fall into the green vinyl-upholstered seat. He reached for a tortilla chip and dunked it into the spicy salsa in the bowl beside it. Stuffing it into his mouth, he let out a satisfied moan.

Dave poked him good-naturedly. "Good thing she never comes to watch the two of us bowl. She'd have a fit."

Harvey laughed at the thought. "She's just trying to keep me alive a little longer, that's all."

"At least you'll bite the dust with a full stomach," Dave said, reaching into a canvas satchel on the seat beside him. He pulled out a folder and pushed it toward Harvey. "Here's what I've got so far from the old station files. It's all on the Davis family and the Youngs. I didn't come up with anything more on your man Statler."

Harvey cursed under his breath and opened the folder. He pulled out several photocopies, newspaper clippings, and a police mug shot of Charles Country Davis. Then he saw an article about Destiny and her mother.

He shuffled through the bits and pieces on Davis's family and came across a clipping stapled to a school photo of a teenage girl. Harvey picked up the article and stared at it.

"My cousin works in records," Dave was saying. "She got a friend in Pittsburgh to dig this up. The girl and her boyfriend were killed when the car they were making out in went into the Allegheny River."

"They were just kids," Harvey mumbled. He wondered where Country had been that night. "What about the mother?" he asked.

"Local call girl. It's all there in the file, you'll see for yourself. Couple of busts for pandering and drunk and disorderly conduct. Not a pretty picture, Harv."

Harvey didn't answer. He studied the photo of Country's sister. The uncanny resemblance between Destiny and the dead girl made the skin on his neck prickle with goosebumps.

"Thanks for getting this stuff, Dave. I owe you for this one." Harvey held the files up off the table as the waitress plopped two huge platters of food in front of them. "I hate to push my luck, but did you locate the facility that's storing my old files?"

Dave polished off his margarita. "Yeah, and I've asked the loading clerk to send them over to your office this afternoon. To my attention, of course. You know we're not supposed to let you have that stuff, Harv."

"I know, and I appreciate it. If I wasn't losing my memory, I wouldn't need them. Hell, if it's not in my computer, I'm lost. I need written notes for every damn thing. Bea gets so irritated with me, tells me I'd forget my head if it wasn't permanently attached. Must be getting old." Harvey stuffed a huge forkful of enchilada into his mouth.

Dave laughed. "Getting old? Hell, you've been old for years. But even if you weren't, Harv, the file you want is at least nineteen years old. I don't remember anything from nineteen years ago. How could *you?*"

Harvey grimaced. "Easy for you to say. Nineteen years ago, you weren't even shaving."

He glanced at the items in the file in front of him again, then closed it up and pushed it aside. He didn't want to look at them now. Too much to assimilate. Anyway, the enchiladas were getting cold, and there was nothing less appetizing than cold cheese-and-chicken enchiladas.

After lunch, Harvey drove back to his office, unsettled. All this digging into his old files could turn out to be a waste of time. The girl's mother's life wasn't any of his business. So what if the woman had had some run-in with an ex-con? It was ancient history. And so what if the ex-con happened to be moving to the same town? San Francisco was a big city, after all. Like Gerri said, it was probably just a coincidence and shouldn't be his concern if it didn't help locate information on Destiny's real father.

Harvey was annoyed that Dave hadn't come up with anything new on William Statler. If the man was still alive, which seemed unlikely, there was no record of him resurfacing in the States. And if there was any interesting information on him, neither he nor Dave had managed to uncover it.

According to the information he'd retrieved earlier, Statler had been an orphan. A ward of the state. Abandoned at birth, with no family at all. Wasn't much to tell Destiny, and he was sure it wasn't what she wanted to hear anyway.

Still, the story didn't hold water. If Statler had been an orphan as his records indicated, why would Alison Young have kept his name off Destiny's birth certificate? Who was she trying to protect?

Harvey glanced at his watch as he pulled into a parking spot in front of his office. It was three o'clock. Gerri was leaving early to drive up to a family reunion in San Bernardino, and he should go home and pack. He had a long drive ahead of him tonight.

Months ago, he'd reluctantly agreed to accompany Bea to the annual Thimble Collectors convention, which was being held this year in Santa Rosa. He hadn't wanted to go. But she told him there were great wineries in Napa Valley, and that after the three-day convention was over, they could go on a wine-tasting tour. She had kissed him and smiled her demure little I'll-make-it-worth-your-while smile, and that convinced him.

What the hell, why not? All these years Bea had stuck by him, put up with the anxiety inherent in being married to a cop, yet never asked him to quit. They'd had precious few vacations. Why shouldn't they have a romantic weekend together?

As it turned out, the trip was a blessing in disguise. He could combine it with his work. Going to the Bay Area gave him a chance to meet with his client, though he'd probably break all his own rules and meet with the client's mother first. He wasn't sure if it was ethical or not, but something told him it was the right thing to do. Maybe the two of them could sit down together and hash it all out, face-to-face. If Statler was indeed dead, with no living relatives, Destiny's search might end right there.

If there was more to the story, he wanted to know it. A hunch told him that handing over the information to Destiny might cause a huge mess. So while Bea was peddling her thimbles in Santa Rosa, Harvey planned to poke around San Francisco.

Gerri was at her desk, typing up a note when Harvey walked in. She stopped and handed him a large manila envelope.

"This package was just delivered for you. Must be the files you were waiting for. Here's the phone number and address of where I'll be in case you need me. I should be back late Monday afternoon."

Gerri got up to hand him the piece of paper. Her clothing rustled enough to send waves of today's bargain perfume into Harvey's nose. Hawaiian Plumeria. The combination of the strong scent and a stomach full of Mexican food was almost too much for him to take.

"Thanks, Gerri. Have a good time."

"You too," she said, pulling on her sweater. "You didn't forget about your weekend with Bea, did you?"

Harvey pretended to be hurt. "Oh, come on! I'm not *that* bad. Of course I remembered. I just came up here to get these," he said, smacking the files, "and to make a phone call. I forgot to tell Dave Sanchez that I'll be gone for the weekend. I have to give him the number of the hotel in case he needs to reach me."

"Oh. I almost forgot to tell you," Gerri interjected. "I picked up those high school annuals for you. They're on my desk."

Harvey looked up at her and smiled. "Great. Now do me a favor and leave. If you wait much longer, you'll hit traffic."

"I'm going. Just take care, will you? You never know what can happen with domestic investigations."

Harvey grumbled as she hurried out the door. All he needed was another woman fretting over what he did. But after Harvey dialed Dave's number, he rummaged through his file drawer all the way to the back. He pulled out a box and unlocked it. Inside was a .45 and a carton of bullets. He knew he should bring them along on this trip.

Dave wasn't home, so Harvey left a message on his answering machine. He glanced at the clock. He had time. He popped open a Diet Coke, opened a new bag of corn nuts, and brought the high school yearbooks over to his desk. He started with 1968.

Destiny got out of school at three and drove to a coffeehouse on Union Street. She sat down in a booth and pulled out her notebook. She was studying her class notes so intently that she didn't notice Country take a seat across from her.

"Hi, doll," he said pleasantly.

Startled, Destiny looked up from her notebook. "Sorry, but I'm waiting for a girlfriend," she said almost as a reflex.

Country smiled but didn't leave. "Hey, ain't you a famous singer? I saw you in the paper, didn't I?"

Destiny blushed, then straightened in her chair, brushing her brown curls back from her face. "I'm a singer all right, but I'm not famous. Just getting started, actually."

"But you were in the papers, right? Isn't your name Destiny?"

"Yeah, that was me. My first gig."

"Well, you got great reviews, lady. This is some coincidence I should run into you."

Country extended his hand across the table. "Country Davis. I own the Stinson Beach Bar. I'm looking for a female singer. You might be the one."

Destiny's eyes opened wide, registering her surprise, and she eagerly took his hand. His grip was strong and warm and his arms were muscular and tattooed. She liked him instantly. Especially his tattoo.

"Nice to meet you," she said brightly. "This is really cool."

"I've got friends at MCA Records, and I think they might be interested in you, too."

"God, this is great!" Destiny squealed. "I can't believe it! Wait'll I tell Marco!"

Country pursed his lips and shook his head. "Better keep it to yourself for now, honey. You'd be surprised how competitive my world is. The less you tell people about it, the better. Until you make a deal, that is."

Destiny's excitement was mounting. "Are you talking about a record deal?"

"I want you to audition for a gig at my place. But like I said, I got friends at MCA. If you're as good as the reporter says, you could have yourself a career. How's that sound?"

"Rockin'! Exactly what I want!"

"Give me your number. I'll talk to the A&R guy I know and have him set something up with you. But remember what I said. Don't mention me to anyone. I don't want to find myself in a bidding war over you before we get to first base, understood?"

Destiny smiled conspiratorially. "No problem."

Country rose from the booth and reached for Destiny's chin, holding her head still as he looked into her eyes. "You sure are a pretty little thing, Destiny. I'll bet that voice of yours will bring the house down."

Destiny blushed again, and he finally released her.

"Thanks, Mr. Davis."

"Call me Country. Everyone does."

Destiny nervously crossed and recrossed her legs, her black combat boots banging the pole under the table. She was exploding inside, but she tried to keep her cool, not wanting this important executive to know she was really a novice.

"I'm psyched that you'd offer to set me up for an audition. I mean, God! What a break. The Stinson Beach Bar is really a happening place."

"Glad to help out, Destiny. And say, if you ever feel like talking, I go to the Lost and Found Saloon to check out new bands every now and then. Feel free to drop by. Meantime, I'll have my guy contact you as soon as he sets things up. Bye, doll."

Destiny grinned as she watched him stroll out of the coffeehouse. *Things are looking up!* she thought. If only her mother could see her now.

Chapter 6

THE *HERS* OFFICES WERE ACTIVE AND HUMMING LIKE A WELL-oiled machine. As Alison walked down the hallway, staffers looked up from their desks, smiled at her, then promptly went back to work. Business as usual. Hers was a familiar face, of course, and her strolls through the halls commonplace. There were now more than a hundred employees at the magazine, a fact of which she was quite proud.

After reaching her own office, Alison sat down and tried to focus on the blue-line copy spread out in front of her. One of this month's contributing editors had written a fabulous piece on successful women artists, the highlight being an interview with a famous eighty-year-old ceramist from Ojai. Much as Alison appreciated the woman's work, she couldn't get through the article. Her secretary, Mariah, walked in with a new design for the political forum masthead and placed it on her already crowded desk, saying the art department needed the go-ahead by the end of the day. Alison looked at her balefully and returned to the copy in front of her.

When the phone rang, she jumped. She peered out her door and saw that Mariah had stepped away from her desk. Alison answered the phone. "Hello."

Heavy breathing. It became a rattling cackle, and her muscles tensed. It was him again. "Piss off," she growled.

"Yeah, talk dirty to me, baby. Gets me hot."

"You're disgusting."

"Destiny thinks I'm wonderful."

Alison bit her balled fist to keep from screaming into the phone. "Liar!" she hissed.

"Soon she'll learn how bad you've been. Do as I say, Ali. I'm *never* gonna leave you or Destiny alone."

"Please," Alison said, her brain searching for some kind of plan. "I need time to absorb all this."

"Your time is up, bitch. I'll be in touch."

The line went dead.

It was several moments before Alison noticed the annoying tone of the disconnected line. She replaced the receiver, her eyes brimming with tears of frustration. She had to warn Destiny that she might have recently met someone who was a raving lunatic. He might be persuasive, might seem to have all the answers, might appear to be normal, but he was really a monster.

Alison felt damp underneath her clothes, as if she'd just broken into a feverish sweat. *What am I going to say to her?* she wondered. She glanced at the clock on her desk, thinking that Destiny was probably not back from school yet. She called Marco's place anyway. At the very least, she could leave an urgent message.

"McCauly's," the voice answered on the other end of the line.

Alison pressed the phone closer to her ear, shocked at the sound of the girlish voice she knew so well.

"Destiny," Alison whispered, forcing calm into her quivering voice. "Thank God you're there. It's Mom."

There was a long pause. "You're so melodramatic, Mom. I know it's you. I do recognize your voice, you know. What's up?"

"I need to talk to you."

"This is not a good time."

"Destiny, please. I know you're mad at me. I know I probably overreacted in the office yesterday, but I have to warn you about someone. Someone who may have approached you. I'm worried about you being around strangers. There's a lot you don't know—"

Her daughter groaned. "That's right, Mom. You think I don't know anything. But you're wrong. I can take care of myself. Don't be so weird. I hate it when you treat me like a baby. Have a little faith in me for a change. I know what I'm doing."

Alison held the phone tightly, her eyes closed. How could she caution her? What could she say? Everything that came out of her mouth sounded so inane now.

"I'm sorry about our fight, Destiny," she said finally. "I love you. I'm just trying to protect you."

"You keep saying that, Mom, but you have to stop! There's nothing to protect me from! I'm not five anymore. There's lots of people out in this world who can give me advice, you know. Not just you! I don't want to fight about this again. I've got finals and a few other *personal* things I'm working on. I'm responsible. I can make decisions. You'll see. Maybe in a few days, after everybody cools off, we can get together."

Destiny hung up. Alison wilted into her chair. A wolf in sheep's clothing was stalking her daughter, and in some ways, Alison had helped put him there.

Destiny's youthful face smiled at her from the silver-framed photo on her desk. Sadly, Alison suddenly realized that Destiny didn't need her anymore. Her daughter had decided she could take care of herself. *A naive notion,* Alison thought. When she was the same age, she had believed she could take care of herself, too, but had been bitterly disappointed. She'd been a lamb in the wild.

Now, a lifetime later, the same danger was lurking about her daughter, but his true identity was obscured. Alison was aware that the most dangerous foe often attacked the mind, not the body. This psychological twist would be how Country would gain her confidence. How could Destiny fight that? Would she want to? Country could easily convince Destiny that he could give her what she so desperately wanted: a connection to her real father.

The phone line lit up, and Mariah's voice broke Alison's reverie. "Collin, line four."

Alison stared down at the blinking light. Collin seemed light years away from her now. Taking a deep breath and unconsciously pushing stray hairs into place, she picked up the handset. "Hi, Collin."

"From the tone of your voice, I'd say you still don't feel very well. Am I right?"

Alison's voice was flat. "Not at all. I'm much better," she lied. "Was your meeting successful?"

"Forget my meeting, Alison. Jesus. You sound about as personal as someone at the dentist's office! What the hell is going on?"

"For heaven's sake, Collin. Nothing! Everything is status quo down here. I'm busy working, that's all. Sorry I sounded so distant."

"So, how's Destiny? Have you two talked, at least?"

Alison fumbled again, reluctant to share any more of the turmoil with him. "Yes, uh, we spoke."

Collin was silent for a second. "And? Look, Alison. I don't know what's wrong with you, but I feel like I'm the odd man out here. I have to pry every tidbit of information out of you. The last few days you've been acting like someone I don't know."

"Don't put all the blame on me, Collin. I'm dealing with a few complicated issues right now, if you'll recall. I'm upset about Destiny moving out, and I don't think you know what that means to me."

"Of course I don't if you won't share it with me! Why are you being so evasive? Am I missing something? I waited for you to call, but of course you didn't. If I hadn't called you, we wouldn't have spoken at all."

"Collin. I don't feel very well, and I've been working. Nothing is different—"

He grunted. "Yeah, right."

Alison felt the room twisting out of focus around her. Her brow was glistening with sweat. "Listen, I have two calls on hold, and I really don't know what you're getting so fired up about. Can't we discuss this when you get back?"

"I think we'd better, Ali," her husband replied crisply. "Something's going on, and I want to know what it is."

Alison hung up as a bolt of pain shot through her head. She should have told him.

Alison knew she should notify the police and report Country's calls, but instead she cleaned up her desk, then left her office. She was in denial, she knew. Part of her hoped she had somehow misconstrued the conversations, that she was somehow mistaken about the threats.

Once again, she stalked the corridors, checking in with each department, wearing a plastered-on smile. Assistants handed her memos as she made her way down the hall, but she barely realized she had taken them. She was on automatic pilot. One of her editors asked a question about the new features and held up a suggested lead-in for the health section. Alison looked right through her. "Leave it on my desk," she managed to croak.

Alison finally realized that any attempt to escape her situation today was a lost cause. Passing by Destiny's old workstation brought on another huge dose of guilt. Maybe after all this blew over, she could convince Destiny to come back. Alison returned to her office, knowing it was just a pipe dream. Destiny didn't want to be here.

Mariah had put on her sweater and was getting ready to leave for the day. "I have a couple of messages for you, Alison. A Mr. Anderson called and said something about setting up a meeting."

"Who's he? I don't recognize the name."

"I thought you knew. Sorry. Oh, and Collin called again. He told me to let you know he'd be home later tonight than he thought."

Alison's shoulders slumped. She rubbed the back of her neck, feeling a knot of tension building.

Mariah looked at her, concerned. "Something wrong, Alison?"

"I'm coming down with the flu," she replied quickly, rubbing her temples. "Is there anything else?"

Mariah handed her a sealed envelope with "Ali" written on the front. "A courier brought this up a few minutes ago."

Alison stared at the envelope.

"Well, hope you feel better," her secretary said, picking up her purse. "I'll see you tomorrow."

"Thanks." Alison went into her office and closed the door. Only a few people addressed her as "Ali," and she knew their handwriting. She tore open the envelope and pulled out the piece of paper inside. The color quickly drained from her face.

"I spoke to Destiny after school today," the note read. "She's the perfect combination of us. The next time I see her I'll tell her who I am. Won't that be great? But first I want to see you. There are a few family matters we need to work out. Meet me at the St. Francis bar at eight o'clock tonight. Don't be late."

It was signed "Country."

Chapter 7

COUNTRY WAS ANTSY. HE RAN HIS TONGUE OVER HIS NEWLY bonded and capped front teeth, enjoying the sensation. The dentist, a friend to local bikers, knew how to get the job done quickly and painlessly. It wouldn't be long before the rest of Country would undergo a transition as well.

He glanced impatiently toward the dock and saw that Jake had finally returned with the stuff he'd ordered. About fucking time.

Jake tossed the large paper bag at Country as he jumped onto the houseboat. "Jesus, what a pain in the ass. I had to go to three different stores to get this shit!"

Country said nothing and went inside to the small bedroom and shut the door. He dumped the contents of the bag onto the bed next to the newspaper article. He paused to study the photo of Alison and the kid.

Soon, he thought. *Soon.*

He stripped down and gazed at himself—lean, muscular, pumped. He flexed his arms, inspecting his rock-hard biceps and forearms. Scars from knife wounds and cigarette burns marked his arms and chest, forming a morbid, sadistic map of the activities in his life. Some he'd acquired at Folsom, but most were self-inflicted. Country didn't feel pain, at least not easily. He enjoyed watching other people squirm, smelling charred flesh as he burned himself. He could do it without even flinching.

Burns and knife scars were not the only identifying points on his body map. The serpent tattoo was a predominant feature, and his arms also bore the purple-colored pockmarks of a regular user.

Country took a razor from the pile of items Jake had retrieved and went to work on his facial hair. Next, he used the professional scissors to chop his hair into a chin-length shag. He exchanged his gold loop earring for a small diamond one. Then he put on the new clothes. The slacks, sports jacket, and lizard-skin cowboy boots suited him fine. He studied himself in the mirror. It had worked. The transformation was complete.

Right out of *GQ* magazine.

When he emerged, Jake did a double-take.

Country took in the cluttered pigsty of a living room and glared at Jake. "Clean up this shithole. It stinks worse than the fuckin' joint."

Jake lit a roach. "Jesus, you're jumpy. Have a joint, man. Chill out."

Country fixed his steely eyes on Jake once more. Jake returned the gaze only briefly, then immediately rolled off the couch and started picking up the empty Coors cans. Country cracked his neck, grabbed the keys to Jake's truck, and pushed open the door. "I'm takin' your wheels."

When Alison arrived home, she was both surprised and dismayed to see Collin's car parked out front. Their quarrel had added another dimension to her uneasiness. Her hands became clammy as she realized she'd have to lie *again* to Collin to get out of the house alone. More lies. Her life was built on them. How could she end the cycle and keep her world from slipping through her fingers?

Her heart thumped as the adrenaline pumped up her system. "Hi. I didn't expect to see you home," she said lamely to Collin as she entered the small alcove of their townhouse.

"I thought it would be prudent of me to catch the early flight after all," Collin explained, an edge to his voice, his face a rigid stare. "Are you disappointed? Were you hoping for a little more time alone?"

Alison was suddenly aware of the strained expression on her face. "Of course not. It's just that—well, I have an appointment tonight, and it's one I can't cancel. I thought you'd be home late, so I didn't think it would matter."

Collin took her hand. He was silent, clearly angry. Alison could see the muscles in his cheeks move as he clenched and unclenched his teeth. "I don't get it. We have some serious issues to deal with, and frankly, you act like they don't matter at all. Can't your meeting be put off until tomorrow?"

Alison felt as if her head would explode. The stress of trying to maintain her equilibrium was more than she could bear.

She extricated her hand from Collin's grasp, a mixture of apology and desperation on her face. "It's too important, and I'm already late. I have no way of reaching them now, and it would be rude and unprofessional not to show up. You know I can't do that. *You* wouldn't."

Collin rubbed his eyes, weary from the flight, the long day, the fighting. "So is that what this is about? Are you getting back at me now for being a workaholic?"

"Don't be ridiculous," Alison retorted. "I don't think you're a workaholic. I just have a meeting I can't get out of. Why are you so upset about it?"

She turned and rushed down the hall, calling back loudly, "These Malaysians hate tardiness! Christ!"

In the bedroom, Alison stripped off her work suit and pulled a pair of slacks and a blazer from the closet. Out of the corner of her eye, she saw herself in the bureau mirror and was shocked at the pallor of her skin. Collin appeared, blocking the doorway.

"You're not acting like the woman I know, Ali. Talk to me, for God's sake!"

Alison took a deep breath and faced him. "There's nothing to talk about. I'm . . . I'm trying to keep all my plates spinning right now . . ." Her voice trailed off as images of her past took center stage. She felt Collin's eyes burning into her, sensing that she was withholding something, but she couldn't bring herself to tell him what it was.

"I don't mean to upset you, Collin, but dammit, no matter what, that seems to be all I do lately."

"I don't want to fight with you, Ali. But that's all we've been doing. Can't Kelly or Sally cover this meeting for you?"

"No!" Alison could feel every muscle in her face grow tight. "I'm just stressed about the time. You know I hate to be late. Kelly has other obligations tonight, and Sally's out of town. I *have* to handle it."

Collin sighed heavily. "Fine." He took his jacket out of the closet. "I'll go with you, then. After your meeting, we can go someplace and have a heart-to-heart talk. I think we owe each other that. In eight years of marriage, we've never been so disjointed."

Alison wanted to cry. Instead, she reached for Collin's arm and pulled him to her. She kissed him, but her lips were cold. Collin recoiled.

She forced a smile to her lips and tried to stay calm. "You can't come. It's with our Malaysian partners' financial majordomo," she lied, "and he's not bringing his wife. You know how these things are. I'll come home as soon as I can, then we'll talk."

Collin knew Alison was manipulating him. She was hiding something from him, for sure. The notion that she might be having an affair dawned on him, and the very thought hurt him deeply.

He'd learned earlier today that he had to go to Seattle tomorrow. He had hoped he and Alison could talk things through tonight, but as she hurried out the front door, he was no closer to understanding their conflict than he was when it all began.

As Alison yanked open the door of the Audi, Collin's mother, Anna, suddenly pulled up behind her. Alison groaned. *Oh, God. Just what I needed,* she thought. Dear, sweet Anna. The woman was in her seventies but had the spunk and verve of a fifty-year-old. Anna Archer was an important force in Alison's life and, under other circumstances, would have been a welcome sight.

But now wasn't the time for a family chat. Anna was even more intuitive than Collin. The woman's appearance only served to make Alison feel even more ashamed of what she was doing.

Alison glanced at her watch. Almost seven-thirty. She had to leave. She was afraid of what Country would do if she didn't show up on time. One more lie wasn't going to change things now, she reasoned. She rushed over to her mother-in-law's car.

"Didn't know you were coming, Anna," Alison said breathlessly, leaning in to kiss the woman, who smelled of lavender. "I'm sorry, but I'm late for a meeting!"

Anna regarded her carefully, perceiving as always Alison's underlying emotions. "It must be a very important meeting, dear, and one you're not looking forward to. You look like you've got the world on your shoulders. I hope you're not overworking yourself."

Alison knew Anna sensed her fear. Next to Kelly, her mother-in-law was the closest person to her, even closer than Collin in some ways. Anna had rescued Alison at a time when safe harbors were hard to find. It was through her that Alison had met Collin, the love of her life. She suddenly felt guilty as hell lying to this woman again.

Alison's hands were moist from nervousness, and she quickly rubbed them dry on the back of her navy blue slacks. She gazed into her mother-in-law's eyes with a look that begged for understanding. "You know how I feel about work, Anna."

Anna got out of the car, pulled her sweater tighter around her, and adjusted the cornflower blue fabric of her dress. Loose tendrils of snow-white hair that had escaped her cinnamon-bun hairdo blew gently around her face, and she batted them aside, smiling with worried eyes at the woman who was like a daughter to her.

She knew Alison wasn't being truthful but allowed her the freedom to hide it, as she had done for the past nineteen years. There had always been something secretive about Alison. As a lonely, pregnant eighteen-year-old, Alison had put on a brave smile, acting as if she had the strength of a woman twice her age. But Anna had known that there was more to Alison's story than she divulged.

With a knowing nod, Anna said, "I know you take your work seriously, Alison dear, but don't let it get to you. Stand your ground."

Alison hugged her gratefully. "I love you, Anna. You always know what to say."

"I'll go visit with Collin for a while," Anna said cheerfully. "See you later."

Alison jumped into her car and peeled away from the curb. As she gunned the motor of her Audi, the only thing on her mind was getting to the St. Francis Hotel by eight o'clock to meet a man she hated.

Anna settled on the sofa, holding a cup of tea spiked with just a spot of brandy to take the chill off. Collin watched his mother pull out her compact and try to stuff her wayward curls back into her bun. He wandered back into the kitchen. He needed a beer.

Reaching into her satchel, Anna took out a large needlepoint canvas and began to thread a long strand of forest green yarn onto her needle. The tension in the townhouse was so thick it felt like steam. She wondered what had transpired between Alison and Collin but kept silent, waiting. She gazed at the family photograph, which sat gleaming in its sterling silver frame on the fireplace, and felt a stab of sadness. Alison was in pain, she knew. And so was Collin. Anna felt deeply for both of them.

Years ago, when Alison appeared on her doorstep to rent the garage apartment, Anna had been delighted and took to the young woman right away. The fact that Alison was pregnant was an added bonus. Anna had become happily territorial, acting as if the baby were her own grandchild, and she had forever treated Destiny that way.

Anna sighed, realizing Collin was not going to start the conversation. She put down her needlepoint and took off her glasses.

"What's wrong, Collin?" Anna blurted out, her face a map of worry lines. "Alison didn't seem like herself, and neither do you, for that matter."

Collin had returned from the kitchen sipping a Corona Light and was staring out the large picture window to the bay beyond. He grunted something indistinguishable.

"Collin? Did you hear me?"

"I'm sorry, Mom. I wish I could give you an answer, but I don't know myself. This has been a strange couple of days. Alison's having a rough time with Destiny."

Anna's eyebrows shot up, and she leaned toward him. "Don't you mean *you* and Alison are having a rough time with Destiny? This is a family, isn't it?"

Collin looked at her, chagrined. "Yes, of course it is. You know that's what I mean."

"Where is Destiny?"

"She moved in with Marco. She and Alison had a blow-out at work. Destiny's been trying to find out about her real father, and it's caused nothing but anger and hurt between them."

Anna sighed. "Destiny's a rebel, just like her mother was. But despite all outward appearances, she has her head on straight. She's nearly eighteen. She's probably ready to try things on her own."

"But Alison's not ready, Mom."

"She might never be. It hasn't been easy for her. She was a single parent for so long. Letting go will be tough. I had a feeling something like this would happen one day."

Collin paced the living room. "I made matters worse. I brought up the subject of having another baby a few weeks ago, and I think Destiny's probably resentful of that. I told her I wanted to adopt her, but she wasn't thrilled with the idea."

He watched his mother carefully, dreading what she was going to say.

"Odd sense of timing, Collin," she said gently, shaking her head. "Of course she'd be resentful. I've always thought you should adopt Destiny, and I tried to tell you so many times. In my heart, she's my granddaughter no matter what you do, but to Desi, that gesture would have meant a lot. I never could understand your reluctance. Life is now, my dear. Don't put it off till later. Later might not come, and you could find yourself with regrets."

Anna absentmindedly wiped her glasses on the hem of her dress, then looked directly into her son's eyes. "I know about regrets, dear," she continued. "I will always regret not having another child, and only too late I realized it was nobody's fault but mine. I was foolish to think I could place all the blame of such a weighty decision on your father's shoulders. That was a cop-out on my part. We are all given choices, Collin. It is up to us to make them. We hope we don't make the wrong ones, that's all, and if we do, we have to be willing to make the appropriate corrections."

Collin stared at her, humbled by his mother's bluntness and clarity. As a youngster, he remembered his father was the one who doled out all the opinions. He had run the family with an old-fashioned autocratic strictness. His mother's thoughts and ideas were almost totally ignored. The relationship between his parents had been one of chilly tolerance. Collin always felt that they were silently serving out some awful prison sentence together. Because of their example, the idea of marriage had been repugnant to him for a long time.

After his father died, his mother found her voice along with her freedom. She went back to school and later started up a successful day care center. For years, in the small hamlet of Larkspur, she was considered tantamount to Mrs. Santa Claus to local kids and parents alike. Mothers came to her from all over town for advice on child care and family issues.

Collin thought it was too much for her to take on and told her so on many occasions. He saw her as the soft-spoken lady of the kitchen until he finally realized that he was acting like his father—independent, aloof, and as hard as it was to admit, just a tiny bit chauvinistic. Now he recognized his mother as a strong-willed individual with a compelling zest for life and a clear-headed way of looking at things.

"I guess our family needs to make a lot of corrections," Collin agreed, staring out the window toward the windy sea.

Alison sped down Marina Boulevard, gripping the wheel tightly. Normally the drive gave her a feeling of respect for the charm of the city, overlooking as it did the Marina Green and, beyond that, the bay. But any sense of beauty or romance was lost to her now. She quickly turned onto Lombard, then onto Fillmore, trying to circumvent traffic as much as possible as she headed for Geary.

During the past nineteen years, Anna Archer had been her nurturer, her guardian angel, her confidante to an extent, and the closest thing to a mother Alison could have hoped for. The woman had been her rock of Gibraltar.

But Gibraltar couldn't help her now. Anna and Collin had no idea what was *really* going on. If they did, she didn't think their first reaction would be a sympathetic one. It would be one of dismay and resentment. Nobody appreciates being lied to.

Alison turned down another side street and found herself dodging around cars and racing through red lights to reach the St. Francis on time. She was overwrought, and it had blurred her ability to make judgments. Her mind was not on her driving.

She pushed down hard on the gas pedal to make it through the intersection of Hyde and Jackson, when the car in front of her abruptly stopped for the light instead of running it.

Screaming, Alison slammed on the brakes and brought her car to a screeching, skidding halt just inches from impact. The driver of the car in front of her turned around and gave her the finger. Alison shrugged apologetically and slumped down in her seat.

While waiting for the light to change, Alison felt herself go through a metamorphosis of her own. Gone was the woman in control, the sophisticated magazine executive, the *good* person who did everything right, followed all the rules, never got in trouble. Gone were her strength, her intelligence, her ability to handle a crisis. Years were erased, and suddenly she was once more that frightened, confused girl who had become a lonely, love-hungry young woman, easily manipulated, easily exploited, easily fooled.

As she sat there in the dark, her car idling, Alison recalled every time she'd run scared from the men in her life. Every time she'd been a fool, acted like an idiot, been abused, controlled, coerced into doing something she didn't want to do.

All those years really hadn't brought her very far. She still had all the old wounds. And bit by bit, Alison felt the wounds reopen until she thought she would bleed to death.

One of the deepest cuts had been her relationship with Graham. The injury he inflicted still lay close to the surface.

Graham Walker was dashingly handsome. Nothing like her first husband, Reed, who was from the literati; a tall, thin, scotch-drinking, closet chauvinist. Before his true personality emerged, Reed appealed to Alison's educational aspirations. Her parents had not been supportive of her desire to go to college. "You learn to type and get your ass into a secretarial position," her dad had always said. "What makes you think I'd waste my hard-earned money on all that math and science shit when you're not gonna use it? You're gonna get married, get pregnant, and clean the house."

That had been her mother's life, not hers. She was going to be different. At first, Alison thought being married to a college professor would guarantee it.

But she was wrong. Before long, it had become clear to her that

Reed was just like her father. He just read more books and had a taste for expensive liquor.

And he had a dark side. As soon as Alison made the mistake of crossing him, he revealed his true colors by hauling off and slugging her. Fortunately, Alison proved to be different from her mother in that she didn't stick around for a lifetime of his abuse. She took her baby daughter and left him.

No. Graham Walker was not like Reed. Graham was muscular, tanned, sexy, and on the surface, incredibly romantic. Everything a young woman could hope for.

Alison remembered the day she met him and thought it ironic that Collin was the one who had introduced them.

She already had a crush on Collin back then, but he was inaccessible and always seemed to be involved with another woman. When Graham appeared on the scene, Alison was ripe for the attention.

Collin's advertising agency did a lot of work with the modeling agency she worked for at the time, and the night she met Graham, Alison had been late for an important meeting with Collin. Rushing into the restaurant, flustered, Alison spotted Collin sitting at a table with another man. She peeled off her coat and joined them. She apologized profusely, but Collin wasn't upset. He stood up, kissed her cheek, and gestured toward their dinner companion. "Ali, meet Graham Walker. He's the photographer we've scheduled for the Macy's shoot."

Alison had been momentarily stunned by his smile. He was unbelievably attractive. He had adorable dimples and the greatest smile lines around his blue eyes, which, she was sure, were flirting with her. The guy was a knockout.

"Very nice to meet you, Graham," Alison said graciously, locking eyes with him and extending her hand. He took her hand, but instead of shaking it, he pulled her toward him and kissed her cheek. Alison blushed and glanced at Collin.

"Watch out, Ali," Collin said jokingly. "This guy's got a reputation. He's a charmer. I'd tell you to lock up the models, but that wouldn't do any good. From what I hear, they'd break the chains just to work with him."

Alison smiled but wished Collin had been more territorial. Graham laughed. "Not true, Collin, but thanks for the compliment." He pulled out the chair beside him, and Alison sat down, wondering briefly if she should sit next to Collin instead.

"I know we've come to see your selections for tomorrow's call-back, Alison," Graham said, his eyes sparkling, "but if it were up to me, I'd throw them all out. None of these models is as beautiful as you. Where'd you find this woman, Collin?"

Collin smiled broadly. "She's something, isn't she?"

Alison lowered her eyes, embarrassed but relishing the compliment. Maybe, just maybe, Collin would finally show some interest in her.

"But you two will have to select the models without me," Collin continued, "because I'm off to Europe tomorrow."

Alison looked up abruptly. Collin was always leaving, and once again, she swallowed her attraction to him and returned her attention to the business at hand. Throughout dinner, Graham kept up a steady, flirtatious play for her. By the end of the evening, she was falling for it.

The photo shoot went well. In the studio, Graham was all business, but Alison observed that he did his job with just the right amount of sexual teasing mixed with compliments, and that made every woman he worked with feel like a million bucks. The smile the cover girl wore was meant for the photographer, and that was the secret to his success.

Over the next week or so, Alison found herself spending quite a bit of time with Graham. By the time Collin returned from Europe, the gossip around the agency was that Alison and Graham were an item. Alison noticed that upon his return Collin acted more reserved toward her than usual, but he never once said anything about her budding relationship with Graham. He merely remained her close friend. A close, *platonic* friend.

The more Alison was around Graham, the more she liked him. He was handsome and funny, with a personality that was larger than life. His brawny physique and modellike face could easily have put him on the other side of the camera lens, but he claimed he had never wanted that. His passion was taking the pictures.

Something about Graham drew people to him. He always seemed *on*. It was the first time Alison had been remotely interested in anyone other than Collin, and she was enjoying the attention.

The night before Graham was to deliver the final photo selections to the ad agency, he asked Alison to help him double-check the latest contact sheets. Leaning over the lightbox together, he put a muscular arm around her as they scrutinized the poses in front of them. The scent of his cologne was intoxicating. Alison thought she also detected the musty smell of marijuana in his hair. She felt him rub up against her suggestively. He gently moved her hair away from her neck and lightly brushed his lips against her ear. Suddenly he snapped off the light and tugged her by the arm into a corner of his studio.

Graham pulled her head back and kissed her lips forcefully. His throaty voice echoed in her ears. "I want you, Alison."

Momentarily on guard, Alison pulled back in surprise but softened when she looked into his eyes. When Graham saw her look of surrender, he swooped her up in his arms and carried her to the couch. Without taking his eyes off her, he slowly undid the buttons of her blouse and ran his hands gently down her breasts. Alison's stomach trembled as he moved his hands down her body, pulling her skirt and panties off in one movement.

She suddenly became self-conscious and embarrassed. He scrutinized her body as if he were memorizing it. Analyzing it. She started to push herself up, but he grabbed hold of her waist and lowered his mouth to her neck, brushing soft, gentle kisses across her skin, making her shiver. She relaxed again, giving in. Slowly, he moved down to her breasts, kissing them until her back arched in pleasure.

Graham was in charge. He moved down her body, spread her legs gently, and took full ownership of her. Alison moaned with pleasure. He looked up, his mouth glistening, lips parted in a self-assured smile. Turning her around, he pulled her buttocks toward him. He let go just long enough to yank his pants off and impatiently kick them out of the way. Graham grasped Alison's hips firmly and sought out the wet place his lips had been only moments before. With an animalistic groan, he thrust his erect penis into her and immediately found a rhythm.

Alison closed her eyes and held on to the couch, feeling the hot, throbbing climax begin inside her, building with each powerful thrust. Graham's moans grew louder. His hips pushed harder until the peak was reached and they exploded, shouting out in unison. Sated. Satisfied.

She had never experienced such an orgasm. Graham had taken her to a new, higher level. But in a short time, Alison would become afraid of heights. She realized early on that Graham was a master manipulator and was apprehensive of where it might lead.

This particular trait was what gave him so much power in the studio. Models would do *anything* for him. His eye for composition was brilliant, and even though he often crossed the line from classy to something bordering on Helmut Newton shock appeal, models were dying to work with him. He was bigtime.

After dating for a couple of months, Graham coaxed Alison into posing in sexy lingerie for him. It was just for fun—a little foreplay. He loved having sexy pictures of her, he said. She was amazed she'd allowed herself to do it. Of course, it wasn't long before he had her posing entirely in the nude.

"Look, Graham, I know this is a turn-on for you, but I don't feel comfortable doing this in front of a camera!" Alison protested. "I have a young child at home, for goodness' sake. I'm not a model!"

"But look at yourself, love," he said with pride when he unveiled some of the photos. "Have you ever seen anyone so gorgeous in your life? Nobody can tell you've had a kid."

Something nagged at the back of Alison's mind. This wasn't her. It wasn't what she wanted. Why couldn't she tell him that? At first the idea had been seductive, but it wasn't anymore. It made her feel used.

Each time Graham took pictures of her, his game changed. First it was sexy one-piece teddies. Then it was garters, bras, and panties. Soon it wasn't just the lingerie he required to get him off, but the staging of what came close to a theatrical production. A miniplay. He started playing out scenes and introducing sadomasochism into them. The photo sessions progressed from handcuffing Alison to dripping hot wax on her body.

Graham was always high on coke when he performed these little acts, but Alison was always sober and straight and increasingly horrified that she was allowing all this to continue.

Despite the fact that they finished off these little photo shoots with lusty sex, Alison's enjoyment of the whole charade soon ceased. It was frightening, and Alison realized too late that she was being passive once again, responding to someone else's whims, obeying orders she didn't agree with, dancing to a tune she didn't know. She was a mother, and she had a responsibility to her daughter. This was not the kind of person she wanted around Destiny, and not the sort of life she wanted for herself.

However, Alison had waited too long to end the relationship. Graham's sexual scenes grew more violent, and Alison had to threaten to call the police to get him to leave her alone.

Graham was killed in a small-plane crash several weeks later, and nobody ever knew what a burden his death had lifted from her shoulders. Alison never had the nerve to divulge the private humiliations she'd allowed herself to suffer and had chalked it up as one more example of what happens when an aggressive, manipulative man takes control of her life. She had learned her lesson. Or so she thought.

The Audi raced down Powell Street toward the St. Francis Hotel. Alison hadn't thought about Graham in years, but the whole nasty episode resurfaced. And she knew why.

Secrets.

She was keeping too many dirty secrets.

Other than Collin, every man in her life had been abusive to her. Until today, she thought she'd finally broken that cycle, but she was wrong. She was still caught up in it. Controlled by it. Now that control threatened not only her, but her daughter as well.

Chapter 8

MAKING HIS WAY DOWN STOCKTON, COUNTRY SPOTTED THE ST. Francis. He turned onto Geary and parked Jake's truck in the underground garage in Union Square.

It was dark. Other than a couple of bag ladies and a bum sleeping on a bench, the square was void of people. Country assessed his surroundings. A large statue stood in the center of the park. The inscription commemorated Admiral Dewey's victory over the Spanish navy at the Battle of Manila Bay in 1898. Who the hell cared? One of the bulbs illuminating the monument was about to burn out, and the flickering light cast an eerie backdrop against the ninety-foot-tall granite column. Despite the shadows, Country saw that a fresh whitewash of pigeon shit covered the statue, and his face broke into an uncharacteristic smile. *How fitting,* he thought.

He found a spot near a lamp post and leaned against it, waiting. On the other side of Geary, a well-dressed woman was leaving Macy's. He studied the sway of her hips, the sleek line of her body, finally focusing on her color-coordinated high heels as they clicked rapidly against the concrete sidewalk. A trolley car barreling down Powell ground to a halt, and the woman climbed on. One more flash of thigh and she was gone.

Grinding out his cigarette with the heel of his lizard-skin boot, Country turned his attention to the front door of the St. Francis. He wasn't here to look at broads.

He thought of Alison and the meeting that would soon take place. Her image had surfaced often during the past eighteen years. Hers, his mother's, and Sara's. His calm evaporated when he remembered his mother and the men who sought her out. Her and his sister. The idea of anyone touching his women set him off.

Country became rigid as blood pumped through the knotted veins in his clenched hands. His eyes glazed over. He would have liked to vent his anger on the first person that walked by, but he resisted the urge. Cracking his neck, he returned his thoughts to Alison, vowing to set things straight.

It was her fault he got busted. When he killed that biker in Jamul, he was thinking about her, that little bitch, and the fact that she'd run off. If she hadn't bolted, he'd have had what was rightfully his.

Country didn't accept experiences, he divined them. He made adjustments easily so that everything that happened to him was under his control. He was in San Francisco now, and that was exactly what he wanted. Ali had made a good life for herself and the kid, and he was ready to step right in.

Destiny looked a lot like his baby sister. Now *that* little girl had been beautiful, too. Sara. Sweet little Sara. *She'd* been a beauty. Too bad about her.

Country had become a man as soon as his dick could stay hard. His mother had seen to that. She loved bringing her friends over to the house to show him off. His mother was only fourteen years older than he was. They were almost like brother and sister.

His father was a mean-assed drunk who did what he pleased with his mother—whenever he was around, that is. She had sought comfort from Country, who was more like a friend to her than a son. He became possessive, but as a young boy he could do nothing to protect her.

His mother was always getting pregnant. Either the babies died, or she'd give them away. Country wanted her to keep them. He wanted to take care of them, not like his asshole of a father.

She finally kept one child because there wasn't anyone around to take her. Sara. Precious Sara was his to protect. His.

When Country got older, his bitch mother pushed him away. He began to hate her then, almost as much as he hated his father. As far back as Country could remember, his crazy, wild-eyed old man had beaten them daily, including his little sister. But his pa didn't just hit her. He did other things. Unspeakable things. It was up to Country to defend her from that asshole's nightly groping, and as Country grew into a man, he was more than capable of doing so. When his old man disappeared one day, no one in their dirt-poor town cared, and no one asked why. Served him right. Country had no remorse.

Sara needed a special kind of affection. The kind only *he* was capable of providing. Country didn't want men around her. One day, Sara started fooling around with the Casper kid in the backseat of his car. That buck-toothed, pimply-faced, redheaded moron from across the street. It pissed Country off. He couldn't bear anyone's hands on his sister. He stalked them, intending to teach the boy a lesson. Things went wrong. He hadn't meant for Sara to die, too, but what was done was done.

He blamed his mother. He wanted to teach the old bag a lesson, too, but she ran off with some salesman. Later, when he learned his mother had died, his only regret was that he hadn't been the one who killed her.

Country pulled another Marlboro out of the pack and lit it. He blew a stream of smoke donuts into the air and refocused on the front of the hotel. A couple of young men in suits and carrying briefcases rounded the corner of Geary and Powell and entered the hotel. They looked like lawyers or accountants barely out of school.

Muffled laughter and the flash of a black skirt caught Country's attention as a trio of young women approached the door. They giggled as the doorman ushered them into the hotel. It wouldn't be long before those three would connect with the horny fresh-faced guys inside. This was a local watering hole, which suited him fine. He'd fit right in.

Country crossed the street, flicked his cigarette into the gutter, and entered the hotel. He settled in at a secluded table in the corner of the crowded lobby bar. A waitress with short blond hair and large breasts appeared. She leaned down, smiled, and asked if he wanted a drink. Country looked directly at her breasts, then at her face.

He didn't smile. He stared at her lips. *She'd be an interesting fuck,* he thought, his eyes cold. "Gimme a J&B on the rocks," he growled.

The waitress stopped grinning and stood upright. She thrust a bowl of nuts and a napkin in front of him and hustled off.

The bar was crowded. Country observed the way people sat, what they drank, how they held their cigarettes. He watched them toss back designer brews, glasses of Chardonnay, and margaritas. The jailbait drank frothy drinks with umbrellas in them, and the underage guys hitting on them guzzled bottled Budweisers.

Settling back in his chair, he picked up a copy of *San Francisco Life* from the chair next to him and started flipping through it. He relaxed his muscles, forced an accessible expression onto his face, and purposefully smiled at his waitress when she brought his drink. Confused at first, she returned the smile. Her demeanor instantly became one of flirtation. She licked her already shiny lips and lingered around his table, adjusting her blouse.

"Nice boots, Mister. I bet you've got a real collection of them at home, huh?"

Country took a swig of his scotch and fixed his eyes on her cleavage. "I'm waitin' on someone, doll."

"I'd never make you wait, baby." The waitress winked at him and sashayed over to the next table.

Country sensed someone new in the bar, someone not laughing, not drinking. Not having fun. He looked around.

Then he saw her. Alison. Damn, she was fine.

She looked the same, except her hair was shorter. She was now a sexy woman instead of a sexy little girl. Her brown hair shimmered under the low-voltage lights, her face flushed, her mouth open, just as he remembered her.

She hadn't spotted him. She walked right by his table, and he inhaled the scent of her. *This* was also different. Expensive perfume. She smelled like a woman now. He closed his eyes and remembered. A hard-on was on the rise under the table and he pushed on it, groaning.

Alison continued to search the bar, her face tense. Country calmly sipped his drink. He wanted to watch her in action for a bit longer. The designer slacks she wore hugged her butt perfectly. Nineteen years hadn't changed her figure. She was still worth a wild fuck.

Alison's heart pounded so hard she could feel it through her blouse. Where was he? He had to be here. She glanced at her watch. Five after eight. Surely he wouldn't have left! Tears burned her eyes, and she bit her lip, forcing a different kind of pain to the surface. Be strong. You *have* to be strong. He can't get the best of you again.

Maybe he'll go away.

She was moving toward the bartender to ask if anyone had left a message for her when she heard it. A popping sound. Cracking knuckles. And then someone uttered her name.

"Ali."

She whipped her head around, peering through the dark toward the source. Someone was in the shadows. She moved forward slowly. She could make out the outline of a man. As she got closer, she noticed the lizard-skin cowboy boots.

The gabardine slacks.

The expensive sports jacket.

She looked at the well-groomed man, confused.

"Hi, doll."

Twenty years rolled back in a moment, and she was walking on the beach in Mission Bay, San Diego.

To her shock, he took her arm and guided her into the chair beside him.

"Don't recognize me, do ya?"

Alison caught her breath. She glanced around at the other people in the bar to see if anyone was watching, but no one was.

Country sat still, staring at her. She didn't want to meet his gaze but couldn't help it. He had that power. A wolf in sheep's clothing. He was still that strong.

But Alison was shocked that everything else about him had changed. His hair, his face. The way he dressed. Like a well-off entrepreneur, in his blazer and designer boots. This was all so different from the bare-chested beach bum of long ago. Looking like this, he could blend in with the crowd. Looking like this, he could be her equal. Nobody would know what a monster he was.

That he looked so normal astounded Alison and added a new level to her fear.

"You look . . . different," she whispered.

Country cracked a smile, but his mirthless eyes remained fixed on her. His gaze moved to her breasts.

"You don't," he said.

Alison's line of vision fell to his hand, which rested on the table near her arm, as if he was ready to grab her if she tried to leave.

Then she saw it. The mark that appeared over and over again in her nightmares. A gaudy, open-mouthed serpent tattoo. The dark blue image was barely visible under his shirt sleeve, but she'd seen enough to make her shudder. She knew the snake tattoo crawled all the way up his muscular arm. She remembered and turned away. His blue eyes were still fixed on her. Those mesmerizing, penetrating, cold blue eyes.

Alison was not sure what to say. She looked at her hands, searching for a way to conceal her anxiety, then glanced around the room to see if she recognized anyone in the bar. But the room was not well lit, and if there were familiar faces there, she couldn't make them out.

"Look at me, Ali. I've waited a long time to claim what's mine."

Alison looked up. "What are you talking about?"

"You're mine, and so is the little girl. Make no mistake about that."

Alison gripped the side of the chair, anger causing her fight-or-flight reaction to kick in. Adrenaline pumped through her body, making the veins in her temple throb and her face flush.

"You're out of your mind, Country. I was never yours."

"Oh, yes you are. You'd have been by my side all this time, but you ran away. Told lies about me. You caused me a lot of problems."

Alison couldn't believe her ears. "Why aren't you in prison where you belong?"

Country raised an eyebrow. "So you kept tabs on me, too, eh, doll? Guess we just can't stay away from each other."

Alison's face twisted into an angry scowl. "I saw it in the paper when I came back to bury my parents. I couldn't have cared less what happened to you, as long as you were punished. They should have locked you up for life!"

"That's not a nice way for you to speak about your baby's daddy."

"Don't you dare call yourself my baby's daddy, you monster!"

Country squinted his eyes into slits as he clenched and un-clenched his fist, nostrils flaring as if he'd been running. Alison watched in awe as he instantly calmed himself, studying her like a snake pausing in front of a victim before the fatal strike. She recoiled, almost by instinct.

But he didn't move toward her at all. He seemed completely in control. He lit a cigarette and drew hard on it.

"Watch your mouth, bitch. You don't want to get me mad. It was your fault I hit that biker. Your fault I hit him so hard. You should never have run away. Should never have told the cops. I found out, you know? I heard you wanted to kill her. Kill our kid. But I forgave you, Ali. I thought about you a lot while I was in the joint. Thought about you and the little girl. Now I'm back, and you're mine, so don't fuckin' piss me off. I told you I'd never let you go."

Alison's eyes brimmed with tears. The craziness of the situation was overwhelming. She needed help. The police would *have* to believe her. Why hadn't she been brave enough to tell them the whole story? She peered into the darkness, wondering if there was a policeman in the bar, thinking about what would happen if she ran out to the concierge to ask for help.

But what would she say? Country hadn't attacked her. He looked like one of the yuppie executives in the bar. He'd talk his way out of it, and she'd look like a fool. He'd still get what he wanted.

She breathed deeply, trying to regain her balance, reminding herself that she was an intelligent executive, capable of running a successful magazine. She could reason with people, use common sense.

But the man sitting across from her didn't fit into a *normal* equation, and she had gone temporarily brain dead. Anger seethed through her, and she lost her temper.

She lashed out vengefully. "I don't know where you get off, Country. You have no claim on me or my daughter. None! I'm married now, and I have a life, unlike you. You stay away from us or I'll call the police!"

People nearby stopped talking and looked in their direction. Alison hunkered down, embarrassed. The last thing she wanted to do was call attention to herself with this man.

Country smiled affably at the onlookers, who turned back to their drinks and their dates. He leaned toward Alison and grasped her hand firmly. She tried to pull it away, but he held it in a viselike grip.

"You want to bother the cops, go ahead. They can't do a damn thing. I haven't done anything wrong, Alison. It'll get you nowhere."

"You raped me," Alison hissed, her face inches from his.

Country was unmoved. "You couldn't prove it then, and you sure as hell can't prove it now, baby. I know the law. I've spent so much time in the joint around scumbag lawyers, I could be one myself. I have rights. Parental rights. You can't keep her from me just because I've done time. I paid my debt to society. I'm a free man now. Rehabilitated."

He let her hand go, but she felt his eyes sweeping over her, tracing her body like a paintbrush. It made her feel dirty, tainted, and violated once again.

"You know the truth, Ali," he continued, curling his voice into a velvety smooth tone. "Look at me. I'm a changed man. I'll get what I want. Don't fight me on this, 'cause I'll win. Tell your so-called husband to take a hike, and get your ass back to me where you belong."

Alison clutched her hand protectively, rubbing it, as if she could remove any trace of his touch. She stared at him defiantly. "You're out of your mind, Country. I have a life with my husband and Destiny. You're not part of it."

Country lit another cigarette, taking a deep drag. He blew out several smoke rings and put the cigarette down, his eyes on her all the while. To her horror, he suddenly leaped forward and grabbed her face with his hands. He planted his mouth over hers, thrust his tongue deep into her mouth, and kissed her forcefully, possessively. Alison quickly struggled out of his grasp, repulsed.

"Fuck your marriage," he said as he sat back down. "I always get what I want, Ali. Nothing and nobody stands in my way. Deep down inside, I know you still want me. I'll get you, and I'll get Destiny."

Alison grabbed a cocktail napkin and spat into it, trying to get rid of the disgusting, stale cigarette taste he'd left in her mouth.

"I could make it easy for you," he added, "but if you want to make it hard, I can do that, too. That's even more fun. Maybe you remember—"

"You make me sick!" She whipped her hand up to slap Country in the face, but he grabbed her wrist and forced it down to the table, bending it back until she winced.

His voice became a menacing whisper. "Like I said, I can make it hard, doll. Just think about what your kid'll say when she finds out that if it wasn't for me, she'd be dead. You were gonna kill her. I'm her father. I'm here to claim her. Think about it. You can tell her about me, make things go easier. Or I can tell her. My way. We'll see what she has to say about it."

Alison yanked her arm away. "Bastard!" she spat. "Stay the fuck away from my daughter!"

Country sat still, cool as a cucumber. "It's not very motherly to talk like that, Ali. And here are all these witnesses who'll remember how nasty you were."

Alison stood up, her chest heaving. Gritting her teeth, she said, "I'm not the same person I was nineteen years ago. You can't manipulate me anymore. If you're so different now, you should be able to understand that I'm different, too!"

She flashed him a spiteful look, turned, and stormed out of the bar.

Country winked at the waitress hovering nearby and shrugged. "I better go calm her down. Bring me another scotch, baby. I'll be back." He put a twenty on the table and casually sauntered after Alison.

Alison hurried through the lobby, her face blotched from anger. What was he thinking? There was no way she was going to give in to his madness.

She looked back at the bar and saw Country striding toward her. She sprinted to the exit and dashed out into the street, nearly causing a cab driver to hit her. Yanking open the door of the taxi, she jumped in. "Take me to 520 Marina View Drive. Now!" she blurted.

Country vaulted forward just as the cab pulled away from the curb. Alison looked back at the tall figure standing on the sidewalk as the cab raced up the street.

He was a demon underneath that slick new haircut and those expensive clothes. She was sure he hadn't changed. Evil was evil. It didn't go away. Or did it?

Tears finally spilled out. She should be going to the police station. She should be doing a lot of things, but she couldn't.

She looked around for her purse and realized she'd left it at the bar. For a moment, Alison thought of having the cab driver turn around but quickly discarded the notion. Country might still be there. She didn't want to risk seeing him again.

Crestfallen and confused, she tapped on the driver's window. "I'm sorry, driver, but would you take me to 1022 Clay Street instead?"

The driver grunted and downshifted. He made a left and headed for Nob Hill. She had to go to Kelly's. There was no way she could go home and face Collin right now.

Country strolled back into the bar and returned to his table. The waitress put a scotch down in front of him.

"Looks like you're having domestic problems, eh, sugar? You ought to get a woman who can treat you right."

Country stared at the girl's boobs. She held up a black leather purse. "Your friend left this behind. Want me to turn it in?"

He snatched the purse and looked at the young face for a long moment. "Nah. I'll take care of it."

"Can I get you anything else?"

Country glanced at her boobs again, reconsidering. He needed a release. He chugged down his scotch. "What time do you get off?"

The girl smiled and looked at her watch. "I took the early shift tonight, so I can get off in a few minutes if I want to."

"Get your coat. I'll be waitin'."

He watched the buxom waitress bounce off and cracked his neck again. She'd be a good diversion. Alison had made him tense. Fuck her for running away. He'd have to break her of that habit. She'd forgotten who she was dealing with.

Rubbing his groin, Country turned his attention to Alison's purse. He reached in and pulled out a shiny lizard-skin appointment book. He flipped it open to the first page. It supplied all of Alison's personal data, though most of it he already had. People were so fucking naive. Why would anyone write down their most personal information on something any fool could steal?

Alison had carefully printed everything about herself right there on the first page. Her address, her credit card numbers, her driver's license, her daughter's name and birth date. Next to Destiny's name, Country noted another address and phone number. Marco McCauly. He remembered the name. Had seen it in the newspaper article. The guy in the band. Destiny's boyfriend. Now this was information he could use.

Country put the book back into Alison's purse. He'd have to teach her not to be so stupid. He'd been away for too long. But all that was going to change. He'd be in charge very soon.

He strolled to the bar and set the purse down in front of the bartender. "My lady friend left this here. She'll probably call for it. Tell her I left it for her."

The bartender glanced at Country, took the bag, and put it under the counter. "No problem."

The waitress reappeared, jacket in hand. The bartender blinked, looking at her, then at Country. He shrugged and set about mixing up another batch of pink ladies for the women at the other end of the bar.

Country slipped his arm around the waitress and smiled, ushering the girl toward the door. He then let his arm snake down her back and planted his large palm on her butt.

Alison's playing hard to get, he thought. He could play games, too. Only he played by his own rules. Outside the hotel, Country steered the waitress across the street toward Union Square, feeling the urge to play rough tonight.

Chapter 9

SAN FRANCISCO WEATHER CAN BE CAPRICIOUS. A WARM, BLUSTERY day can turn into a nippingly cold night, even at the onset of summer. By the time the cab driver pulled up in front of the house on Clay Street, the famous San Francisco fog had enveloped the hilltop neighborhood in a grayish blanket of cottonlike fluff. The air had become cold, moist, and dense. Alison should have been chilled to the bone, but she was not even cognizant of the weather.

She was sweating and flushed when she ran up the steps of Kelly's well-cared-for Edwardian and pounded on the door.

"Kelly! Open the door. It's me!"

Footsteps clapped against the oak-floored hallway of the charming house Alison knew so well, and she felt the warm rush of heated air as the door opened. Kelly gawked at her. "What's wrong?"

"Could you lend me five bucks to pay the driver?" Alison was breathing hard as she gestured toward the waiting taxi. Kelly didn't hesitate. She grabbed her purse from the antique hall tree in her foyer and yanked Alison inside. "Get in here. I'll pay him. It's freezing out there."

Alison wandered into the living room of her best friend's house, peering around carefully to see if Kelly's husband or sons were home. She didn't see anyone. She felt a throbbing in her wrist and looked down at an angry purple spot that had formed. Rubbing it absentmindedly, she suddenly remembered how it got there. The tears began to fall as she sat down heavily on the sofa. Kelly blew back into the house, flapping her arms against the chilly night air.

"Alison! My God, what the hell happened? Did you have another fight with Destiny? Or Collin?"

Alison wiped her face, smearing her makeup. "Not with Collin," she said, almost in a whisper. "And I haven't talked with Destiny long enough to even call it a fight. This is worse. This has to do with someone I never thought I'd see again."

"Well, you look like you've seen a ghost."

"I've not only seen one, I've spoken to one." Alison turned her bloodshot eyes on Kelly. "He's back, Kelly. The man who raped me is back."

Kelly took Alison's hands and squeezed them. A look passed between them that transcended time.

"God, Ali. How in hell did he find you?"

"He started calling yesterday, demanding to see me. Then he said he'd seen Destiny, and threatened to tell her everything if I didn't meet with him. He says he's seen Collin, too." Alison allowed her shivering body to collapse against her friend's.

The words came rapid-fire out of Kelly's mouth. "Why didn't you tell me? God, I can't believe this! What are you going to do? Did you call the police? Have you told Collin?"

"I can't." Alison got up and walked to the bay window. She stared at the street traffic below. For the rest of the world, life was normal. People below walked arm in arm, heading for cozy little townhouses, wonderful dinners. Perfectly safe. Perfectly happy. But not Alison.

Kelly pulled a tissue from the Kleenex box and handed it to Alison.

"I went to the police yesterday, but I nearly choked on my own tongue," Alison explained. "I got the sweats. It was as if I were still a kid. I hated being there. I don't trust them to help me. They didn't before."

"Things are different now, Ali."

"Maybe so. But my story was never proved, remember? What can I say he did now? He just called me. He hasn't harmed me. What are the police supposed to do?"

Kelly wrapped a lap blanket around Alison's shoulders and tried to reassure her friend. "Don't let yourself lose the ground you've worked so hard to cover all these years, Ali. Don't you think it's time to tell Collin?"

"I'm not ready to tell him. Destiny, either. Everything is falling apart, Kel."

"You've got to get a grip, Ali. You need help."

Alison choked out a laugh. "Get a grip? I'm barely holding on by my fingernails. I'm totally screwed! I have a psychopath breathing heavy over the phone, a daughter who doesn't want to talk to me, and a husband who at this moment probably thinks I'm fooling around. I can't just blurt out to them that I lied about everything they know about me from A to Z, and that by the way, Destiny's real father is a rapist!"

Alison's eyes suddenly darted toward the telephone on the desk and she ran over to it. "And I left my purse in the hotel bar. Dammit!"

"You met him in a bar?" Kelly asked.

Alison didn't answer. She punched in the number for the St. Francis and asked to be connected to the lobby lounge. "This is Alison Young. I left my purse on the floor at one of the tables. Could you check to see if it's still there?"

"Just a minute, ma'am," the voice on the other end said. "I'll ask the bartender."

Alison curled the phone cord around her finger nervously, staring at the floor. Kelly waited by her side, concern and confusion on her face.

The voice came back on. "We have it, ma'am. The bartender said it was turned in by the man you were with."

Alison sighed in relief. "Thanks. I'll pick it up later."

She hung up the phone and made eye contact with Kelly. "Everything I've built up over the past nineteen years is going to be destroyed, Kelly."

Alison started pacing around the room. She paused to look at herself in the mirror above the fireplace and noticed her smeared makeup. "Look at me," she said. "I look like hell."

"I think you need a brandy." Kelly went into the kitchen and poured them each a shot. She remembered having to do the same thing nineteen years earlier, and the still-vivid memory made her shudder.

Alison sat on the sofa, numb. Had she overreacted?

When Kelly came back with the drinks, Alison took hers gratefully. Then she related the details of the last few hours. Kelly stared at her, amazed. When Alison was finally talked out, she looked imploringly at her friend of twenty-five years. "I can't believe it's happening all over again."

"It's really imperative that you go to the police," Kelly insisted.

Alison shook her head. "Nineteen years is a long time. I've buried the truth for so long, I don't know how to begin to tell anyone. Especially Collin and Destiny. I've never been myself because of it. I wish I could be more like Marlene Burkette, but I can't. This has always been a part of my past that I can't face. And now he shows up."

Alison grabbed a pillow and moved to the floor by the fireplace. Staring into the flames, she whispered, "He could shatter my whole world."

"He's a sleazebag." Kelly interjected.

"Problem is, he doesn't *look* like a sleazebag anymore. He looks normal except for those damned insane eyes."

Kelly pushed her granny glasses up higher on her nose and shook her frizzy curls in frustration. "What is it that makes us so damn reluctant to call out for help? He's stalking you, for God's sake!

Remember when we were kids? It didn't matter if we got beaten black and blue, we never went for help. We used to run and hide when our fathers fought with our mothers. We cringed with each slap. Each broken dish. Each scream. We were scared shitless. But we never got help. The whole mind-set sucks, Ali."

Alison looked up, a flash of the old fire in her eyes. "We didn't go for help because we knew, like our mothers did, that it wouldn't get us anywhere!"

The two women had witnessed many a fight between their respective sets of parents. Both of their fathers worked in construction, but Kelly's dad was often out of work. He took his resentment out on his family with brutal regularity. Once he had hit Kelly so hard, he slammed her into a wall. The impact broke her arm. She ran screaming down the block, but not one neighbor wanted to get involved. Her father dragged her back into the house. He finally let Kelly's mother take her to the emergency room.

Alison had plenty of her own war stories. The fights were hideously etched into her memory.

She rubbed the back of her neck. A tension headache was forming knots at the base of her head. She could almost feel the blood vessels constricting, limiting the blood flow to her brain.

"Country's crazy," she said. "He thinks he owns me *and* Destiny, and he wants to tell her who he is. It scares me to death. He could *make* her believe him. He could twist the truth so I'd look like nothing more than a manipulative liar."

Kelly's voice was firm. "Destiny won't believe it."

"You don't know him. He can finesse his way around the legal system, and with Destiny being so hungry for knowledge about her father, who knows?"

Alison stared at the red-and-orange flames and the white-hot ash accumulating at the bottom of the wood stack. "She looks just like him, Kel. Right down to his blue eyes."

"Oh, God."

"Christ, I've been lying to my family for a lifetime." The tears started flowing again.

"You did what you had to do, Alison," Kelly reminded her.

"Maybe I did the wrong thing." Alison wrapped her arms around herself, head down.

A long silence followed. "Tell them what happened, Ali," Kelly finally said, her voice gentle. "What you did years ago, you did to survive."

Alison rubbed her throat nervously, trying to dislodge the painful lump stuck there. "A lifetime of lies is hard to forgive. How are they ever going to trust me again? Where does the lie end and the real me begin? I'm not even sure I know who the real me is. How can I expect my family to?"

She forced herself to breathe deeply, hoping all her years of yoga practice would come to her aid. This was *her* mess. In the back of her mind, she'd always known she'd have to deal with her past. But at this moment, she didn't have a clue how.

Alison got up and went to the mirror to straighten her hair and clothing. She spied a copy of *Hers* on the entry table and was grateful for the temporary distraction. "By the way, how's the cover coming? I forgot to ask about it today."

Kelly regarded her thoughtfully. "It looks great. I'll send you a layout of it tomorrow."

She came over to Alison and hugged her. "I can't believe you, Ali. You're in the middle of a crisis, and you're still worrying about the business."

Alison gazed at her, eyes glistening with emotion. "I guess Destiny was right. I'm the queen of compartmentalization. I can't let the magazine fall apart just because I am."

Kelly shook her head reprovingly. "Don't shortchange yourself. Compartmentalization is another word for being organized, responsible, accountable. I'd call that being strong."

Alison wasn't so sure. It wasn't how she felt right now.

She looked at her friend with hollow eyes. "Would you drive me back to the St. Francis so I can get my purse and my car? It's time for me to go home."

Chapter 10

THE LIGHTS WERE ON. ALISON LOOKED AT HER WATCH. TEN-thirty. Of course Collin would be waiting up for her.

Alison unlocked the front door of the townhouse and entered. As she feared, Collin was on the couch, waiting, not smiling.

"How was the meeting?" he asked flatly.

"A real pain in the ass."

Collin's eyebrow arched. "I thought you *liked* the Malaysians."

Alison gave Collin a perfunctory smile. "I just met this guy," she said, avoiding eye contact. She felt shaky and weak, as she reached for an apple from the fruit bowl on the kitchen counter. It just occurred to her that she hadn't eaten all evening.

"It was one of Mr. Jambhala's new financial advisers," she continued, working the lie.

"Another one?" Collin asked, his voice sharp.

"Our *usually* silent partner wanted his newest adviser to meet with me personally."

"I'm surprised this meeting didn't take place at one of your famous cocktail parties. At least then he'd have gotten some press out of it."

Alison gritted her teeth. Collin was getting too technical. Of course he was right. Her monthly cocktail gatherings were becoming a highlight of the city's social calendar.

She headed toward their bedroom, saying, "Funny how things work out, isn't it?" She heard Collin utter a mumbled reply.

Alison pulled a terry-cloth robe from her closet and slipped out of her slacks and blazer. She threw them into the hamper and closed the lid, worried that the cigarette smoke from the bar would permeate the room. She wanted to climb into the bed and pull the covers over her head.

But Collin was still sitting in the living room, on the same couch he'd been sitting on when she arrived, stern as stone. Alison donned the bathrobe, walked back out to the living room, and curled up next to Collin on the sofa. She began fiddling with the needlepoint pillow beside her. "How's your mom?" she said finally.

"Enlightening. And more liberal than we are," he said crisply. "She understood Destiny's point of view and took the fact that she'd moved out in stride. By the way, she asked me to tell you she's going to make the cake for Destiny's birthday, so don't order one."

Alison's shoulders slumped. Her daughter's eighteenth birthday was a mere ten days away. An event that should have been a milestone was in danger of being lost in the shuffle. She suddenly remembered the earrings she'd hidden in her closet a month ago. A pair of diamond studs. She meant to give them to Destiny as a keepsake. Alison had precious little of her own mother to cling to and had always regretted it. She didn't want Destiny to suffer in the same way, though at the moment she doubted her daughter wanted anything from her.

Collin sighed, and Alison's eyes met his for a moment.

"Mom voiced a couple of opinions that really cut to the chase, Ali. Destiny will sort things out, if we give her the chance. She'll come around eventually and realize that you really just want the best for her. We need to be more accepting. Let's call her and get over this quarreling. Our family has to be stronger than this."

Alison didn't know how to respond. Her precious, stubborn, beautiful daughter had moved out in anger, and she couldn't bring herself to accept it. It was too close to her *own* life passage for comfort. *This is how mistakes are made,* she thought. Mistakes that can ruin your life.

Alison squeezed her eyes closed to hold back the tears threatening to burst from them. What was she doing? Collin was groping for a way to make sense of her behavior, and she wasn't giving him any ground to stand on.

Finally, Collin rose from the couch, a look of resignation on his face. "I give up, Ali. We're not getting anywhere. Maybe when I get back from Seattle you'll be ready to talk."

Alison sat up. "You're going out of town again? But you just got back!"

"That's right, Ali. Just like you, I have meetings I can't cancel. I'm leaving early in the morning. I'll sleep in Desi's room tonight so I won't wake you."

"Don't be silly, Collin. You don't have to do that."

Collin paused. "I think I do."

He started walking toward the hallway. Alison leaped up but froze in the middle of the living room. What could she say that would make things better? Collin had no idea what was raging around them. Now she was afraid not only of Country, but of Collin as well. After everything that had happened, she was afraid Collin would abandon her, too.

It looked like all her fears would be realized.

On the other side of San Francisco Bay, in the dark shadows of the Sausalito docks, a decrepit houseboat rocked in the murky waters.

No amount of coke or booze could make Country reach his desired state of satisfaction. He gazed down at the waitress from the bar, sweating and writhing beneath him, groaning like a pig, and was suddenly bored with her. She was not the one he wanted tonight.

Placing both hands around her neck, he squeezed and shook. She stopped groaning. He watched curiously as her eyes popped open and stared at him in horror. He found her feeble attempts to pry him loose amusing. She thrashed about, kicked, clawed his face with her nails. But he was much too strong to be pushed aside by her, even without an injection of "vitality."

The woman stopped resisting, then stopped breathing. Country came quickly and rolled off. He carried her lifeless body outside onto the deck, tied an old anchor around her neck, and calmly pitched her overboard.

He lit a cigarette and listened to a distant foghorn as it bayed at unseen ships at sea.

Chapter 11

THE DRIVE UP THE COAST TOOK MUCH LONGER THAN HARVEY HAD expected. Bea dozed off on the way from Santa Barbara to Carmel, and he was relieved. It gave him time to think, and he needed to think.

Harvey had finally found Statler's name in a yearbook. For some reason, the boy's formal graduation picture had not been included. Harvey pored over the yearbook, searching for sports photos or other candid shots, and eventually found one that included Statler.

The William B. Statler in the photo had black hair, black eyes, and very dark skin. He was also African American.

Harvey had checked and rechecked the spelling of the name, and there was only one William B. Statler. It had to be him.

Once Harvey had a face to go with the name, he sought out more information on the young man. Posing as an investigator from the veterans insurance claims office in Denver, he called the Veterans Building in La Jolla. Harvey made up a story about a bogus insurance claim and was immediately given all the particulars he had been denied at North Island.

William Benjamin Statler, born July 10, 1950. (No birth certificate on file. Abandoned at birth. Ward of the State of California.) Stationed on the USS Independence, *1968 through 1969. Listed Missing in Action in Saigon until 1972. New status: Killed in Captivity. Body returned to U.S. February 1972. Interred in Veterans Cemetery,*

San Diego. Religion: Christian. Ethnicity: African American.

Bill Statler, football hero, track star, valedictorian, posthumous recipient of the Purple Heart, was black. Unless all his black genes were recessive, this man was not Destiny Young's father.

Harvey was beginning to have a bad feeling about the whole situation. His files had proven that his nagging intuition had been right. He *had* met his client's mother years earlier. A meeting initiated by her as a result of her encounter with Country Davis.

But his file on that meeting was sketchy at best. No formal charge had been made. If it wasn't for the fact that during his first year as a detective, he'd taken notes on every possible case shoved under his nose, there wouldn't be any record of his having met her at all.

Police file or no, Alison had clearly lied about the identity of Destiny's father.

Harvey looked over at his sleeping wife and was suddenly grateful for their normal, boring life. Bea's hand had slipped down to the armrest between them, and he saw the tiny chip of a diamond ring on her finger. She'd gained some weight over the years. Her ring finger was swollen up around the sides of the thin gold band, and Harvey doubted that she could take the ring off. But it didn't matter. As far as he knew, Bea hadn't taken that ring off once in their whole marriage.

He'd been so poor when he'd bought it for her. Even though it was cheap, he still had to pay for it in installments. But she'd never asked for anything more. She was as protective of that tiny diamond as if it had been two perfect karats. He caressed her hand softly, not wanting to wake her.

Beatrice Ann had been a real beauty when they'd married. She was still a good-looking woman. A bit larger, but then, so was he. He knew she'd bought some new lingerie for this trip because he'd seen the Broadway charge bill, and he couldn't wait to see it on her. Maybe someday he'd buy one of those Winnebagos and the two of them could just take to the road.

Harvey drove along Route 1 past Big Sur, Carmel, and Monterey, along the rocky coastline of California, trying to forget about the case, to enjoy this time alone with his wife.

They arrived in San Jose and checked into a motel for the night. They were both tired, but the vacation mood had settled in, and he and Bea acted like honeymooners for the first time in years. He was glad he'd booked them a room at the Flamingo Resort Hotel in Santa Rosa, hoping their playful mood would continue.

The next morning, as they drove through San Francisco, Harvey's mind returned to the business of being a private detective. He had at least one more job to finish before he could even contemplate cashing in on his pension plan and buying that Winnebago.

He stopped at a gas station in the financial district to ask directions and placed a call to Destiny. He got the answering machine. He didn't like leaving messages on machines—you never knew who would listen to them—but in this case he had no alternative. He didn't know when he'd get a chance to call her again.

They went through the rainbow-painted tunnel leading into Marin County, and Harvey pointed out the turnoff to Sausalito, mentioning to Bea that he'd booked himself a room at the inn there. He didn't feel guilty about working during their minivacation. Once Bea got busy with her thimble friends, she wouldn't even miss him. Besides, she was being a good sport, especially since he had offered to stay in Santa Rosa a couple of extra days after her convention was over.

It was dark by the time Harvey drove by the Santa Rosa Veterans Memorial Building, where the convention was to be held, but the street lights illuminated the huge banner strung up outside the building. Bea's face lit up.

"There it is, Harvey. The convention hall! Isn't it grand?"

"A sight to behold, honey," Harvey said, his voice dripping with sarcasm. "Truly extraordinary!"

Bea poked him in the ribs. "Let an old lady have some fun. I'm just happy to be here!"

Harvey tweaked her cheek. "You're not old, Bea," he said, winking at her. "You're just getting warmed up."

Bea smiled at him, her cheeks turning a rosy color.

Harvey turned onto Fourth Street, pulled up to the Flamingo Resort, and checked them in. They made a reservation for dinner at the hotel restaurant, then headed up to their room. The clerk at the front desk came running after him, waving a slip of paper.

"Mr. Anderson! I forgot. A message came in for you this afternoon."

Harvey took the note. It was from Dave. He reached into his pocket, took out some change, thought better of it, and pulled out a dollar instead. He stuffed it into the clerk's hand. "Thanks."

Bea was holding the elevator door open. "Anything wrong?"

"Dave called. I'll try to reach him before we go down to dinner."

Martha Barnathan, an old acquaintance of Bea's, approached them in the hallway. After the proper introductions were made, Bea and Martha continued to chat. Harvey went into their room to call Dave.

"Hey, Dave. Did you miss me?"

"Just wanted you to know I'm burning the midnight oil for you, buddy."

"Tell me."

"Your man's been ID'd by a guy named Gus Baker, one of Mac's parolees. Baker has to check in with Mac every week and happened to mention Country's name. Apparently Davis has been hanging around a place called the Stinson Beach Bar."

"Where the hell is that?"

"In Stinson Beach, of course."

"Don't be a smart-ass."

Dave chuckled. "You asked for it. It's just north of the city, Detective. Ask around. You'll find it."

Harvey wrote the name down on a notepad next to the bed, smiling. "Everyone's a comedian. Anything on the family yet?"

"Nothing. Maybe tomorrow. I'm waiting on some information from my cousin."

"Thanks. Catch you later."

Later that night Harvey went to sleep with a knot in his stomach.

The steady drumbeat could barely be heard outside the garage, and the music accompanying it was completely inaudible. Marco and the other band members had soundproofed the place to keep the neighbors from calling the police every time they practiced.

Inside, the pulsing rhythm of the bass guitar poured out of the Marshall speakers, laying a foundation for the melody that Destiny sang in a husky, breathy voice. The middle verse required her to use her full range, and Destiny reveled in it. She was developing an impressive style—she could feel it—and she loved having the opportunity to test it.

This was their best song so far. Marco and the band planned to make a demo the following week, and they were spending a lot of time tweaking it, adjusting the track to make sure it was perfect before they recorded it. He had already told them he planned to make some changes in the lyrics.

Destiny vamped on the final verse, improvising a few licks of her own. Afterward, Ben, Chain's drummer, clapped his drumsticks in a salute. He always practiced without a shirt, and his tattooed chest glistened with sweat from the rigorous set. "Awwwl right, Destiny! Nice ending. It's different but cool."

"Thanks, Ben. I hope the record company thinks so!" Destiny threw him a towel, then took one herself to mop her face. She thought about her chance meeting with the man named Country, and how proud the group would be if she secured a record deal. She was dying to tell Marco but remembered the man's warning and kept silent. *I'll tell him as soon as I get more details,* she decided.

Destiny looked at Marco, waiting for his opinion on the session. He unplugged his guitar, thoughtful. "Not bad, Des. Work on your vibrato a little. It's not consistent. And I'm not sure about the scat you did at the end, because I might want to change the last verse. But basically I like where you're going with it."

She nodded. It stung to hear criticism from him, but she respected his opinion. He'd been doing this for a long time.

Marco set his Gibson on the stand next to his Fender and picked up a large bottle of Evian. He guzzled half of it and set it down to help Ben unplug the rest of the equipment. Destiny stepped carefully over the tangled masses of AC cables but accidentally tripped on the microphone cord, which in turn tipped over the Evian.

In horror, she watched as water spilled out onto the floor near the amp. An AC cable that wasn't plugged in to the second receptor was dangling from Ben's hand, and his shoe was within inches of the spreading water.

Ben saw it and leaped back. "Whoa, watch it! The amp's on!"

Destiny grabbed a towel and quickly mopped up the water before it touched any cables or Ben.

Marco glared at her. "Be careful, Des. Jesus!"

"Sorry." Destiny blushed.

The band members packed up their gear and headed out. Ben slapped Marco on the back. "Good set. Later, bro."

"Yeah, take it easy, Ben," Marco replied. "You too, Derik. Catch you later."

Marco took Desi's hand and led her up the back stairs to his apartment, but she could tell he was brooding. The small space was cluttered. They passed through the kitchen into the living room, stepping over Desi's duffel bag, which was lying open in the middle of the floor with her stuff strewn around it. Marco glanced at it, a slight frown crossing his face. Destiny noticed it and immediately put herself on guard.

Letting go of her hand, Marco snatched up the duffel bag and dropped it in a corner on the way to the bedroom. Destiny trailed back and started picking up the items that had been spread out on the floor. "Sorry," she said again.

"No big deal. It's just kind of cramped in here, ya know?"

Destiny felt awkward and suddenly out of place, like a child who'd just been scolded. Living with a boyfriend would take some getting used to.

Marco called out from the bedroom, "Are your folks cool about this? You want to call them?"

Destiny swallowed hard. She wasn't ready to call them. She was trying to forget about the fight, her birthday, everything. And graduation. God, she still had to go through graduation. A few weeks ago, she had been really excited about it. She and her friends hadn't talked about anything else.

But things had changed. Ever since she'd decided to find out about her dad, her life had been a mess.

"Don't worry," she said finally. "They know I'm here. Anyway, I put your number on my answering machine."

Marco brushed passed her. He grabbed a can of grapefruit juice and a granola bar from the kitchen. "Whatever," he muttered, walking around the apartment, gathering up his books and backpack.

Destiny heard him humming the first few bars of the song they'd just rehearsed. She recalled his comment about working on her vibrato. Everything he said today seemed to be a criticism. What happened?

Last night they'd been so close. Why was it so different this morning? She felt fragile and wanted him to be more supportive. He was distant, almost cold. *He must have a lot on his mind,* she thought.

Nibbling on her lip, Destiny looked around the room and saw

several file folders spread out all over the floor. She rushed over and self-consciously started putting them into a neat pile. When she was done, she sat down on a pillow and opened the top folder, which was labeled DAD SEARCH. She took out the fax from Harvey Anderson and reread it, moaning.

"What's that?" Marco asked as he slung his backpack over his shoulder.

"It's from the detective I hired. I talked to him yesterday. By the way, he asked me to thank your father for him. He doesn't know how to get in touch with him."

Marco nodded. "Yeah, well, if I see him, I'll give him the message." He looked down for a moment, a shadow passing across his face, then walked over to her. "So what's up? He have any news for you?"

"Not yet," she said, sighing. "I thought this would be a quick, one-day job. Now it looks like it might take a while."

Marco moved her hair out of her eyes and touched her cheek. "Don't stress it. What difference does it make if you find out about your old man today or next week? You'll have all summer to check it out."

"But I feel like I've been waiting for years to learn something about him. Now that I've started the search, it's like I opened up the floodgates. It's caused a lot of friction between me and my mom. Now I just want to get it over with. I don't want to be in this fight with her forever. The sooner I find out what I want to know, the sooner I can get on with my life."

Marco kissed her, then headed for the door. "I have to go to class. I might not be home tonight. Got some heavy cramming to do. And I want to rework that last song. I'll probably crash at Derik's."

Destiny looked at him, her eyes pleading. "Can't you come back home tonight? Please? I just moved in. I'm not used to being alone."

He frowned. "Don't start, Des. I don't mind living with you, but don't tie me down. I don't want to start keeping a time sheet or anything."

Destiny felt a sarcastic retort about to emerge but bit her tongue. She didn't want to get into a fight with Marco now.

"Fine. Whatever." Destiny flipped an errant curl out of her face and watched him leave. *Men are just as moody as women are,* she thought. *Maybe more so.*

Destiny glanced at her watch. She might as well leave, too. It felt uncomfortable being alone in the apartment. There was one last final ahead of her, and she decided to go to the library to study.

She was just closing the door when the phone rang. She ran back inside to answer it, hoping it was the detective. But it wasn't. It was a voice she didn't recognize.

"Is this Destiny Young?"

"Yeah. Who's this?"

"My name's Gus Baker. I do A&R for MCA. Country Davis told me to call you. You're the singer, right?"

Destiny couldn't believe her ears. The second time in so many days that she'd been called a *singer!*

She tried to sound calm and professional. "Yeah, I guess so."

"I'd like to talk to you about a possible album deal on our label. Can you come to the Fior d'Italia Restaurant tomorrow at one o'clock? Know the place?"

"Yes. It's in Washington Square. I go there all the time. Do I need to bring anything? Music? Lyrics?"

"If you're the chick from the newspaper, we already know you're good. And I listen to Country. He knows a good thing when he sees it. If he wants you to audition for a gig at the Stinson Beach Bar, you must be hot. We'll talk about the audition at the meeting. Okay with you?"

Destiny was smiling so hard her cheeks hurt. "Great," she said, thrilled. "I'll be there!"

She hung up the phone, jubilant, trying not to scream out loud. Her first gig as a singer! It was unbelievable. Closing her eyes, she imagined herself strutting across some stage somewhere with hundreds of fans watching her, clapping and screaming. Destiny wrapped her arms around herself and squeezed, straining to hold her emotions in check. She didn't want to get overconfident. This was only the first meeting, after all. But somehow she knew she'd get the job.

It was kismet. She didn't need her mother's contacts. She was going to do just fine on her own. This would be proof positive to her mom, Collin, even Marco, that she was committed to her career.

Destiny grabbed her backpack and the spare apartment key and flew out of the apartment. There was a bounce to her step as she descended the back stairs. She thought about how happy Marco would be when she told him the news.

Destiny spent a couple of hours studying at the library, then went to pick up her cap and gown. She couldn't wait to tell her best friend, Caroline, what was going on, and she was thrilled when she ran into her in the hallway near the lunch quad. Caroline had jet-black, short-cropped hair that was spiked with hair gel. Her right ear had seven earrings dangling from it, and she sported a tiny heart-shaped tattoo on her ankle. She and Destiny had been friends since grammar school.

"I can't believe you moved out, Destiny," Caroline said incredulously after Destiny filled her in on the latest. "You're the first out of all of us!"

"Yeah, well, I'm not thinking about it that way. It's not how I would have planned it. Marco's been great about it, but my mom's not very happy."

"What mother would be? Mine would flip out."

"You know my mom and I haven't been getting along lately. She's really upset that I've been trying to track down my real dad."

"Have you heard anything yet?" Caroline asked excitedly.

"No. But I do have some other good news," Destiny said slyly, tugging up her thigh-high socks. "I'm auditioning for a singing job at Stinson's that might even lead to a recording deal."

Caroline's dark brown eyes grew round. "No way!"

"Isn't that rad? I can't believe it myself. I got a call from an A&R guy from MCA, and I'm meeting him tomorrow!"

"That is rockin', Des!" Caroline grasped Destiny's hands and shook them vigorously. Suddenly tears came to her eyes. "This feels so weird. I can't believe we're graduating. Everybody's going off to different colleges and moving on. What's going to happen to us?"

Destiny gave her friend a hug. "Don't get all maudlin on me, Caroline. I'm not going anywhere. I haven't told my mom yet, but I sent in all my application forms to San Francisco State. My SATs are pretty high, and my grades are good enough. I'm pretty sure I'll get in. We'll still be together."

Caroline wiped at her eyes and smiled. "Thank God. What made you change your mind? I thought you were put off by the whole college thing."

"I was. I had it in my head that sitting in classes all day would screw up my chances of making it as a singer. But look at Marco. He does it. Watching him has convinced me that I can do both. If I get lucky enough to make a hit album and go on the road to perform, I'll worry about the logistics of it all then. In the meantime, I'm keeping my options open."

Caroline picked up her backpack and slung it over her shoulder. "I've got to go. My last science final is in five minutes. Good luck with the audition, Desi. You might be closer to making that album than you think. I won't call and bug you about it, 'cause I know it'll make you nervous. But let me know as soon as it's over, okay? We'll celebrate."

Destiny gave Caroline a high-five. She turned and walked across the quad toward the parking lot and her motor scooter. As she climbed onto the scooter, she felt someone touch her shoulder from behind. Destiny jumped and whirled around.

"Country! God, you scared me." She paused, her brow furrowing. "How'd you know I went to school here?"

Country took a drag on his cigarette, then blew smoke through a thin smile. "I make it my business to know everything about the people I care for, Destiny."

Her face broke into a grin. This guy made her feel like a million bucks. "By the way, thanks for following through with your promise," she said, remembering the phone call. "Your A&R friend called me, just like you said he would. We're meeting tomorrow. I can't thank you enough for this opportunity."

"I told you I can make it happen for you. You can count on me."

"I don't know what to say!" she gushed. "It's like a dream."

"Just keep on dreamin', baby. And remember that I can make 'em come true. See ya."

Destiny could barely contain her excitement as she watched Country saunter across the street to where his Harley was parked. She nodded in approval as he kick-started the bike and continued to watch him until he roared down the street and out of sight. He was strong and to the point. She couldn't wait to tell Marco all about him. Instinctively, she knew this man would play a big role in her life.

Later that evening, she was on the apartment floor studying when she heard a key turn in the lock. Destiny felt uneasy but was instantly relieved when Marco walked through the door. He had come home after all, a private triumph for her. *He must really care about me,* she thought. She'd prepared dinner just in case. Turkey meatloaf and baked potatoes—the first meal she'd ever cooked for him.

Destiny was glowing. She'd decided it was okay to tell Marco about the audition. She sprang to her feet, flushed with anticipation. Marco was silent as he entered the apartment. He seemed to be in a sour mood, unresponsive, grouchy. He dropped into his worn-out chair and started plucking his guitar.

Her good spirits dissolved. "What's wrong? Can't you at least say hi? I mean, wow. I made dinner for you, cleaned up the place, and you're practically ignoring me! What gives?"

Marco looked up, jerked his hair out of his face, and returned his attention to the song he was playing. "It just wasn't my day, okay?" he said, irritated. "Traffic coming back here was a bitch, and my bike broke down. I spent the last hour in the shop only to find out it's gonna cost me a month's salary to get it fixed. That means I won't be able to get that new synthesizer. I should've just stayed at Derik's."

Destiny put her arms around his neck. "I'm sorry, baby. I'm glad you came back. Maybe I can cheer you up a little. I have some good news! I got a call today to audition for a real gig. An A&R guy from MCA Records, no less. So maybe I can help with the new synthesizer."

Marco gave her a dubious look. "Yeah? Where's the gig?"

"At Stinson's! Isn't that awesome?" she squealed.

He put down his guitar. "Who's the guy? You've sung with our band only once, twice if you count the Career Day thing. Where'd he hear you?"

Destiny thought she detected jealousy in his voice, and suddenly she felt self-conscious.

"He saw that article about my mom and me in the paper," she continued, her voice becoming softer. "Says they're looking for a female singer for the club, maybe even for a record deal. Wants me to audition. I'm supposed to meet him at Fior d'Italia tomorrow at one to discuss the details."

"How'd he get this number?"

Destiny thought it was better not to tell Marco about Country just yet. She was sure he'd be jealous of a guy coming up to her at a coffee shop. "Uh, I left it on my answering machine at home, remember? That's okay, isn't it?"

Marco shrugged. "If you say so."

His suspicious tone bothered her. "What's wrong with you?" Destiny said, feeling hurt. "I thought you'd be happy for me."

"If it's legit, I'm happy for you, but it seems weird. It sounds like some guy's just hitting on you."

He turned away from Destiny, anger on his face. She tugged on his muscular arm, forcing him to look at her. "I never met this guy before, okay? I can't help it if they want me to audition. He called me out of the blue. What was I supposed to do?"

Marco got up and grabbed his guitar and his keys. "Just what you did, I guess. I don't know. It's your life."

He opened the back door and glanced back at her, his face set in a hard grimace. "I need to be alone. I'm going down to work on some songs."

Destiny was wounded but defiant. "You've got it all wrong, Marco," she called after him.

Marco sat in the garage studio alone, working out a song. He felt at home among the guitar stands, synthesizers, and speakers. It was his world. His fight with Destiny had inspired him. A bitter moment in life could translate to pure genius on the written page. He took advantage of it. It wasn't unusual for him to use unhappy incidents as fodder for his music. He knew that many a famous songwriter did the same.

The song he was working on was coming together better than he'd expected. He'd already sent a cassette of the band's latest demo to Jo Cox, owner of Belladonna Records, but thought he might send this song as well. It was going to be better than the rest, he could feel it.

Chain was on the verge of breaking onto the scene. Every time they performed, they got a positive response. Destiny could be part of it. He didn't understand why she would consider going off on her own now.

Marco thought the man who offered Destiny the audition was making a play for her. Who wouldn't? She was beautiful, sexy, and a little naive. He didn't want her to get hurt, but he also didn't want to rain on her parade. There was always that slight chance that his intuition was wrong. He had to tread carefully. Artists were sensitive, as he well knew.

Marco scribbled down another verse to the song. He and Destiny had some problems, but then again, nobody said relationships were easy. Take his mom and dad, for example. But Marco believed life was about working things out, and he was willing to do that. Destiny was worth it.

The verse was finished. Marco made a cassette recording of the melody so he could work on it later. He thought about Destiny's meeting tomorrow afternoon. Marco decided he should check out this A&R guy after all.

Chapter 12

ALISON AWOKE TO AN EMPTY HOUSE. TRUE TO HIS WORD, COLLIN had departed before dawn. Again. At first she was angry and blamed him for her distress. She felt backed into a corner, and she hated it. She'd spent most of her childhood feeling that way and loathed going through it again. Memories flooded her brain, memories of violent fights between her parents and the constant fear and humiliation she'd endured.

She and Collin rarely exchanged angry words. Sadly, Alison admitted to herself that her lies had brought them to this point. Collin was not the most demonstrative father, nor the most forthcoming in sharing his feelings, but he was not the reason for the decay of their family life. *She* was.

In the past, lies had been Alison's refuge for everything. She needed them for her very survival. The lies she'd told had helped her become the strong woman she was. Now her lies had come full circle. Instead of protecting her, they were hurting her and everyone she loved. There is no free lunch, she realized. It was time to pay the piper. But she was damn sure she wasn't going to pay the full price.

Alison desperately needed to find a way to get the upper hand on Country before the truth finally leaked out. She didn't want to be the victim again. That was the old Alison. The new Alison was going to take charge of this situation.

She got dressed and went to the office. Once she was at her desk, she shifted into her disciplined work mode to avoid giving in to her panic. Listening to the low-level buzz of activity out in the hallway, she forced herself to think logically. What was she missing? How could she use the strength and business savvy she'd accumulated over the past nineteen years to her own advantage?

In her late teens, she had dealt firsthand with her fight-or-flight impulse and had chosen to flee. Since then, she'd acquired more skills and had learned to be more resourceful in getting herself out of predicaments. She needed those skills now.

Alison stared at the predictable movement of the Flying Windows screen saver on her computer monitor until her eyes blurred. Just before she shut the computer down, she had a flash of inspiration. Research. Of course. Why not use the resources at her disposal? Perhaps answers were closer to home than she thought.

Quickly logging on to the office networking program, Alison accessed the on-line message service. Breaking into Destiny's private E-mail box was not something she'd ever considered doing before, but today she felt justified. Perhaps this was the way Country had communicated with her. She hoped Destiny would forgive her. Though she'd already racked up a long list of things she needed forgiveness for, one more item wouldn't break the camel's back, she decided.

After two incorrect attempts at a password, Alison succeeded. The password was MUSIC. She kicked herself for not having guessed it right away. It was her daughter's passion, after all. A storm cloud hovered in Alison's mind at the realization of how deep the chasm between Destiny and herself had grown.

Alison scanned Destiny's latest messages. She felt like a hacker, but this infraction was the least of her problems. Reaching into her drawer, she took out a butterscotch candy and popped it into her mouth. She continued sifting through her daughter's E-mail messages until she found something noteworthy. But it wasn't an E-mail from Country. Destiny had been communicating with a private detective from San Diego with the initials H.A.

Dismayed, Alison was at the same time filled with a sense of pride. Her daughter, for all her fervor and defiance, had been brilliantly resourceful. *Maybe she really is growing up,* she thought.

Alison sent H.A., private investigator, an E-mail message, hoping with all her heart that he was sitting at his computer, ready to receive it.

Archer Advertising had just secured Green's Coffee Stop, a public company on the rise, as a new account. The purpose of Collin's Seattle meeting was to present Archer's proposed campaign to the client. The coffeehouse chain had spread like wildfire, taking over much of the Northwest and spreading east and south quickly, and Collin had been pleased his firm had been selected to handle their advertising.

The presentation was already under way. Collin's team had developed a unique strategy that was receiving plenty of enthusiastic nods from Green's board members. Despite his usual hands-on style, Collin was clearly distracted during the meeting.

Seattle was cold, wet, and gloomy, reflecting Collin's mood perfectly. It had been raining all morning. His attention was continually drawn to the large window in the conference room. The persistent patter of raindrops sounded like small, wet chamois beating gently against the glass. He watched the drops as they drizzled down the glass, blurring the view of the pine trees and bay beyond. His constant commuting between cities hadn't bothered him before; there were times during the year when he spent three weeks out of every month abroad. But today, traveling left him disturbed.

At work, Collin was used to resolving problems quickly. He had an employee roster of more than two hundred people and managed them well. But the fact that he could handle conflict in the office didn't mean he could handle it on the home front. That had become crystal clear.

A pang of guilt struck as he thought about Alison and Destiny. His true feelings were basically off-limits to everyone but himself. Destiny was right when she said he didn't know her. He could counter that by saying she didn't know him either, but it wasn't her fault. He simply hadn't allowed it.

Collin's own father had been strong-willed, had thrown his weight around. His overbearance made life difficult for both Collin and his mom. As a result, Collin learned to handle unpleasant issues by pushing them away and giving himself time to regroup.

However, distancing himself hadn't worked with Destiny. He and his stepdaughter had been politely avoiding each other since her teens, and his Johnny-come-lately adoption attempt wasn't the panacea he'd hoped for.

The rain was letting up, but dark, ominous clouds hung low on the horizon, promising more storms. The weather seemed to be a forewarning of more unfavorable events at home as well. *I could sure use a racquetball game right now,* thought Collin. He wanted to pound the living daylights out of that ball and get rid of some of his angst.

If things were going to be resolved between Alison, Destiny, and himself, he needed to jump into the fray and take his rightful place in the family. He couldn't wait around for Alison or Destiny to invite him in.

Bea flounced off to the convention, and Harvey headed into town. He felt the weather change as he drove south through St. Helena, past miles and miles of grapevines. The air was warm and dry and smelled slightly dusty, mixed with a variety of tree and shrub fragrances.

As he neared Mill Valley, the air grew decidedly moist and several degrees cooler. Harvey was grateful. Driving past the majestic pines of

Mt. Tamalpais, he inhaled the sharp scent of the sea as he neared the famous San Francisco Bay.

He drove through the tiny port village of Sausalito, locating the Sausalito Inn at the corner of El Portal and Bridgeway. The inn was charming, though a bit whimsical for his taste. It was, for the most part, a California Mission design with red tile-capped bay windows. But the exaggerated parapets gave the building a crownlike appearance, as though it were a facade on a movie set. The hotel and the town surrounding it were pleasant and quaint, and if the circumstances had been different, Harvey would have enjoyed exploring it with Bea. But he was alone, and he wasn't sight-seeing.

Inside the inn, he asked the receptionist to cancel his reservation and suggest a hotel in the city. The young woman recommended the Hyatt on Union Square and made a reservation for him, giving him a placemat-sized map of San Francisco and marking a path straight to the hotel in red ink.

Harvey opened his jacket pocket to put the note away, not realizing he'd exposed the gun in his holster to the girl. When she gasped, he followed her stare and adjusted his jacket. He smiled apologetically. "Sorry, Miss. Don't worry, I have a license to carry it."

His justification didn't put her any more at ease, so he thanked her and quickly departed. He wanted to get checked in at the Hyatt and visit Alison. Their conversation couldn't take place over the telephone. It had to be face-to-face.

Washington Square, enclosed within Powell, Filbert, Stockton, and Union Streets, has been described as one of the finest parks in the United States. The early neighborhoods surrounding it bore enviable addresses. It was an earlier version of Pacific Heights.

The lowest point between Telegraph and Russian Hills, Washington Square was reserved as a park by Jasper O'Farrell in 1847 but was spared from the ongoing trend of converting parks into playing fields. It also escaped becoming the green icing atop an underground parking garage, which had been the fate of Union Square.

In the 1860s, the park was the only patch of green that city dwellers could easily walk to. Originally nothing more than a square of mowed grass, the square had been surrounded by a low board fence. But over the years, it had been lovingly cherished and pampered. When Columbus Avenue was cut through the southwestern corner, the park was landscaped with lawns and rows of fragrant Christmas trees.

The centerpiece of the park is a statue of Benjamin Franklin, bestowed upon the square in 1879 by prominent Prohibitionist H. D. Cogswell. The dry taps at the base of the monument are whimsically inscribed with the words "Cal Seltzer," "Vichy," and "Congress," but, of course, provide only plain water.

Day and night, the square is full of people from all economic and social walks of life, and they all interact in perfect harmony. Retired men sit and chat on the benches facing Union Street, Chinese-American families bring their children to play in the sandbox in the northwest corner, and young people congregate on the central lawn or hang out at the outside tables of the Fior d'Italia Restaurant.

Located on Union Street, Fior D'Italia is the oldest Italian restaurant in San Francisco. The place was already famous for its fried calamari, house Sangria, and reasonable prices even before William McKinley was elected president in 1896. It was a favorite gathering place for Destiny and her friends, and she was glad the lunch meeting had been set up there. This time of day, the park and restaurant were crowded, but the outside tables accommodated the overflow. Gus Baker had reserved one of these.

Destiny looked like a star. Her tight Levi's and shiny black combat boots had practically become her trademark look. Today she'd added a tight white Lycra bodysuit that hugged her young form provocatively, and she knew it. She had purposely applied a darker shade of red lipstick and had outlined her eyes in black. She was vamping. Selling herself. And she felt great.

When she approached the outdoor patio of the restaurant, she noticed a man sitting at a table by himself, reading *Billboard*. She was sure he was Gus Baker. He wore stone-washed jeans, fashionable short black Guess? boots, and a white T-shirt under a black vest. A cell phone rested on the table next to his tall glass of beer. *Well, he looks like a record executive,* she thought. Even though she couldn't see his eyes behind his Ray-Bans, she was certain he was watching her.

He stood up and waved her over to his table. Taking off his glasses, he introduced himself as he eyed her lasciviously.

"You look hot, Destiny. You could really rock my world. If you need a man in your life, you just call me."

Destiny blushed. "I just hope I get the job. I can't believe what a break this is for me!"

"It'll mean steady bucks, too," Gus said, leaning in close to her breasts. "Not bad for a newcomer, eh, sugar?"

She smiled awkwardly and sat down. The roar of an engine caused Destiny to look up just as Marco arrived on his motorcycle. She bolted from the table and ran over to him.

"Thanks for coming, babe," she said excitedly. "I hoped you would. I'm really sorry about what happened this morning."

Marco eyed Gus Baker skeptically, then kissed Destiny squarely on the mouth. He placed a cassette tape in her hand. "Don't worry about it. I've been writing a new song. I thought we could work on it together. Later."

Destiny clutched his hand possessively and led him back to the table. She introduced him to Gus. The two exchanged dubious glances.

Marco began interrogating Gus about local artists, other record labels, and promotion possibilities, testing him. But Gus cleverly avoided giving straight answers. He shrugged, made noncommittal statements, and eventually turned the conversation back to Destiny and the gig she would most likely get at Stinson's.

Oblivious to their sparring, Destiny was flushed with excitement. "This is so cool! I'm going to make a living doing what I love most. Wait'll my mom finds out. I told her I could do it!"

Marco leaned toward her. "I don't mean to burst your bubble or anything, but aren't there any other people auditioning for this gig?"

Destiny shrugged, looking at Gus for an answer.

"I'd guess we've got nine or ten girls lined up," Baker calmly lied. "I'm not sure yet."

"What about backup?" Marco asked. "Shouldn't she have her band with her? We work together."

Gus lit a cigarette. "We'll provide the backup. We don't want a bunch of extra people hanging around. Gawkers get in the way."

Marco shook his head. *A lot this guy knows about music,* he thought.

Gus was losing his patience. "It's our policy, man," he said gruffly. "We just want a singer, okay?"

He stood up, signaling the end of the lunch. "Look, Destiny, if you're pulling out, just say so. We'll get someone else. But Country said—"

"No, I'm in," Destiny interrupted, panicked. She hadn't told Marco about Country yet. She touched Marco's hand in a conciliatory gesture, intertwining her fingers with his. "You thought I should get more serious about my commitment, right?"

Marco sighed. "It's your life, babe. Go for it."

"I'll be at that audition, Gus," Destiny said eagerly. "Just tell me when to show up."

"Smart girl. Be at the bar tomorrow night at nine." He plunked down a couple of twenties on the table and headed for his car.

Destiny rushed after him. "Should I bring a tape or something? Any special song I should prepare?"

Gus grinned. "Hell, I don't care. Sing 'Desperado.' Shit-kickers love it."

"You got it," Destiny said.

Gus cast a last glance at Marco, who was standing beside the table, staring him down. He jerked his head in Marco's direction. "And make sure you come alone, sugar."

Climbing into his dark green Land Rover, Gus peeled away from the curb and sped off.

Across the street, Country had observed the entire scene from a park bench next to the groundskeeper's kiosk. The gardeners had just finished trimming the park trees, providing him a view of the tall, twin spires of the two Roman Catholic churches on the north side of the square. He had walked the square for an hour before Gus's meeting with Destiny took place, and the inscription on the facade of one of the churches had caught his eye: "The glory of Him who moves everything penetrates through the universe, and is resplendent in one part more, and in another less."

This is the less, Country thought, watching Destiny head back to the table and put her arms around her long-haired boyfriend. Marco's hand slipped down into Destiny's back pocket. The intimacy of their behavior made Country stiffen. He cast a last glance at the pair, then left his perch to stroll across the park to the place where Gus would be waiting for him. Now he had two obstacles to deal with, not just one.

Marco climbed onto his Harley as he questioned Destiny. "Who was he talking about? Who is this Country guy?"

Destiny looked away, busying herself with the straps of her backpack. "Oh, he's a partner or something. I don't know for sure." She pulled out her change purse and fished around for tokens.

Marco nodded, not wanting to appear possessive or jealous. "So where are you going now, Des?"

"My grandmother's. I haven't talked to her since I moved out. I don't want her to think I'm mad at her, too. I might stay overnight. That okay with you?"

He nodded again. "By the way, I checked the answering machine. Your mom called a couple of times, and also that private detective. He wants to meet you tomorrow sometime. He left a number."

Destiny was elated. "Finally! I can't wait to hear what he's found out."

Marco donned his shades and kick-started his bike. He pulled her toward him for a kiss. "Going after this gig is your thing, Destiny, and I'll stay out of it. But if you ask me, that guy is after you. He doesn't seem straight to me. Be careful."

Destiny bristled. "Don't worry. That's just his style. I'm lucky they noticed me, Marco."

"I won't fuck it up for you," he said, touching her cheek. "See you at *our* place tomorrow."

As she watched him drive away, Destiny felt both happy and ashamed. She should have told him about Country, but she'd done as Country had requested. She didn't know why, because he was a perfect stranger. But something about the man intrigued her. He seemed to know what she needed, what she liked. He was understanding and very knowledgeable.

But Marco was her boyfriend, and she loved him. Right after the audition, she'd tell him about Country so there wouldn't be any more secrets between them.

The Powell Street trolley clanged, slowing down minimally as it neared the corner. Destiny slung her black leather backpack over one arm and jumped on.

Alison poked at her pasta salad, unable to eat more than a couple of bites. She glanced numbly at her computer screen. The cursor was blinking, waiting for her to continue. She'd gotten no response from the private detective yet, though she kept jumping onto the Net, sending him message after message so that she'd know when he logged on.

She'd nearly finished writing her monthly From the Editor column, though she was sure she'd have to scrap it and start over. It was supposed to be a mere three columns of copy, not much by her normal criteria, and usually a cakewalk for her. But coming up with something useful to say today was nearly impossible. Her mind kept wandering. She wondered how she'd manage to get through her interview with Marlene at the end of the week.

It was ironic that she'd chosen to do a piece on rites of passage for this month's column. The subject had been selected months ago, but it couldn't have been more appropriate. Breaking away wasn't always a painless process.

She was just about to run the article though spell check when Mariah ushered a strange man into her office. "He was determined to see you, Alison," Mariah explained.

Alison pressed F10 on her keyboard and relegated the unfinished piece to a disk. She stood up as the man walked toward her, his hand extended. As she took his hand and shook it firmly, she felt the air in the room shift, become warmer. She looked over at the window, which was already open, wondering why she was having trouble breathing.

Today she'd worn one of her few truly expensive suits, a light beige Giorgio Armani she'd gotten on sale. Although it fit her perfectly, it suddenly felt uncomfortable. She tugged at the hem of the jacket as she moved out from behind her desk, staring at the stranger.

Something about him seemed familiar, in a discomfiting way. Maybe it was the blue suit he was wearing, or the squeak of his black leather shoes. The way he kept one hand in his pocket, rattling his change. The scrutinizing look on his face. Something.

But at the same time, everything about this person was unfamiliar and out of place. He didn't belong in her world, she felt sure of that. What was he doing here?

"Sorry to barge in like this," he began, then paused, as if she should respond. "I guess you don't remember me. We met many years ago. In San Diego."

Alison, a look of confusion wrinkling her face, glanced at Mariah. "You can go now," she said. "Hold my calls."

Mariah nodded, closing the door behind her.

Apprehension rose in Alison's chest. She could smell the gum he was chewing and unconsciously took a step back. She felt warm, but her hands were ice cold. Still, she removed her suit jacket and draped it behind her chair, each movement requiring a more than normal amount of concentration.

He was staring at the photos of her family on her desk. She quickly readjusted them to face another direction and flashed him an impatient look.

"Excuse me," she said finally. "I didn't catch your name."

"Harvey Anderson. Formerly of the San Diego Police Department. I was hired recently by your daughter to locate her father."

Alison felt the blood rush into her brain. Her eyes twitched from the pressure and instantly her head throbbed with pain. The initials H.A. suddenly had meaning. She *did* remember him. Each word the man said cut a little deeper into her psyche, and Alison began feeling dizzy.

She gripped the edge of her desk and slowly guided herself into her chair. She did not take her eyes off him.

"Detective Harvey Anderson?"

"Yes, ma'am. Do you remember me now?"

Alison inspected him carefully, forcing deep breaths into her lungs. He was large, but not as big as she remembered. He had been lean and cocky when she'd first met him. His hair, what was left of it, was gray now. The man she remembered had a Marine-like crew cut. Now he was almost bald.

A host of memories flooded her brain, and Alison suddenly recalled the size and characteristics of the room where she'd first seen this man. She thought about the water cooler against the pale green walls, and the cone-shaped paper cups that filled a brown plastic trash can beside it. She remembered a gaggle of men, all wearing short-sleeved white shirts and ugly ties, all sporting black or brown leather shoes and black or dark blue slacks. Their pockets bulged with plastic pen holders, and they all wore guns. The overpowering smell of cigarettes permeated their clothes and hair and tainted their breath, making her want to gag.

Jolting herself back to the present, she was fully aware now of who he was. Not remarkably, she still despised him.

"Yes," she said. "I remember you."

Alison stared at him as if he were a ghost, and she wished he was. He represented everything about the legal system that didn't work. Everything she loathed. Feelings of anger and hurt washed over her, and her voice took on an edge that didn't mask her feelings.

"I left you an E-mail an hour ago," she said brusquely. "I didn't know who you were, of course. I just broke into my daughter's system and stole your address, hoping you could assist me. But I don't think you'd be much help after all. I want an investigator who has a heart. What are you doing here, Detective?"

Harvey put his hand on the chair opposite Alison but didn't sit down. "It's been a long time, hasn't it?"

"Try a *lifetime*," Alison corrected.

Harvey felt Alison's animosity and couldn't blame her for feeling that way.

"I guess I'd better cut to the chase," he continued. "I came here to talk to you about the reason Destiny hired me: her father. When was the last time you saw him, Mrs. Archer?"

Alison leaned toward the detective, her voice a furious whisper. "First of all, I go by the name of Alison Young, and Destiny's father was listed as MIA eighteen and a half years ago. He was probably killed in action."

"He was," Harvey replied, "in 1972."

Alison froze.

Harvey went on without missing a beat. "But he wasn't Destiny's father, Ms. Young, and you know it. Your daughter told me everything you told her. You did a good job of selecting a phantom father, but I managed to dig up contradictory facts. If I give this information to Destiny, as I was paid to do, she's going to be unhappy with you."

He studied Alison's pale face. "You would have had no way of knowing that William Benjamin Statler was an African American, unless you spent as much time as I did poring over all those yearbooks."

In Alison's brain, electrical signals were being issued frantically, telling her body to run, to save itself. But she didn't move.

"I couldn't take the responsibility of dropping this information on Destiny," Harvey explained. "I opted to come to you first. It's against all the rules, but I feel like I owe you that much, at least."

Alison felt as though she was being sucked into a maelstrom. Harvey Anderson was the first cop she'd talked to nineteen years ago. But he hadn't helped her. He and the other officers had been just as bad as her dad. Closing her eyes, she saw the scene as if it were yesterday.

Alison, her meek, sorrowful mother, and her bitter, accusing father. The police officers had kept them waiting. They'd stood around the water cooler, looking at her and whispering. Every so often they laughed at something they all found hilarious. Alison thought they were laughing at her. They stared at her long, braided hair, her love beads, her peasant blouse, her bell-bottom jeans. In their eyes, she was the enemy. She could still remember the cold, unfeeling surroundings, the dark wood floor in the outer hallway, the beige-speckled twelve-by-twelve linoleum floor in the inner offices. The mint-green walls reminded her of antiseptic. She could still remember how afraid she'd been, and how uncaring and disinterested they had behaved toward her.

The humiliation still burned. To them she was nothing but some hippie who probably deserved exactly what she'd gotten.

"Nice of you to have a conscience now, Detective," Alison said in a voice barely above a whisper. "You didn't have one nineteen years ago."

"I'm not the same guy I was nineteen years ago."

Alison turned away from him and stared out the window, silent.

Harvey shuffled uncomfortably from foot to foot, acutely aware of the squeaking of his new leather shoes. He wanted to kick himself for wearing them, but Bea had asked him to get a new pair for the trip, and he'd obliged her. Right now, facing someone he had hurt long ago, he wished he could crawl under a rock. He felt about as small as a rugrat.

He remembered his days on the force when he'd been an unfeeling, chauvinistic fool. He and the guys all acted as if they were more important, more intelligent, more significant than women. They all decided that hippies were useless ingrates, a bunch of spoiled kids with loose values and no morals.

Domestic violence was almost completely ignored except in extreme cases, and even then police officers usually assumed the women deserved it. After all, women needed a slap now and then to keep them in line.

And as far as they were concerned, date rape was a charge that had been trumped up by women as an excuse for their own loose behavior. Cops didn't lose any sleep over cases like that. That had been the temperament of the station when Alison had come through.

Then Harvey recalled what had finally turned him around. It happened a year or so later. Bea, his new wife of two years, had never really seen his bad side until he got furious one day and raised a hand to her. He didn't hit her, but he had been willing to, and the realization shook him to the core. She had been tough and had held her ground, saying he had no right to lay a hand on her or any other woman. That very day Bea threatened to leave him. She told him that if he wanted to save their marriage, he needed to get counseling, which he did.

Soon afterward, he was investigating a particularly gruesome case that finally made him realize what assholes men could be. A "harmless" drunken sailor, enjoying a little R & R, had beaten a young hooker senseless and left her for dead in an alley. The girl had been eighteen and, as it turned out, a runaway. Looking at her battered face and watching her parents break down and cry at the sight of her had turned him around. Nobody deserved that kind of treatment.

From then on, whenever he went out on a 415F—a family disturbance call—that involved a woman who had been beaten, he made a point to speak with her. He tried to convince her to make a formal statement and gave her numbers of crisis centers and shelters that could help her get out of her situation.

Alison kept her back to the detective, determined not to let him see her weakness. She remembered clearly how he had overpowered her so many years ago. She couldn't forget that every direction she turned, she was met with unyielding misunderstanding. Her weakness then had been her young age and her fear of the system.

Though she was older now, she still feared the system. Sharing her story meant she'd have to trust the very man who had betrayed her. She couldn't bear relinquishing control right now, but her emotions got the better of her and she let the tears fall.

"You should have believed me, Mr. Anderson," she said softly.

"You couldn't prove it at the time, Ms. Young. What could we do?"

"You never really listened to me."

Harvey nodded. "I know. And I'm sorry. Please believe me. Tell me what happened. This time I'm listening, and I'm here to help, if I can."

Alison turned and looked at the baby picture of Destiny on her desk. "Please sit down, Detective," she said. Returning her gaze to the window and the cloud-covered sky, she went back in time.

It was the end of the summer of '69, and Alison had been among the handful of college-bound students who still clung to the few remaining days of their summer leases at the beach. She was sad that her vacation was almost over, because now she'd have to return home, and home was a violent, suffocating place.

Alison had enjoyed the freedom of living alone for a month. The solitude had helped her get over the heartache of losing her boyfriend, another part of her life her father had ruined. He'd been so nasty, he'd scared the guy off.

She didn't look forward to going back to face her father's viciousness and the endless fighting between her parents, but she didn't have enough money to move out permanently. Using part of the money she'd saved for college to pay for the beach lease was a big sacrifice. It was worth it, though. She'd made some new friends and had a good time. She still had enough saved up for her first year of college, and getting an education was a top priority for her. Alison was determined to get out of the rut her mother was in. She was sure it would improve her life.

On one of her last nights at the beach, Alison had dinner with one of the guys she'd met during her stay there. He was just a friend. She chose to go home alone, planning to walk along the beach and enjoy the solitude of the star-filled night.

As she walked out of the Gas Light, a local pub and pool hall where she had become a regular, she stopped and stood for a moment, breathing in the cool night air. She continued down the deserted alley. Soft breezes ruffled her long, wavy brown hair, blowing stray strands into her face.

Dressed only in bell-bottom jeans and a gauzy peasant blouse, she shivered slightly in the chilly air. But Alison relished the dampness, the smell, everything about the seaside, knowing she would miss it.

When she reached the end of the alley, she heard someone call her name from the dark recesses of a nearby building and was startled. She could barely make out a figure in the shadows. As she drew nearer, she saw it was one of the bikers she'd met on the beach. She relaxed, relieved to see a familiar face. He was leaning up against the building in his bell-bottoms and peacoat, bare chest showing through.

"Hi, Country," she called out. "How's it going?"

He didn't answer.

She came closer, noticing that he looked strange. His head was hanging down, his eyes half-closed. He mumbled something she couldn't understand and swayed back and forth sluggishly. He seemed drunk.

Alison felt uneasy. "I gotta go now," she said, backing up.

He stared at her, his blue eyes suddenly intense. Her discomfort turned to fear, and she whirled and quickly walked away. She heard a movement. He was following her. Alison broke into a run. To her horror, he sprinted after her.

Barely audible sounds escaped her lips as she tried to outrun him in her worn-out flip-flops. She looked about frantically, searching for signs of other people, but there was no one. What stopped her from screaming out loud, she would never know. She kept thinking, *This is a beach community. This was* not *supposed to be happening.*

Her heart raced as she ran down the sparsely lit side street; her temples pounded as adrenaline coursed throughout her body. She hoped to reach the main street, but suddenly he was right behind her, grabbing her by the hair and yanking hard. Alison fell to the ground, scraping both her knees. She yelped in pain and scuffled to her feet. Maintaining his grip, Country whipped her around and slapped her hard.

"You little bitch," he growled, slapping her again.

Alison gasped, the pain from the blows making her breathless. "Why are you doing this?" she screamed as she struggled and twisted against his powerful, unyielding hands.

He loomed over her, his face wicked, angry. "You're gonna be punished!" He struck her again.

The slaps stung, making her face hot and red. She tasted a trickle of blood from a cut on her upper lip. She was crying. Why wasn't somebody coming to help her?

He stared at her, eyes glazed, lips pulled back in a sinister grimace, arm raised to deliver another powerful slap.

"No," she whimpered, "please don't hit me again. Leave me alone."

"You were comin' on to that guy tonight, but you belong to me, you two-timin' whore."

Alison stared at him. "I barely know you."

"You're gonna get to know me real good before this night is through, bitch. You're my woman!"

Alison lurched away from him as he raised his hand to strike. But Country's fist came down on her face again, and the world went blindingly white. He dragged her down a darkened walkway, pushing her into his dilapidated beach bungalow. She smelled the sour odor of alcohol on Country's breath and thought of her father.

He shoved her through the paint-cracked door. "Get in there."

"Don't! You're having a bad trip."

"Damn right I am." He pushed her toward the bedroom. "Now get over there." Country picked her up and threw her onto the bed.

"No! Somebody help me!" Alison screamed, her voice hoarse from crying. No one came.

"Shut up! You're gonna learn a lesson, bitch!"

He pinned her down with his muscular arm. A purplish blue serpent tattoo crawled up his forearm to his shoulder. Leering at her, he opened his fly and climbed on top of her. He held both her arms apart, immobilizing her. Alison screamed but Country forced his tongue inside her mouth, muffling the sound. The stubble of his beard scratched her skin raw. She wrenched her face from side to side, trying to yell, but he wrapped a beefy hand around her neck to stifle the sound. When she couldn't breathe, Alison realized he could kill her, and she stopped struggling. He released her neck and she gasped for air. She didn't have the strength to stop him from forcing himself on her. As she looked into his eyes, she nearly gagged from fear.

"That's more like it, bitch," Country said with a smile as he wrenched her jeans off and forced her legs apart. He stared at her, brought his face down to hers slowly, ready to clamp down on her throat again if she moved. He thrust his tongue inside her mouth again, slobbering all over her face. Alison cried softly as he tore open her blouse. He ran his hand over her body, harshly grabbing her breasts. He pinched her nipples so hard her body arched in pain. He laughed and did it again. As she arched up, he pushed her legs even farther apart and forced himself into her.

This time he couldn't quiet the scream. He enjoyed hearing her cry out. It fueled his thrust. With each cry, he pounded harder. Like the howl of a wounded animal, Alison's scream pierced through the night, but Country didn't stop. He thrust deeply, brutally, savagely.

Country's fury left his body along with his sperm. As his lust flagged, he relaxed his grip on her. Alison lay petrified and humiliated. She knew she should try to run, but fear kept her plastered to the bed. She wanted to make herself invisible.

He rolled off her and lay beside her, one arm holding her tightly. Alison closed her eyes and prayed.

Suddenly she heard male voices outside. Someone was pounding on the door. "Hey, Country! Ya through? C'mon, man. We got a beer fer ya."

Three of Country's biker friends entered through the unlocked door. Alison tensed, fearing they'd rape her, too. But they just looked at her and laughed. Country smirked at Alison as his friends dragged him off the bed. Laughing, he said, "Meet my new wife."

They laughed again and carted him out of the suffocating room, leaving Alison on the bed like a pile of rags.

Alone in the dark, she found her clothes and slowly crept out of the bedroom, shaking uncontrollably. The men were sitting in the shabby living room, sucking on a joint. She looked at them hollow-eyed as she inched her way to the door. Country stared at her. "Don't go far, doll, ya hear?"

Alison backed out of the house, bleeding, bruised, humiliated. At first her fear kept her from running. But as she got farther from the house, her fear turned into outrage and she started to run, tears spilling down her cheeks. She never went back to her leased apartment. She ran to her car and drove away from the beach forever.

Although she remembered little about the drive, Alison later found herself at the home of the only person she could turn to—her best friend, Kelly McAllister.

Kelly threw open the front door and stared wide-eyed at the rumpled figure on her porch. "Alison? My God!" she gasped.

Alison collapsed in the doorway, crying in deep, heaving, primal moans. "I've been raped," she choked between sobs.

Kelly quickly pulled her inside and fetched her a brandy. Alison settled down on the sofa, shoulders slumped forward. Kelly and her husband, Kurt, exchanged glances. "We've got to call the police," she said.

"No, Kel. I can't go through it. Not right now."

Kurt reached out to touch her, but when Alison jerked involuntarily away, he pulled his arm back.

"The longer you wait, the worse it's going to be," he said. "The cops have to take a . . ." He frowned as Alison's eyes weakly met his and his words trailed off.

After a moment he continued, "They have to get the evidence if they're going to get this guy."

Alison looked away. "I can't. You know my dad. He'll go nuts. He'll say I was stupid to have been there in the first place. I don't want to relive it."

Kurt looked at Kelly. "She should at least go to a doctor."

Alison looked at both of them pleadingly. "No. Please. I'll be okay."

Kelly nodded solemnly. "Whatever you want, Ali."

Alison spent the next few days with Kelly, nursing her wounds. Her parents weren't expecting her back until the end of the week, anyway. When she finally arrived home in her beat-up old Volkswagen, the atmosphere was as gloomy as she'd remembered.

Jack Young glanced up from his TV chair. "Decided to come back, eh? Finally get those wild ideas out of your head?"

Alison put her luggage down by the door. "My lease was up, Dad. School starts next week, remember?"

He picked up his cigarettes from the coffee table, lit one, and took a closer look at her, noticing the trio of quarter-sized pale blue bruises on her neck and the cut over her eye. He gestured toward them with his cigarette. "What happened?"

Alison hesitated. "I fell down the porch stairs at the beach house."

"Drunk, eh?"

"No. I just tripped and fell."

He shook his head and sat back down in front of the television, mumbling under his breath. "Crazy hippie kids." He turned back to his television show, dismissing her. He polished off his beer and burped. "Rita! Get me another beer, will ya?"

Alison spun around as she heard her mother enter the room. "Hi, honey," she said softly to her daughter as she set a beer down on Jack's TV tray. Alison caught her and hugged her tightly. There were new bruises on her mother's arms, and Alison knew nothing had changed.

"What happened to you, Mom?" she asked, already knowing the answer.

Jack glowered at them both. "None o' yer business! Ya wanna come in here and butt into my affairs?"

"She's just come home, Jack. Please don't shout at her."

Jack burped rudely and returned to his television program. Alison and Rita shuffled off to the kitchen, hugging each other in silence. Rita smoothed her daughter's hair, noticing the bruises on her neck. Alison peered into her mother's sad brown eyes, searching for some faint sign of happiness in them, but there was none.

"Tell me about it, Mom."

"Oh, it's nothing, honey. We just fought about my wanting to have a Tupperware party here. That's all. He'll get over it. You know he's always against things at first."

"It's no way to live, Mom," Alison whispered. "I swear to God."

Alison had enrolled at the local community college and tried to throw herself into her studies, but as the weeks passed, she realized something was seriously wrong. Finally she paid a visit to the college infirmary. During the humiliating examination, Alison looked up at the ceiling awkwardly, clutching the sides of the table for balance.

Dr. Morrison regarded her silently for several minutes. "What happened, Alison?"

"What do you mean?"

"It looks like someone ripped you apart." He sat up and put the cold metal instrument in the sink. "It also looks like you're pregnant."

The color drained from Alison's face.

"I'll take a blood test to be sure," he continued, "but I'd guess you're about six weeks along. You can sit up now."

She swallowed hard and bit the inside of her lip, futilely trying to blink back tears. Alison feigned denial at first, but Dr. Morrison finally prompted her to tell him the whole story.

"Why didn't you go to the police?" he asked, concern in his voice.

"I was afraid. I wanted to forget it. Anyway, I thought my dad would kill me."

"Nice guy, your dad."

"I was afraid everyone would think I brought it on myself." She lowered her eyes and added, "I sort of knew the guy who did it."

"Sort of knowing a guy doesn't mean it wasn't rape, you know." The doctor closed Alison's file and looked at her. "This wasn't your first sexual experience, was it?"

"Why do you ask?" Alison was indignant. It was none of his business.

"Because I'd guess that's another reason why you didn't want to report it. Perhaps you thought you had to be a virgin to be raped. Is that possible?"

"Maybe," Alison replied vaguely. She sat hunched over on the examining table, crying. "I only had one boyfriend," she explained, "but we broke up at the beginning of summer. My dad hated him—wouldn't let him in the house." She returned her gaze to her folded hands.

"I think you should go to the police," the doctor said. "The only way you can have a legal abortion is to go to the police and tell them what happened."

Alison buried her head in her hands, giving in to her grief. She had never considered what she would do if she were pregnant.

At dinner that night, she sat quiet and withdrawn. She waited until her father had finished eating. "Can I talk to you both for a minute?" she squeaked. "It's really important."

"Hurry up. The game's on." Her dad settled back in his chair and frowned. "And this better not be about money."

"It doesn't have anything to do with money, Dad. It's serious. Do you remember when I came home from my vacation?"

"What about it?"

Alison looked at them for a moment, afraid to say it.

"I was raped." Alison looked down. She couldn't bear to see their faces. "I just came back from the doctor. He told me I'm pregnant."

The silence seemed endless. Jack glared at her, anger etched on his face. "Ya know, I remember saying I'd sit here and say 'I told you so' if you went and got yourself into trouble. Well, that's what you get."

Alison felt the abyss opening up beneath her. "Dad, I was raped," she repeated, her voice a little more firm. "I was beaten up and raped. Doesn't that mean anything to you?"

"You were living alone, for God's sake. What the hell did you expect? You practically goddamn asked for it. All this talk about free love and peace and all that shit . . . hippies hangin' all over each other, smokin' that dope."

He stood up, lit a cigarette, took a long drag, and blew the smoke into the air. "Well, now ya got it," he said, stomping off toward the living room.

Alison called after him. "I'm going to the police tomorrow. I want you and Mom to come with me."

Jack grabbed his jacket from the closet and yanked open the front door. "Yeah, yeah. Just don't mention this to anyone, hear? I'll be damned if the whole fucking neighborhood knows my daughter is a slut," he said. He slammed the door behind him.

Alison stared at the door. "I knew you wouldn't understand," she said.

The officer at the information desk had directed Alison and her parents to a detective's office. Without looking up, a man said, "I'm Detective Harvey Anderson. Take a seat. I'll be with you in a minute."

They settled into the folding chairs across from his desk and waited in silence as he strolled over to the water cooler to talk to some other detectives. Alison flinched as she heard them laughing. She decided that the white-shirted, close-cropped, pompous-looking detective was the last person she would want to confide in. Unfortunately, she was not given a choice.

Anderson finally came back and sat down. After she told him about the rape, he said, "I'll need you to look at some pictures, Miss Young."

"Mug shots?" Jack asked.

"She's got to identify the rapist."

Alison flipped through several pages of scruffy-looking men when she found his photo.

"This is him. But I thought his name was Country."

"So you knew him?"

"Yes, kind of."

The detective raised an eyebrow, shaking his head. "We'll try to pick him up for questioning, but you have to file a formal complaint identifying him as the one who assaulted you. You'll have to testify at a trial."

Alison tensed.

"I'm assuming you're going to ask for a legal abortion, but you can't get it without the judge's okay. First you have to prove this guy raped you."

Alison felt sick to her stomach. She wasn't sure if it was from the pregnancy or the detective's attitude. "I'm not sure I can do that," she whispered.

Anderson shrugged. "It's up to you. Go home and think about it, then when you're ready to press charges, give us a call."

Alison closed the book on her private memory and sat quietly. There were no more tears. Just self-deprecation and remorse for errors in judgment she had made in her past.

"I couldn't press charges, Mr. Anderson. I guess you don't remember the chronology, but your police department never located Country. He vanished into thin air. Yet he managed to locate *me* and telephoned my home many times, threatening to kill me if I got the abortion. He was demented. He thought he owned me.

"But by that time it was too late for me to have the abortion, anyway. I was too far along. When I could no longer endure my father's seething enmity and the bitter humiliation, I left town and came here to start a new life."

Harvey sighed. "You created a phantom father for your daughter. Someone she could look up to."

Alison looked at him, a level of determination in her voice. "I did what I had to do. I was not about to have my daughter grow up ashamed the way I was. You think I want her to know she has a monster for a father?"

Harvey held his hands up in a gesture of surrender. "Believe it or not, I'm not your enemy. I'm here to help you, if I can, and please, call me Harvey. When was the last time you saw Country Davis?"

She felt her hands grow cold and clammy. "At the St. Francis, last night."

Harvey's eyebrows crunched together, causing deep wrinkles to furrow his brow.

"He's already made contact with Destiny. The man is clever, resourceful, and doesn't *look* at all dangerous. But I know he still is. I can feel it."

"Have you told your husband about him?"

"No. I haven't told *anyone* about him in nineteen years."

"Go to the police and tell them he's threatened you, even if he hasn't. You must let *someone* in on this."

"I'm letting you in on it. For now, that will have to be enough. If you're serious about wanting to help, I need proof that he's dangerous so I can use it to explain all of this to Destiny. Can you get it?"

Harvey nodded, digging around in his jacket pocket for a business card. "I have a guy working on that. Country's got a past. A nasty one. His prison record alone is grisly. If I were you, I'd get your daughter the hell out of town."

"I will lose Destiny completely if I try to bully her or bend her to my will, Harvey. I don't have the nerve to just blurt out that she may have recently befriended a murderous psychopath who also just happens to be her real father! I need another angle. Destiny's search for her father is just the tip of the iceberg. She has already lost faith in me. If I don't handle this the right way, I'll push her completely over the edge."

"I promise I'll do what I can, Alison." Harvey quickly caught himself. "May I call you Alison?"

Alison finally allowed a weak smile to bend her lips, and she nodded.

Harvey turned the business card over and wrote down the E-mail address of Dave Sanchez. "This is my contact on the force in San Diego. I'll ask him to E-mail you a copy of all the data he retrieves on Davis. You might be surprised by what he digs up. Feel free to contact him on the Net."

Alison took the card. "I appreciate it."

Harvey rose to leave, extending his hand to Alison. "I know that hindsight is twenty-twenty, but I sure wish I could turn back the clock on this one, Alison. I'm deeply sorry about what happened to you. I hope you believe that."

Alison looked into the man's eyes and found honesty in them. "Thanks."

"I've got a lead on where Country hangs out, and I'm going to go talk to him. If you need to reach me for any reason, I'm staying at the Union Square Hyatt. I'm planning to meet with your daughter there tomorrow evening at about seven-thirty."

Alison nodded gratefully as the detective left her office. *Soon this will come to a head,* she thought, and she braced herself for the inevitable.

Kelly poked her head into Alison's office and observed her friend deep in thought in front of her computer.

"What're you working on, Ali?"

Alison looked up, grateful for the chance to stretch her muscles. "Come look at this, Kelly."

Alison told Kelly about meeting the detective and explained that Harvey had put her in touch with a police officer in San Diego. She was exchanging E-mail messages with the man now.

"I'm waiting for him to download some files for me," Alison said, glancing at her watch. It was after three. "With this information down on paper, it'll be a little easier to confront Destiny with the truth."

Alison stretched her arms and moved her head back and forth to release the tension.

"I'll sit here and wait for the files, Ali," Kelly offered. "I can print it out and bring it to the house later. Maybe now you'll take the detective's advice and go back to the police station."

Alison closed her black leather briefcase and slung her DKNY handbag over her shoulder. "I'll do that, although it may not be necessary anymore. Anderson is going to talk to him, and he's a retired cop. But I appreciate your waiting for the files. It shouldn't be much longer. I'll see you later."

As Alison walked the short distance to her car, she realized that if she actually convinced the police to get involved, it could mean publicity and embarrassment for her whole family. *Before I shatter their world completely,* she thought, *they have to know what's going on. I can't avoid it any longer.*

Earlier, Alison had called Marco's apartment several times in an attempt to reach Destiny, to no avail. Now she drove up and down the streets around Destiny's high school, searching for her daughter's motor scooter, hoping to catch a glimpse of her. She didn't see the bike, and there was no sign of Destiny.

With Harvey Anderson on his way to deal with Country, Alison could no longer delay what she had to do. Collin would be in Seattle until the following morning, but she needed him now.

From her car phone, she dialed Collin's hotel in Seattle and left word on the hotel voice mail that she was coming up to join him. Maybe during the hour it took to fly there, she could convince herself that telling Collin the truth would be the beginning of a new trust between them, instead of—as she feared—the beginning of the end.

Chapter 13

THE MEETING OVER, COLLIN AND THE OTHER REPRESENTATIVES from Archer Advertising and Green's Coffee Stop exchanged pats on the back, expressing a mutual desire to move forward on the ad campaign. Collin bade a swift farewell to his staff and made haste to the lobby, where he phoned his hotel's message center. He was pleasantly surprised to discover that Alison had called and was flying up to join him. She had finally come around.

This is what we need, he thought as he rode back to his hotel. Some time alone. They had to set their work schedules, deadlines, new accounts, and magazine covers aside—at least for a night—and focus on what was really important: their family.

Alison rode the elevator to the tenth floor of the Four Seasons Hotel, reciting her opening line over and over. *Collin, I've lied to you from the moment we met.*

No, she couldn't just blurt it out like that. How should she say it? She wasn't sure.

Alison walked slowly along the lush beige carpeting, searching for Collin's suite number. It was a lovely hotel, and in spite of the dire circumstances that had brought her here, she regretted not being able to travel with her husband more. Would she ever be able to rectify that?

She blinked rapidly, catching herself before her emotions got the best of her. After Collin heard what she was about to tell him, he might not want anything to do with her again, much less ask her to travel with him.

Bracing herself, she rapped on the door of his suite.

Collin opened it, smiling broadly. "I can't believe you're here, but I'm glad you are."

Alison allowed his strong arms to engulf her, needing his comforting embrace to prepare her for what lay ahead.

She searched his gray-blue eyes, seeing both empathy and longing in them. She ran a hand through his sandy-blond hair. It had begun to go gray around the temples, a transition that only added to his good looks. She wanted to stay in his arms forever.

Collin breathed in the familiar scent of Alison's perfume. "This is more like it. I needed this, Ali. I need you. I hope you know that."

Alison gently dislodged herself and led him to the sitting room sofa.

"I have to talk to you, Collin."

"I know. We have to make some changes so we can get our family back on track."

Alison shook her head sadly. "There's more to our family problems than you know, Collin."

"Oh?"

She sighed deeply. "God, I don't know how to begin. I feel like a walking time bomb whose time has run out. If I don't cut the fuse, I'll explode."

Collin's face grew anxious. "You lost me. What are you talking about?"

Biting the inside of her lip, Alison gathered her strength. "I know how much you value honesty, Collin, but I haven't been honest with you. I've hidden something from my past, and it's affecting our present."

Alison watched Collin grow apprehensive. She could feel the

temperature in the room rise as the tension grew dense enough to touch. He folded his arms across his chest, waiting.

"I'm listening, Alison."

"Almost everything you know about me is false, Collin. I'm living a lie."

"That's a broad statement, Ali. Are you sure you're not just overreacting to all this?"

"I'm not overreacting. The lie started with Destiny's real father. He wasn't killed in Vietnam like I told you. He's not really dead at all."

Her husband frowned. "Oh." He paused. "Do you know where he is?"

"Yes."

Collin's body stiffened, and Alison saw his face morph into a rigid glare. "That explains your bizarre behavior lately. He's back in your life, isn't he?" Collin stared at her, his face flushed. "You're having an affair," he stated flatly.

"God, no!" Alison said, shaking her head adamantly. "It's nothing like that."

"Then what? Are you still in love with him? Is he just a friend?" Collin got up and paced the floor, anger replacing his confusion. "Great. This is great. Just as I thought we were going to work things out as a family, I suddenly find out I'm not even part of it."

"Wait! It's not what you think." Alison tried to reach out and grab him, but when she approached, he backed away.

"Okay," she said, her heart pounding. "There's no easy way to explain this. I'll just spill it all out. The man *raped* me," she said with somber finality. "And Destiny is his daughter."

Collin looked at her in disbelief. Silence.

"I need a drink," he suddenly said, heading toward the minibar. He poured himself a shot of vodka. Tossing it back, he faced Alison. "I've known you for eighteen years. Why in God's name didn't you tell me this before?"

Alison shook her head, tears brimming in her defiant eyes. "I never thought I'd have to. But then he reappeared, and he wants to tell Destiny who he is. I can't let that happen. He's an awful man. A monster! I never thought I'd have to face him again."

"I need a minute to digest this, Alison. All this time I thought Destiny's father was a war hero, and so does she. You've drilled that story into both of us, all these years. You'll forgive me if this is a little hard to accept. How you came up with this William Statler fellow. Your descriptions of him made me feel like I knew the guy. Did you just conjure him up out of thin air?"

"I saw his name at the cemetery," she said steadily. "He was an orphan from San Diego. The perfect combination for me." Alison bit the inside of her lip again and sighed heavily.

"I can't believe you've kept this from me for eighteen years," Collin said.

Alison sat nearly paralyzed on the sofa. She wiped at her tears and forced the words out. "Let me try to explain it, Collin. My parents didn't believe me when I told them about the rape because I didn't tell them about it until I discovered I was pregnant. I *knew* the guy. Not very well, but I knew him, and I was ashamed to admit it. By the time I told them, my bruises had healed, so they weren't convinced it was rape. But, believe me, it was rape, and I was hurt. Emotionally *and* physically. Most of those wounds still haven't healed."

Collin stared at the floor, shaking his head. "I'm sorry it happened to you, Ali. I don't mean to minimize it, but I still can't understand why you didn't tell me about it. I thought you trusted me. I assumed that all these years, we were building a life based on mutual respect."

Alison felt the last of her inner strength ebb. The pain of telling the truth was unbearable.

"I reinvented myself when I moved to San Francisco, Collin. The person I created hadn't been raped. She was a fantasy, don't you see?"

Collin chose not to look at her. Alison continued feebly. "I couldn't get an abortion. It wasn't legal in those days."

He didn't seem to be listening. "Jesus, Ali. Did you think I was such a jerk? Did you think I wouldn't understand?"

Alison clutched at her Kleenex, fumbling for the words an intelligent woman of the world should be able to say.

"Everyone I told acted like a jerk, Collin. I was just a kid. I couldn't be sure that anyone *would* understand. God, the police assumed I'd brought it on myself, just as my father did. The cops couldn't find my rapist because he went underground. But *he* found *me* and threatened to kill me if I had an abortion! I was the victim, dammit, but the authorities and my dad made me feel like I was the criminal. My mom couldn't do anything to help me. She was too busy trying to save her own neck in our household. All I wanted her to do was stand by my side . . ."

Her voice trailed off. Alison gazed at Collin's incredulous expression and shook her head. "I wouldn't wish that kind of fear, pain, and humiliation on anybody. I was only eighteen. I didn't know what to do or where to turn. I certainly didn't want my baby to know that she was the product of a horrible, violent act.

"My dad told me I got what I deserved," she continued. "I was frightened and felt cornered, so I ran away to San Francisco. I made up a whole new past, omitting the truth completely. When I rented your mom's garage apartment, I was a totally different person. And that is the person I had to show to everybody. You included."

Collin's face was a mixture of empathy and anger. She couldn't bear to look at him.

"I never saw my parents alive again," she added softly, staring down at her hands. "They were killed in a car accident just after Destiny was born."

"At least I knew that much," Collin muttered.

"I never had a chance to resolve things with them. Besides Kelly, your mom was the only friend I had for a long time."

Collin took her arms and pulled her up to face him. "Mom loves you, for God's sake! What made you think she wouldn't care about what happened to you in the past?"

"I'd already spun my story," Alison insisted, pulling away again. "She had accepted me as the new person I'd created. Don't you see? It had to be that way. I couldn't bear having anyone think of me as an outcast, a bad person. I didn't want her to think that the rape was my fault. I'd almost begun to believe that myself, that I was the one to blame. I didn't want her to think my baby was less than perfect. Because of the lie, your mom believed me to be a normal girl who'd gotten caught up in the devastation of Vietnam. I could live with that."

Collin sat down heavily in a corner chair.

"Anna nursed me back to emotional health. She was my surrogate mother. How could I possibly tell her the truth after all she's done for me? What good would have come from it?"

"She's not a shallow person, Alison. My mom, of all people, would have accepted it."

Alison was quiet for a moment. Deep down, she knew Collin was right. But her thoughts returned to Country and the danger he posed to them all.

"When I went back to San Diego to make funeral arrangements for my parents," she went on, "I learned that the guy who raped me was in prison for manslaughter. I was relieved. At least he was serving time for something. I had hoped they'd keep him there for life. But that didn't happen. He wants Destiny to know he's her real father and claims he has that legal right. I went to the police but froze up. Memories of how I'd been treated the first time around overwhelmed me and incapacitated me. Besides, I didn't know what to tell them. He hasn't harmed me—that is, he hasn't in over eighteen years."

She felt drained. "I need your help, Collin."

"Why are you asking for my help now?" Collin said, bitterness in his voice. "Seems you had things all worked out without me."

His stinging words only added to her growing frustration. "I was young, Collin. Don't you understand how awful it was for me? I was pregnant! I made a mistake, maybe, but it was the best I could do at the time. All I can say is, I'm sorry I lied to you."

Collin didn't look up. His gaze was fixed on a spot on the carpet.

"Making up the lie was the only way I could live my life with any self-respect," she said imploringly. "But now everything is falling apart."

Collin's face showed signs of strain. "I'm sorry, too, Alison, but I can't seem to move beyond the fact that you lied to me for eighteen years. I thought you knew me better than that. I wouldn't have judged you . . . I wouldn't have thought any less of you. But I guess you never thought I was worth the risk. I'm sorry you feel that way."

"Collin, please don't—"

"I really don't know you, Alison, and you clearly don't know me. I'm hurt, and frankly, I'm stunned by your behavior. Here I was, hoping we could expand our family, hoping I could convince Destiny that I've always loved her, but you never thought me man enough to understand that you were once attacked."

Alison was at her wit's end. "It was *rape*, Collin!" she repeated vehemently. "He *raped* me!"

She watched helplessly as Collin's face retained its chiseled rigidness.

"I get it, Alison. You were violated, but I've never given you one reason to believe I'd react negatively," he said, his eyes glistening. "You know how I feel about you."

Alison was near tears. She couldn't believe what she was hearing. Why was she still trying to explain herself?

"Please understand, Collin. Not only was I afraid of how you'd perceive me, but I was also worried that you'd think less of my daughter. Your relationship with Destiny has always been strained. What would it have been like had you known she was the child of a psychopath?"

Collin shook his head. "I would have dealt with it, okay?"

"It was my only defense, Collin."

"Defense? Against me? That does it. If you've always thought you had to defend yourself against me, I don't know what future we could possibly have together. You clearly don't think I'm worthy of your trust."

Collin picked up his jacket and headed for the door of the suite. "Well, despite what you must think of me, I won't leave you to handle this guy alone. When we get back to San Francisco tomorrow, I'll go to the police and get a restraining order. I'll get my lawyer to check into your rights as the mother, and believe me, I'll do everything in my power to get this guy out of your life so you can put this nightmare behind you."

He paused, then said crisply, "I'll get another room for the night. I don't think either one of us should be sleeping with strangers."

Collin cast a final sad and angry glance in her direction, then walked out, closing the door behind him. Alison stood alone in the middle of the room, tears streaming down her face. His words were like a slap in the face. Her worst nightmare had come true. She was losing the very family she had sought so desperately to protect.

Chapter 14

COUNTRY ADJUSTED HIS SUNGLASSES AGAINST THE GLARE OF THE sun as Gus drove the Land Rover away from Washington Square. He stared out the window. Remembering how Marco had touched Destiny made him think about Sara.

Retrieving the page he'd torn out of Alison's address book, he flung it into Gus's lap. "I think we should give that Mexican punk his *own* private audition."

"Who knows if he'll even go there, man?"

"What the fuck. You got something better to do?"

Gus felt the pimply effect of gooseflesh on his skin at the tone of Country's sarcasm. Obediently he steered the car toward the Castro.

Destiny caught the two-thirty ferry to Sausalito. She had phoned her grandmother from the dock, knowing that Anna would pick her up, as she had done a hundred times before.

Destiny had been so pumped up about her meeting today that she hadn't even thought about the fight she'd had with her parents. But as she stood on the top deck of the ferry, looking out toward Tiburon, the reality of it settled in.

Relishing the exhilarating feel of the wind on her face, she struggled with her contradicting emotions. Outwardly, this was her moment of glory. She was on the way to becoming a professional singer. It was a dream come true. And she was sharing it all with the man she loved. Nothing could be better.

But she couldn't fully enjoy her good fortune. The problems with her mom and Collin overshadowed everything. The quest to find her father had mushroomed into a battle that Destiny had never intended. She wasn't sure the end result would be worth it.

The ferry bobbed in the churning sea, and a group of grammar school children on a field trip squealed with delight. It reminded her of visits she and her mother had made to the city when she was growing up. She and her mom had been extremely close then; "a private club," they used to say to each other.

What would she do if the detective she'd hired found living relatives of her real father? Would she be able to build as many wonderful memories with them as she had already done with her mom, Collin, and Grandma? Would she want to?

Later, sitting in her grandmother's green-and-yellow-checked kitchen, Destiny wolfed down two oatmeal-and-raisin cookies and Anna's specialty, a mug of hot, sugary cinnamon-apple tea. The small room was warm and inviting. Whenever the family got together, they'd invariably end up congregating here, even though they'd practically have to sit on one another to do so.

Anna had listened patiently while Destiny filled her in about the fight with her parents, about moving in with Marco, about the audition. When Destiny fell silent and pensive, Anna knew her young granddaughter still had something on her mind. She could see Destiny was grappling with mixed feelings, so she didn't push her.

"I'm trying to find out about my real father," Destiny said finally. "Is that going to change how you feel about me? Would you disown me?"

"Are you crazy?" Anna said, wrinkling her nose and smiling. "I don't care if you find out your father is the man in the moon! It doesn't matter to me if we're blood relatives or not. You're *my* granddaughter, plain and simple. End of discussion. You've been special to me since the day you were born, Destiny. You don't have to feel guilty about wanting to know about your real father. No matter what happens, it won't change a thing for me."

Destiny frowned. "Then why doesn't my mother feel the same way? She freaks out whenever I bring it up. I've had to go to extremes to get any information out of her at all. Her parents aren't alive, so I can't ask them. She has no brothers or sisters. It's just us. Why doesn't she want me to know if I have any other living relatives? I don't get it. It's not fair."

Anna nodded her head but didn't respond. Instead, she touched Destiny's cheek, then brushed her curls aside to admire her granddaughter's newly added earring. "This is a new one, isn't it?"

"Yeah. Three holes in each ear now."

"You kids have fortitude. I nearly fainted having just one," Anna said, trying to lighten Destiny's mood.

"My parents don't understand me, Grandma. That's the bottom line."

Anna sighed. "Your mom is just overprotective, like a lot of mothers. I don't know why she's reluctant for you to dig into your real father's history, but perhaps she's just afraid of losing you. I have a deep love and admiration for your mother, Destiny. She's a strong-willed woman. She's had to be. She shouldered the full responsibility of raising you for a long time. Maybe she just can't bear to share you with anyone else."

"What about Collin? He's not very good at showing he cares about me. Did my mom tell him to be that way?"

Anna took off her bifocals and wiped them on her apron. "No way, darling. Collin does care about you. Unfortunately, he learned his behavior while he was growing up. Collin has a hard time expressing his feelings. When he was a child, his dad discouraged it. His father was in total control of our household and our lives. I didn't have much of a voice. I didn't offer opinions because my husband always discounted them. After he died, I learned that what I had to say had value, and slowly I rediscovered my self-esteem. Collin was happy for me, but by then he was already a teenager. Old habits are hard to break. But I know he loves you and your mother very much, Desi."

"But I'm not his real daughter, Grandma. He didn't have a choice. He had to take me because he married my mom. He wants his *own* baby now."

"Finding out about your real father won't change how he feels about you. Trust me." Anna wagged her finger emphatically to make her point. "You belong here, just as your mother does. She may not be my real daughter, but I couldn't love her more if she was, and that goes for you, too. Another baby in the family will be just that— *another* baby!"

Anna looked around her neat little kitchen and grew nostalgic. "I can still remember when your mother brought you home from the hospital. This whole place was overflowing with baby things: your swing, your bottles, your toys. Your mom was young, like you, but she was a good mother. You always came first for her."

Destiny took the last cookie, picking out the raisins carefully. "Mom thinks I'm so fragile. Like, I'm *graduating*, you know. I can take care of myself," she said confidently.

"She's trying to shelter you from some of the hardships she suffered. Give her time. She'll come around. We all do, you know."

Destiny gave Anna a big bear hug. "Thanks, Grans. When I talk to you about things, you always make them seem so easy. You're the best."

She moved to the sink to deposit her plate, then turned and flashed a smile. "Be back in a few minutes. I'm going down to the 7-Eleven to get a *Billboard* and check this week's Top Ten."

Wiping her mouth on her arm, she hurried toward the door, calling back, "Just wait, Grans. One of these days you'll see my name in there!"

"Don't stay away too long," Anna warned. "We have reservations at the Larkspur Inn, remember?"

"I'll be back in time to take a shower before dinner. Don't worry."

Anna heard the screen door flap shut. She stood at her kitchen window, gazing out at the empty garden swing, remembering days long ago. She had always known it would just be a matter of time before Alison would start sharing the dark secrets she harbored. Now, after eighteen years, it appeared the time had come.

Chapter 15

MARCO PARKED HIS BIKE AT THE CURB IN FRONT OF HIS APART-ment. He'd stopped at the market to get bottled water and a bag of apples, all the fuel he needed for the next few hours. He planned to finish that song and work out some of the chord changes before they made their demo.

He unlocked the garage, put his backpack and the bottled water on the floor, and went upstairs. As he walked through the tiny apartment to the bedroom, he detected the lingering scent of Destiny's jasmine perfume. Glancing at the small photo of her perched on top of the JBL, Marco got the inspiration for another set of lyrics for his song. Living with a woman might take some adjustments, but for Destiny, he was willing to make them.

As Marco thought about her, he became even more convinced that he should be at that audition with her. It bugged him that the two men had approached her the way they did. He still thought the whole thing seemed bogus. He'd go to the bar and stay in the background. And if they couldn't handle him being there, screw 'em.

Gus and Country cruised down the deserted street. "Soon as I deal with this little prick, I'll see about obstacle number two," Country said, laughing to himself.

His companion started to laugh along with him, but Country threw him a demoralizing look that shut his mouth. Country cracked his knuckles roughly. He jerked his head toward Marco's motorcycle. "There's his chopper, man. Pull over."

Gus glided the Rover to the curb.

Country pulled a Marlboro out of Gus's pack and lit it as he nodded at the apartment. "Perfect place for a quiet little chat. Let's go."

He and Gus climbed the back stairs leading to the small apartment. The door was ajar.

"Anybody home?" Gus pushed the door open. "Hey, Marco. Amigo. We wanna talk to you, man."

Marco appeared in the doorway of the bedroom, frowning at the two men standing in his kitchen. "What the hell are you doing here?" he shouted, glaring at Gus. "And who's the creep?"

Gus shrugged. "Don't get steamed. We got the address from Destiny."

Marco cursed under his breath, thinking how naive she was. "She's not here," he said gruffly.

Country walked over and pushed Gus to the side. "Chill out, man. Gus told me we'd slipped up, that's all. He said you had a hot-shit band—the one the chick sang with. I wanted to check you out."

Marco eyed them suspiciously. "What for?"

Adjusting his body into a relaxed pose, Country said, "The girl bragged about you, man. I thought, hell, I'd better take a listen. We could use your band, too, you never know. Don't wanna miss out on a good thing."

Marco moved past them toward the kitchen door. "I thought you were looking for soloists."

Country sauntered around the room casually, noticing the photo of Destiny, wanting it. "We are," he said dryly. "But I'm not in town very often, and since I'm here, I thought I could kill two birds with one stone. Know what I mean?"

"Suit yourself. Come down to the studio and I'll make you a copy of our demo. If you like the band, call me." He headed out the door.

Country followed Marco, snatching an apple from the counter. He motioned for Gus to follow. Inside the cluttered garage, Marco turned on a light and began pushing equipment out of the way. Gus tugged on Country's arm, whispering, "What are you gonna do, man?"

Country glared at him, his eyes steely hard. "Are you as stupid as you look?" he hissed back.

Gus backed away, and Country returned his attention to Marco, who had flicked on the amp. He waited patiently while Marco set up his tapes to make a dub of his song. When the music started to thump, Marco picked up his guitar and played along, grooving to the music. "Destiny's my inspiration for this one," he said, shouting over the track. "She'll sing the hell out of it when it's done. She's my good luck."

Country nodded, a fake grin on his face. As Marco closed his eyes, rocking with the music, Country moved toward him. *Your luck is about to run out, asshole,* he thought.

Harvey sat down on the hotel bed and kicked his shoes off. They hurt like hell. He hoped his feet wouldn't swell up now, and cursed himself for not bringing his old shoes with him.

Meeting the mature, adult Alison Young had been dispiriting. He felt partly responsible for what had happened to her, though he knew he couldn't have stopped the rape from occurring. He might have helped her during the aftermath, however, and knowing that made him feel guilty as hell. But he was going to help her now, and that was what mattered. With Dave's assistance, Alison could get a hard copy of Country's lurid past. With ammunition as strong as that, she should be able to persuade Destiny that Country was a dangerous man.

Still, Harvey sensed that waving around proof of the ex-con's corruptness wouldn't be a permanent solution to the current risk. It might help convince Destiny to steer clear of him, but getting Country to leave them alone was another story.

Lying back on the white starched pillow, Harvey considered his options. He knew Alison couldn't bring legal action for the rape charge; a statute of limitations stood in her way. And he couldn't get the police to haul the man in without sufficient cause. This wasn't his town. It'd be tough to pull favors here.

But he was an ex-cop and still knew how to interrogate a perp. He'd use that to his advantage. When he paid Country a visit, he'd throw around a few veiled threats, convince him that he could make his life a living hell if he didn't back off. Harvey was sure Country wouldn't relish the idea of cops watching his every move. Being in the joint for so many years must surely have fostered some amount of reverence for the power of the justice system.

Harvey hauled himself off the bed. His stomach was growling, and his minibar wasn't stocked with anything more substantial than a bag of potato chips. He left another message on Destiny and Marco's answering machine about meeting him at his hotel the following evening, and went out into the foggy night air to catch a cab. He'd decided to treat himself to dinner at the Wharf.

He was in no hurry to match wits with a madman, but before he met with Destiny tomorrow, he wanted to have something compelling to tell her.

Chapter 16

At the Sausalito dock the next day, Destiny kissed Anna good-bye. "Thanks, Grandma. You're my touchstone. No matter what, you always make me feel better."

"Sometimes all it takes is a hug and an ear," Anna said, smiling. But her smile couldn't hide the worried expression on her face, and Destiny caught it.

"Don't worry about me, Grans. I'll be fine. Marco is a really cool guy."

Anna studied her granddaughter's blue eyes, wondering if her real father had had them, too. "Oh, I'm not worried about Marco and you. I know you two'll be okay. I was thinking about this investigation of yours. Try to keep an open mind about whatever you discover. Okay? And no matter what happens with that detective, remember that I will *always* be your grandma."

"I will. I'll be sure to call you as soon as I find out something."

Anna hugged her again. "By the way, good luck tonight, dear. I know how much this means to you."

Destiny flashed her a vibrant smile and dashed down the ramp as the ferry's horn sounded the final call. Filled with anticipation, she leaped aboard the ferry. She couldn't wait to get home and start warming up so she could practice for the audition. She hoped Marco would be there when she arrived.

The ride across the bay was swift and invigorating. As she stood on the deck, her face damp from the mist of the crashing waves, her attention momentarily turned to the ominously quiet prison island of Alcatraz across the water. She shivered involuntarily, wondering about the underbelly of society that ended up in such places. She turned away abruptly, looking instead at the dock at Fisherman's Wharf and the safe life she led in the city.

Disembarking, Destiny rushed through the crowd and grabbed the Powell-Hyde trolley, hoping to get to her bank branch before it closed. Now that she was living with Marco, she wanted to show him that she could shoulder her share of the expenses and had decided to split the rent with him. All part of her plan to be an independent, responsible adult.

Standing on the edge of the trolley car, Destiny leaned away from the pole like a kid on a carousel. She felt excited as the cable car plunged downhill from Powell Street and Nob Hill to the financial district. Hopping off at Powell and Montgomery, she saw that her bank was closed due to remodeling and was mildly annoyed. She trudged over to the BART station at Montgomery and Market. She'd go to the Twenty-third Street Bank of America instead.

BART stations were generally boring, white-tiled, unattractive places, and the Montgomery-Market station was no exception. But several of the stations in the mission district were more interesting because they sported aboveground murals, some of which were meant to send biting messages to the powers that be regarding the .5 percent sales tax used to finance BART. Others were more culturally inspired, depicting the present-day Latino population of the district.

The Bank of America branch at Mission and Twenty-third Street boasted such a mural, created by Chuy Campesino, Luis Cortazar, and Michael Rios, titled *Raza History*. Destiny thought it was beautiful. She loved the crowded scene, the dark-skinned men and their eager faces, working hard, studying, struggling, surviving. As she made a withdrawal at the express window, she thought about Marco and his ambitious goals and was determined to be as driven. *He's someone worth emulating,* she thought proudly.

It had taken her over an hour to get home. By the time she arrived, she was exhausted, but she was happy to see that Marco's chopper was parked out front.

Leaping up the back stairs two at a time, she burst through the door. "Honey, I'm home!" Giggling at her campy choice of words, she threw her bag on the floor and walked through the kitchen into the small living room. It was quiet. That was unusual. Whenever Marco was home, there was always music playing.

"Marco?" She moved through the room, assuming he must be in the bathroom. "Babe?" She rapped her knuckles on the door, but the bathroom door wasn't latched. It swung open as she knocked, empty.

"Marco! Where are you?" Nothing. Then she realized he was probably down in the garage, rehearsing.

She grabbed an apple from the bag on the counter, wondering why Marco hadn't put them in the fridge. Munching on it, she made her way down the stairs. The city trash collectors were at work, and the noise of their truck blocked out almost all the other sounds on the block. Destiny wrinkled her nose at the disgusting diesel fumes.

She knocked loudly on the garage door. "Marco?" Testing the knob, she found it locked. She cursed softly. "Hey, Marco? Derik? Anybody in there?"

Disgruntled, she kicked the door, grumbling under her breath. *He must have gone somewhere with one of the band members,* she thought. But now she wouldn't be able to rehearse, because she didn't have a key to the garage.

Despite her earlier resolve not to crowd him, Destiny was annoyed. He *knew* this audition meant a lot to her. Why couldn't he be here to at least help her go through her songs? She was miffed. He was probably mad that Gus told him not to come along with her.

Destiny climbed back up the stairs, singing her scales. What the hell. She'd just treat the neighborhood to some outrageous vocals in the shower.

She pushed Play on the answering machine as she stripped out of her clothes. There were messages from her mother, but none from Marco, which irritated her even more. She wasn't going to let that spoil her mood, though. Harvey Anderson left messages about setting up a meeting, which lifted her spirits up again. She'd have just enough time to see Anderson before going to the Stinson Beach Bar. Destiny was giddy at the prospect of all her goals being fulfilled at once.

Plugging in a cassette of the band's demo, she contemplated her scant wardrobe for the perfect outfit. She was going to rock Country's world and get herself signed to a record label tonight, she felt sure of that. Country was cool. She knew he liked her. He looked at her in such an adoring way. And they were on the same wavelength, too. In the short time she'd known him, he had tuned into her wants and hopes, and it seemed like he understood exactly how she felt. *He won't be sorry he's given me this opportunity,* she thought.

As Destiny sang her heart out in the shower, all she could think about was the audition, and making Country proud of her.

Alison and Collin drove home glumly from the airport in separate cars. The morning had been unbearable. They hadn't been able to get an early flight due to inclement weather in Seattle. To add to their frustration, a lightning storm in the area threatened to keep them there another day. Power and phone line outages plagued them until one in the afternoon.

Finally, the storm let up, and flights resumed. They managed to get on a two-thirty plane that would arrive in San Francisco by about four. They spoke to each other in tight, clipped sentences, and only when necessary. The tension between them was palpable. Alison had thrown up twice on the plane, a result, she was sure, of the anxiety she felt.

Driving home during rush-hour traffic, Alison yelled obscenities at the empty seat beside her, venting her frustration and sadness. She dreaded thinking about the possibility of her life changing forever, yet it definitely had, and those thoughts wouldn't leave her alone. Almost as a reflex, she picked up her cell phone and dialed her office to listen to her private voice mail. As she'd suspected, it was full of messages, most of them internal. Though she'd spoken to Mariah several times before she got on the plane, she hadn't been able to connect with Kelly or Sally, and she felt guilty about it. She never disappeared for twenty-four hours without warning.

"That was the quickest trip in history," Kelly quipped when Alison finally got through to her. "When did you decide to fly to Seattle? I stopped by to deliver that printout for you last night and was surprised you weren't home."

"I flew up there on an impulse and told Collin everything."

"That must've been some conversation. How'd it go?"

Alison sighed wearily. "Not well. He feels betrayed. I always knew it would be disastrous if this news came to light. But let's not talk about it right now, Kelly. I have to get home and try to get a hold of Destiny. And I'm sure my fax machine has been working overtime. Mariah promised to send me everything that was pending so I could get to it tonight."

"I've made my own contribution to that pile," Kelly admitted. "The Beauty and Fitness section is two pages longer for the holiday issue, and I want to get your comments on it."

"I'll look at it as soon as I get home."

"I'm so sorry about all this, Ali," Kelly said gently. "I'm sure Collin will realize what a jerk he's being after he cools off."

"He's not being a jerk," Alison replied. "He's just hurt. Who's to say I wouldn't react the same way if the shoe was on the other foot? I just hope Destiny won't."

"I should have a long talk with the two of them. If they only knew what you looked like that night."

"I have to handle this my way, Kel."

"I know. By the way, I left that printout in your mailbox. I looked through it, Ali. It's nasty. When you show his record to Destiny, she'll want to stay as far away from him as she can."

"I hope so, Kel. With all my heart, I hope so."

Alison hung up and immediately dialed Marco's number. She got the answering machine again.

Determined, she proceeded to call all of Destiny's usual haunts but couldn't locate her. Even her best friend, Caroline, didn't know where she was.

There was one last place she could try, and Alison quickly realized it should have been the first. She punched in the number.

"Anna, it's me."

"Ali. I was just thinking about you. Destiny spent the night here last night."

"Thank God. I was worried."

"She's fine, dear. Confused and upset about what's going on, but basically fine, so don't worry."

Alison wondered how Anna would react when she found out what was *really* happening. "May I talk to her?"

"She left a couple of hours ago. We had a wonderful visit, though. Last night we went to the Larkspur Inn for dinner. She loved it."

Alison remembered the place well. When she'd first come to live with Anna, she'd worked as a receptionist at the Larkspur. After Destiny's birth, she had continued to work there part-time and brought the baby in to show her co-workers on many occasions. They had celebrated Destiny's first birthday there.

"I'm sorry I couldn't have joined you. I haven't been to the Larkspur in years."

"It's just as charming as it ever was. Destiny wanted me to help her celebrate. She has an audition for some kind of a singing job tonight. She's very excited about it.

Alison felt her stomach muscles quake. "Oh?"

"Are you all right, Ali? You don't sound like yourself."

Destiny hadn't shared this information with her, of course. Her music career had been the cornerstone of their argument.

Alison began to sweat as a hot flash engulfed her. "God, Anna," she whispered, "everything is falling apart."

"Come now, Ali. Moving away from home isn't the worst thing that could happen. You were on your own at her age. Try to see it from her perspective. As much as she fights you, she's trying to *be* like you, can't you see that? She's searching for her independence, that's all."

Alison remembered the price she'd paid when she went looking for independence, and thought the cost too dear. "Thanks, Anna," she mumbled. "I'm sure you're right."

The streets of San Francisco were a blur as Alison drove the rest of the way home.

The moment she walked through the door, she sensed something wasn't right. The air smelled of stale cigarettes. Alison quickly opened the living room window, wondering where the stench had come from. When she went to the kitchen, she saw the shattered glass and gasped. Someone had broken into her home. She stopped moving and listened fearfully, thinking the intruder could still be in the house.

But there was no noise, no movement. Alison backed out of the kitchen and rushed down the hall to the bedroom. When she saw the shredded underwear and smelled the acrid odor of urine, she bolted for the phone and dialed 911 just as Collin came in the door.

Later, after the police had left and the broken window had been boarded up, Collin, after getting several assurances from her that she was okay, went to meet with his lawyer to get a restraining order against Country Davis.

Alison sat in the kitchen, wanting to vomit. She didn't want to touch anything. Her skin crawled just being in the room. There was no proof, of course, but she knew Country had been the one to violate her home. She wanted to scrub the place from top to bottom, so repugnant was the thought of him roaming through it. The pure evil of his actions penetrated straight through to her soul. He was getting his way after all. It didn't matter that she'd told Collin the truth. Country was at large, and he had the upper hand. Once again, he knew how to get to her, and the message he left was crystal clear.

At least now the police were involved, which, if nothing else, was a comforting thought. They had entered Country's name in their report as a possible suspect and promised to check him out. There was also the possibility that Harvey Anderson would be able to locate Country as he'd promised, and then certainly he would alert the police.

Her watch read six-forty. Anderson's meeting with Destiny was in less than an hour, a detail she'd neglected to share with Collin. Alison planned to be a part of it. She carefully placed the dozen or so faxes from her office into a file in her briefcase to address later, after her hands had stopped shaking.

Then, seeking solace the only way she knew how, Alison pulled out her photo albums and diaries and flipped through them. Reflecting on her memories, she desperately missed the closeness she'd always shared with her daughter.

Destiny had been so cute as a baby, and wild, even then. Her frisky personality, though captivating, was difficult to control. Her sparkling smile begged for trouble, and her blazing blue eyes invariably gleamed with mischief. There was also a defiance and an underlying anger in Destiny that had, from time to time, given Alison pause. Where did all that intensity come from? When she considered the answer, she shuddered. The genetic connection to Country Davis had always been troubling to Alison. What were the hidden characteristics he and their daughter might share?

But no matter what kind of creature had fathered her, Destiny would always be pristine and perfect in Alison's eyes. Screw genetics.

As for the wild side, how could she expect her daughter to be any different than she had been as a child? Alison's biological footprint flowed through her daughter's veins, too.

Destiny wanted to live her own life. Anna's sage observation that Destiny was using Alison as her role model was probably correct, but she trembled at the virtual mirror images she imagined her daughter's life and her life to be, and hoped the similarity in their paths would stop before Destiny got hurt.

Before she put the album away, she glanced at her wedding portrait and felt a stab of pain. Was it over? It had taken a long time for her and Collin to make a commitment to each other, but once they'd finally done it, their relationship had been solid. Until now. How could lightning strike every part of her life at the same time?

Alison stacked her journals on the kitchen table for Destiny, hoping she could convince her to come home sometime soon to read them.

Air whistled around the edges of the boarded-up window, making it impossible for her to forget about what had happened. The phone rang, making her jump. The answering machine picked it up as she sat glued to her chair. There was no message except a low, dry cackle, then a click. Him again. Calling to gloat.

Alison felt rage explode throughout her body in a violent spasm. She couldn't remain in the house a minute longer. She stuffed the printout into her purse and headed for the Union Square Hyatt.

Harvey had stopped at the Mill Valley Cafe to ask for directions to Stinson Beach and was happy to learn it wasn't going to be too tough to find. He'd spent the day at the library on a computer, pulling up newspaper clippings from twenty years ago, reading every item published about Country's sister's death. He hadn't come away with much that he didn't already know, except a gut feeling that Country had killed her. It didn't bode well that Country was trying to develop a relationship with Destiny Young. The resemblance between the two young women was striking.

Driving along the winding Panoramic Highway, he rolled his window down and breathed in the fresh smell of ponderosa pine mixed with salty sea air. There was nothing but trees and rocky cliffs on this part of the road, and it wasn't well lit. He'd learned from the concierge at the Hyatt that Stinson's Bar had achieved a cultlike popularity with the college crowd, and he wondered how. The highway was nothing more than a skinny two-lane road over the mountains, full of treacherous curves. A long way to go for a good time.

But as he entered the small community of Stinson, he understood. It was a private enclave, off the beaten track, and probably not frequented by the police as often as the city clubs would be. If you wanted to sit out in the woods and smoke pot, this was the place to go.

The area was rustic and unspoiled. Harvey liked it immediately. The road that curved around the mountain overlooking the ocean had driveways cutting into it, tagged with mailboxes set into brick columns. These columns marked the entrances to tree-lined access roads, the houses beyond hidden from view by dense foliage. Harvey suspected these homes all had ocean views. Once again, he began to think of his imminent retirement, though he knew this area was too expensive for him.

Continuing farther into the hills of Stinson, he spotted lights burning in the cabinlike structures nestled in the hills. These were older, less expensive homes, probably more in his price range. But parked outside of some of them were oversized choppers, the kind driven by hard-core enthusiasts. This looked like old biker heaven.

Finally, Harvey saw the road sign announcing the Stinson Beach Bar and pulled into the dirt driveway. Several yards down the road, he stopped short in front of a large sign posted on a tree that read: BAR CLOSED FOR INVENTORY. COME BACK TOMORROW.

Peering through the trees, he saw lights on inside the bar. He'd already come this far. The least he could do was ask if Country was there. Harvey parked his car under a tree in the side parking lot. Once his eyes had adjusted to the darkness, he glanced around at the authentic-looking surroundings. It was like an old saloon. He imagined loud music playing and young people milling about on the ranch-style porch, drinking beer. He wondered why the management would close the bar down on a weekend.

Harvey headed for the entrance, thinking the night was strangely devoid of human sounds. But animals and insects made up for it. He listened to a cacophony of dogs, crickets, and other night creatures as they barked, chirped, and croaked out their incessant symphony. The sounds gave the place an even more isolated ambience, making him feel slightly uneasy about coming here alone.

He climbed cautiously up the steps to the porch, the lanterns above him casting patches of gold across the wood-planked floor. The light spilled down the steps, painting a ghostly silhouette of the tables and bales of hay dotting the side yard.

Almost by instinct, Harvey patted his side, touching the lump that was his gun. He was glad he had it.

Pushing through the doors, he found the place deserted except for a bald man standing behind the bar, smoking a cigarette. Harvey approached him, a sociable smile on his face, but the man held up a finger and jerked it toward the door.

"Can't you read, buddy? We're closed tonight. Beat it."

Harvey sized up the character in front of him and fell into his country bumpkin act. "Hey, I been drivin' all day to git here, Mister. Came t'see an old friend. I cain't just turn around and leave without at least sayin' hello!"

"I don't care if you've been driving all week, ace. We're shut down. Come back tomorrow."

Harvey walked toward him, stalling. He cast a quick glance at the closed door behind the bar. "I'm sure muh friend would wanna talk t'me. Cain't ya just check 'n' see if he's here?"

The man glowered at him. "Look, asshole. I don't need to check to see if anybody's here. I told you we're closed. Now get the hell out!"

Harvey was undaunted. "His name's Country, and I ain't leavin' till I talk to him."

Slick stopped short. Suddenly he wasn't sure what to do. He looked back nervously at the closed door. Finally he knocked on it, whispering loudly, not taking his eyes off Harvey. "Country? There's a guy here to see you."

After a moment of silence, the door opened and Country emerged. He glared at Slick, who moved quickly aside. "You're an idiot, Slick. Anybody ever tell you that?"

Country glanced at his watch as he approached Harvey, cracking his knuckles loudly. "I got no friends in this town, buddy. What the fuck you want?"

Harvey pulled out his identification and held it up, thinking it might buy him a margin of safety. "I want to talk to you."

Country eyed him for a moment, then moved casually toward the pool table. He stood in front of the cue rack, examining all the cue sticks carefully, taking his time selecting one.

"I don't waste my time talking to cops. Especially ex-cops. We're closed tonight. Even you slimeballs can read. Come back when you got a warrant, asshole."

Country took down a stick, checked its weight, and passed it from hand to hand, stroking it. It was heavily weighted on the handle. He glared at Harvey, then grabbed the chalk cube and began to rub the tip of the cue in it.

The detective watched Country's every move. Strolling toward the pool table, he pulled his jacket back to expose the gun harness. Country saw it and continued chalking his pool cue.

Harvey glanced around the room, spotted the framed photo of Destiny on the bar, and picked it up. Country looked up, anger flashing in his eyes. "Put that down, pig. It ain't nice to touch things that don't belong to you."

Harvey put the photo down and moved closer to the pool table.

"You don't follow your own advice much, do you, Country? I know that girl. She's cute. Looks just like your sister, doesn't she?"

He walked a little closer, his voice becoming sarcastic. "Oh, but she was more than your sister, wasn't she?"

Country regarded him briefly with no expression. He returned his attention to chalking his cue. "Get out, cop."

Harvey didn't move. "You killed her because you wanted her to yourself, didn't you? Just like you wanted Alison. Remember her?"

Country walked around the table, lining up a shot, ignoring Harvey.

"Did Alison remind you of Sara, Country? Is that why you raped her?"

Slowly, Country turned his steely eyes toward Harvey, his nostrils flaring slightly. "You're gettin' on my nerves, old man. I told you to get out."

"I know you killed Sara."

Country chuckled. "You got no proof, pig. Nobody was there 'cept that slimy Casper kid, Sara and me. Their car slid into the Allegheny River." Country grinned as he racked up the balls, lined up his shot, and broke them with a loud crack.

Harvey moved closer. "I'm warning you. If you keep harassing Alison and her daughter, I swear I'm gonna nail you."

The burly man looked directly at Harvey, his voice low and condescending. "You're not gonna nail me, you old fuck. You're a has-been. A private dick. You got nothing. For the last fucking time, get the hell out of here!"

Country took a step toward Harvey, and slid the cue stick down so that he held it at the narrow end. Then with frightening speed, he whipped the cue around, whacking Harvey in the head and pitching him onto the pool table. Harvey groaned, blood spurting out of one ear. He instinctively put his arms up to protect his head, but Country brought the heavy-handled stick down again, cracking his nose. Blood splattered onto the worn-out green felt.

Slick drew back, repulsed.

Country tossed the bloody stick into the corner and stood still, breathing slowly, studying the unmoving figure sprawled across the pool table. "Cops really get on my nerves."

Slick shook his head, disgusted. "Jesus, man. No kiddin'."

Country pulled out a cigarette and lit it, inhaling deeply, not looking at Slick. He blew a series of smoke rings into the air, then jerked a thumb at the bloody figure. "Throw him in the cellar. We'll get rid of him later."

Grabbing Harvey by the scruff of the neck, Slick dragged him to a doorway at the side of the bar. He threw the detective's limp body down the stairs into the dark cavern of the cellar. Slick walked back to the bar, breathing hard and sweating, his face pulled down in a frown. This was not what he needed in his life right now. Leaning against the bar, he eyed his friend cautiously, realizing he'd made a mistake allowing him to move in. Country was staring at the picture of Destiny, oblivious to Slick's scowl.

"Get me some gage, man. I want to chill out till the girl gets here."

"I could use one myself," Slick said. "Jesus, that pig was a heavy son of a bitch. Think I'll have a joint and hit the road."

He dug into his stash, pulling out a bag of Acapulco Gold and some rolling papers. After taking some for himself, he handed them over. Country locked eyes with him, a mirthless smile turning up the corners of his mouth as he rolled a couple of bombers, licking the edges carefully.

"You're gonna stay put till my little fish gets here. I'll tell you when you can leave. Got it?"

Slick was pissed but was careful not to show it. He merely grunted in response and lit up his own joint.

Country took the small framed photo of Destiny from the counter and touched her lips tenderly. Fetching himself another bottle of Bud, he gestured toward the bloody pool table. "Clean that up. We've got an audition soon, remember?"

Firing up his joint, he took his beer and disappeared into the office.

Slick looked at the bloody pool table, irritated. All of a sudden he couldn't wait to be far away from this place.

Alison hadn't heard from Collin, but then, she hadn't expected to. He'd told her that he was going to talk to his lawyer and had planned to go to the police station after that to see if he could get someone to patrol their street.

Printout in hand, Alison entered the Hyatt lobby and located the courtesy phone bank. Harvey Anderson wasn't in his room. She checked with reception and was told he hadn't checked out, so she settled in the lounge to wait. Ordering an iced tea, she kept an eye on the entrance. Her heart was thumping in anticipation of what she would tell Destiny.

She left her surveillance spot to visit the courtesy phones once more and spotted her daughter marching through the lobby.

"Destiny!" Alison dropped the phone and ran to her. "I've been trying to reach you all day!"

Destiny frowned. "What're you doing here, Mom?"

"I came to see Detective Anderson, and to see you. It's urgent that we talk!"

Destiny's eyes went round with anger. "You've been talking to *my* private detective? How could you? Can't you let me have anything for myself? I just checked at the front desk, and they said he's not here. What did you do? Talk him into dropping my case?"

"Of course not. There's more to all this than you think. We have to talk about Country, you and I."

Anger flashed in Destiny's eyes. "Great. So now you're having me followed. Is that it? This is so typical, Mother. As soon as I do any-thing for myself, meet someone who's interested in my career, you think you can discredit them, invalidate them. Well, I'm not going to listen this time, okay?"

"Destiny, he's not what you think. I have to tell you something about him. Something really bad."

Her daughter glanced around the hotel impatiently. She looked dressed to kill in black leather pants, motorcycle boots, and a tight white crop top. Alison took her arm and tried to usher her to a more secluded area. "Please sit down with me. It's not easy for me to do this. If Harvey Anderson were here, he'd be on my side, believe me."

Destiny yanked her arm away. "I'm not interested in talking with you, Mom. I've got an audition tonight that is very important to me, and I need to keep my mind on that! I'll catch up with Harvey later, and fire him! He's supposed to have been working for me, not you! I can't believe you'd try to control even this!"

"That's not what this is about, Destiny. You have to believe me, Country's a dangerous man!"

"Look, Mother," Destiny retorted, saying "mother" with nasty sarcasm. "You have a thing about me and men. You think you can edit my life to make it fit into your version of a perfect manuscript, just like an article in your precious magazine! I'll find out about my father no matter what you do! At least Country was understanding about that!"

Destiny turned abruptly away from Alison and ran.

"Destiny! Please!" Alison called after her.

Ignoring her, Destiny ducked through the lobby bar. Weaving deftly through the after-dinner cocktail crowd, she cut across to the Powell Street exit and slipped out the door.

Alison rushed after her, dodging around the same people in the lobby, but her maneuvers weren't as swift. She shouted Destiny's name, bringing an admonishing glance from the concierge. She cursed under her breath, wanting to flip him off.

The crowd closed back in on the path Destiny's mad dash had made, and Alison was forced to cut a new course. She swerved to avoid a table adorned with a huge crystal vase, slipped, and stumbled, dropping her purse and its contents all over the floor.

"Dammit!" Alison quickly scooped her compact, wallet, and lip-stick into her handbag, cursing again as she searched for her pen. A woman knelt down to help collect her things. "Are you okay?"

Alison gave the woman a hollow-eyed look, her heart pounding in her chest. "Yes," she lied. "Sorry. I should watch where I'm going." Brushing off her khakis, Alison hurried through the front door, but Destiny was long gone.

Chapter 17

COLLIN NOW UNDERSTOOD HOW NERVE-RACKING A POLICE STATION could be. Even if you weren't guilty of anything, the atmosphere was intimidating, the people so official. It had to have been hard for Alison to face them again, especially if she'd had a bad experience with cops before.

Realizing he hadn't told his mother anything about what was going on, Collin punched in her number on his cell phone.

"Hi, Mom."

"Hello, Collin. Is everything sorted out between you and Destiny?"

Collin sighed. "You have no idea, Mom." He described the events of the last twenty-four hours, telling her about Alison's secret life, and most notably, his reaction to it. "It's a shock, I know," Collin added after he'd finished.

"It's horrible, Collin. To think that poor little girl has been harboring that dark secret all these years. I can't imagine how hard it must have been."

Collin was a bit perturbed. "Aren't you even a little upset that she lied to you?"

"What's really upsetting is how *you* handled it," Anna pointed out.

The impact of her statement stung. "Yeah," Collin said softly. "I blew it. I know."

"I always knew there was something she wasn't telling me," Anna said. "It was in her eyes. A kind of sadness that even the smiles of her baby couldn't cure."

"Well, I missed it," Collin said. "And when she finally told me, all I could think about was myself. I got stuck on the fact that she didn't think me worthy of her trust."

Anna sighed heavily. "And at the moment of truth, you weren't."

Collin closed his eyes, feeling bruised by the truth. "You don't mince words anymore, do you, Mom?"

"I spent too many years swallowing my opinions, Collin. I'm too old for that now. The truth is, I've tried to tell you for years that no matter what, your family should come first. Every one of us has secrets, Collin. Everyone makes mistakes."

Collin looked at the cross section of humanity represented in the busy police station and silently agreed.

"I understand why she did it," Anna added. "The love of a mother is unbelievably strong. There's an animal instinct in us that just overrides logic sometimes. All she was trying to do was protect her child. Telling a lie of such magnitude, she'd have to believe it herself to pull it off."

They spoke a little longer, then Collin hung up, humbled. Alison had reached out to him, and he hadn't been there for her. Now it was up to him to set things straight.

Alison had struck out twice. Every opportunity she'd had to tell Destiny the truth had come and gone, leaving her choking on her secret each time. As she raced her Audi up Geary, reality finally sank in. The hard, cold fact that she had thrust her daughter into harm's way slapped her in the face. She had to overcome her own insecurities and expose the lie while she still had a chance. The time for discretion was long past.

In her hand, she gripped the printout Kelly had left for her. If she could just get Destiny to look at it, she was sure the facts would convince her that Country had been lying.

The most disturbing part of the E-mail from Harvey's police buddy was a copy of a newspaper photo. It was a high school picture of Country's eighteen-year-old sister that had appeared in the paper after she and her boyfriend were tragically killed. The deaths were suspicious, and foul play had not been ruled out. Country had been suspected of the crime but was never charged due to lack of evidence.

Alison had gasped when she first saw the photo. The dead girl could have been Destiny's twin.

Damn him, Alison thought. Damn Country to hell for coming back into their lives.

Alison sped through the Mission District, searching for Marco's address. She would tell Destiny the truth even if she had to hold her down to hear it.

Finally locating Clipper Street, Alison recognized Marco's motorcycle. A light was on in the second-floor apartment, and she thanked God Destiny had come back here. Scrutinizing the neighborhood, Alison regretted not paying attention to where her daughter had been coming for the past several months. Now she understood why Destiny had never encouraged her to know; it was not the sort of neighborhood Alison would have liked to see her frequent.

The night had descended like a shroud. It was pitch black, the moon not yet risen in the sky. On this stretch of street, there wasn't a street lamp, and the neighborhood was dreary and quiet except for one dog who had parked itself in front of the garage below Marco's apartment. Scratching at the door, the dog was sniffing and yapping incessantly.

She climbed the wooden stairs to the second floor and rapped on the door. No answer. She rang the old doorbell and knocked again. Still no answer. Trying the door, she found it was unlocked. "Destiny? Marco?" she called out. "The door's open. Can I come in? I need to talk to you."

Alison walked in slowly, embarrassed to enter Marco's home uninvited. She would have preferred to visit here under different circumstances. She hadn't made an effort to get to know Marco in the year he'd been dating Destiny, and suddenly she felt guilty. She had loathed her parents' unyielding attitude toward her own friends, yet she had nearly duplicated the same behavior.

Looking around at the small, cluttered space, she reluctantly remembered the summer she had spent at the beach, the summer she had spent trying to establish *her* independence. The ratty little rental had looked very much like this: tiny kitchen, old stove, stained porcelain kitchen sink. No conveniences. Emancipation. God, if she'd only known.

"Destiny?" Alison stepped through the small living room, and peeked into the open bedroom and bathroom. Empty. They weren't home. Destiny hadn't come back here. Where in the hell did she go?

She walked back through the apartment, frustrated. She hadn't wanted this for her daughter. She'd hoped Destiny would choose a traditional path: a dormitory, sororities, fun things. All that a regular college experience could offer her. All that Alison hadn't had herself. This place had none of that. No warmth, no comforts, barely any furniture. It was Marco's place. A bachelor pad.

Still, despite her own reservations, Destiny probably loved the place. The apartment was devoted to music. Tape recorders, huge speakers, guitars, a small keyboard, all hooked up to a sound system that looked expensive and state-of-the-art. *This* was what her daughter wanted. Not the magazine business. Not an office job. The message was loud and clear. Destiny had plans for her own future, and if Alison wanted to be part of it, she'd have to learn to accept them.

Leaving the door unlocked, Alison exited the apartment. The little dog was still barking at the garage door. Feeling sorry for it, she walked over, knelt down, and rubbed the dog behind its ears. She noticed a sliver of light coming through a crack near the bottom and could make out faint sounds of music. Maybe Marco and Destiny were inside. She'd overheard Destiny talk about a garage studio.

Alison pounded on the door but got no response. All she heard was the continuous, soft beat of the bass line from within. The door handle had a simple, cheap lock. Alison thought she could jimmy it open with a credit card. Pulling a MasterCard from her bag, she slipped it into the doorjamb and slid it up and down, just like she'd seen so many times on television. The latch popped. She opened the door and entered. The dog scooted past her.

"Sorry I broke in here, but—"

Alison stopped in horror. Chaos. A choked scream escaped her throat, and she looked around wildly, half expecting whoever had done the damage to be hiding nearby.

As she scanned the room, her stomach tightened. Alison nearly gagged as her mind digested what she was seeing. Guitars and music stands were pitched over on their sides. Her eyes fell on a large tarpaulin. A leg and part of an arm were sticking out from under it.

Was it Marco? She wasn't sure. Where was Destiny? What had happened here? Alison's heart pounded in her chest as she backed out of the garage. She had to get help. She ran back up to Marco's apartment. She couldn't stop shaking as she dialed 911 for the second time tonight.

"911 police emergency."

"Please help me. I've found someone in a garage. I think he's been killed." Alison began shaking uncontrollably. "I don't know where my daughter is!"

"I need your name and your address, ma'am."

"This isn't my home," Alison whispered.

"Give me the address you're calling from."

Alison got a grip on herself and repeated the address of Marco's apartment, glancing around the room, trying to keep her mind focused. "Please hurry," she said, her eyes settling on a handwritten note near the phone.

"Officers are on the way," the voice said. "Stay where you are."

Alison hung up. She grabbed the note. It was written in Destiny's hand. "Come to the audition tonight, babe. I don't care what Country says. I can sing better with you by my side. Just show up at Stinson's Bar as soon as you can."

Alison's heart thumped harder. As sure as the sky was blue, Country had arranged this audition.

What did Country plan to do? Kidnap her? Or worse? Alison ran out and hurried down the stairs past the garage. She couldn't wait for the police. She had to get to the Stinson Beach Bar.

Trembling, she asked God to forgive her for leaving the poor man lying in the garage, but she could not allow Country to take her daughter. She may not have had the strength or the sense to fight him off the first time, but fear could not paralyze her now. Destiny was not going to become his victim, too.

Alison gripped the steering wheel, driving fast but controlled. She hadn't been to church in years, but she hoped God wouldn't forsake her, and she mouthed every prayer she'd ever learned. She punched in Collin's cell phone number and prayed he'd answer.

"Hello?"

Alison was crying but forced words through her tears. "Collin! I went looking for Destiny and Marco at their apartment. Someone's been killed!" Alison wiped her tears from her face as she sped along Van Ness Boulevard.

"What? Alison, you're talking too fast. Slow down. Who's been killed? Where's Destiny? Where are you?"

"Someone in Marco's garage—I don't know who. I don't think it was Marco. But I couldn't wait to find out. I think he's got Destiny. I have to stop him!"

"Alison!" Collin's voice roared over the phone. "Do *not* go anywhere alone! Wait for me. I'll get the police."

"I can't, Collin. I can't just let him take her!"

"Alison, tell me where you are. Pull over and I'll come get you!"

"Just get the police to come to Stinson's, Collin. Please!" Alison hung up and pushed down on the gas as she headed across the Golden Gate Bridge.

Collin bolted out of his lawyer's office, his impetuous, stubborn attitude dissolving into intense regret in a matter of moments. What was wrong with him? He should never have left her.

All his adult life, he'd been devoted to his business, placing its importance higher on the scale than anything, including his family life. Before he married Alison, he'd enjoyed a parade of noncommitted women with whom he could play after hours. After their marriage, he came to understand that true love was far better than anything he'd experienced so far and was worth the wait. He had cherished Alison even more because she had not tried to change him. She was as driven as he was, if not more so. Theirs had been a perfect union. And he had almost thrown it all away.

Collin called the police again and told them what Alison had relayed to him. He finally got through to someone who admitted that she'd taken a 911 call from the Mission District, and he convinced the officers that the break-in at their townhouse, the death in the garage, and the threats his wife had been receiving were most likely from the same man. The police officers promised to check it out.

Collin raced his Porsche across town, cursing himself. His wife and daughter were in danger, yet he had been too self-indulgent to really see it. Based on his egotistic reaction to Alison's plea, he didn't deserve her trust. He only hoped he'd get another chance to prove himself worthy of it.

Destiny parked near the entrance of Stinson's, checked her face one last time in the rearview mirror, and went inside.

She loved the place instantly. The lights were low and cast a golden glow over the room, which smelled like sawdust and beer. A Tammy Wynette song was coming from a jukebox in the corner, and she noticed a nice-sized stage on the far side. Destiny imagined it would be a great place to perform and couldn't wait for Marco to show up. Her gaze came to rest on two men behind the bar. She didn't recognize one of them, but the other one was Country. She put on a winning smile and walked toward them.

Without taking his eyes off her, Country whispered, "You can take a hike now, Slick."

"About fuckin' time," Slick muttered. He put on a leather jacket and strolled out of the bar, casting a long glance at Destiny as he passed.

He leaped immediately onto his chopper, kicking it over and revving it forcefully. He wondered briefly if the cop was still alive and cursed Country. Dead or alive, beating up a cop on his property wasn't his idea of keeping a low profile. The bar was in his name. This kind of trouble could land him in the joint.

As he was about to leave, two of the local bikers roared up on their machines and jerked their heads toward the make-shift "closed" sign. "What the fuck's going on, Slick?" one of them asked. "You never closed this joint before, man."

The other biker, a smaller man, rolled his bike right up to Slick's. When he spoke, the stud piercing his tongue was visible. "Yeah. I was gettin' ready for a couple of brews and a babe. This is gonna spoil my plans, Baldy. I don't take that kinda shit sittin' down."

Slick spat in the dirt beside the road, knowing they wouldn't want to tackle Country tonight. "An ex-con in there's got a private gig with a chick tonight, boys. He's good people, and he's paid the price, if you know what I mean. Don't piss him off by ignorin' that sign. C'mon. I'll buy ya some beers in Mill Valley. It's a good night for a ride anyway."

Later, Slick bought a round of brews at the small Mill Valley bar, glad to be away from Country for a while. Friend or no friend, the stupid fuck had gone off the deep end and would surely be made to pay for it. But Slick saw no need to get dragged down along with him.

Destiny admired the way Country was dressed. Hip, lizard-skin boots, perfectly worn-in jeans with just the right amount of fade, and an expensive-looking shirt under a soft black-leather jacket. A Marlboro cigarette dangled from the corner of his mouth.

He took her hand and squeezed it. Shyly, she looked down at her boots. He gazed at her as if he were memorizing her. Finally he released her and squashed out his cigarette.

Destiny surveyed the bar, self-conscious. There was nobody else in the place, which seemed odd.

"Am I early or something?" she asked.

Country winked at her. "Not at all. You're right on time."

"Aren't any other girls auditioning tonight? Gus said—"

Country cut her off, his voice steady. "Forget Gus. You're it. This audition is for you, baby. I'm the only one you need to worry about."

Destiny smiled awkwardly, uncertain what he meant. She felt her stomach flutter and thought she was getting a case of stage fright. *I can't get cold feet now,* she thought.

Taking a cassette tape out of her purse, she handed it to Country. "Here's a backing track for 'Desperado.' Where would you like me to sing?"

Country's eyes cruised her body again, lingering first at her lips, then moving slowly down her neck to her breasts. God, she was like Sara. He shifted in his chair and took a long look at the line of her legs. Her leather pants were tight, leaving nothing to the imagination. His nostrils flared and he began breathing heavily.

"Uh, Country," Destiny said nervously, "I'm sorry to sound so dumb, but aren't there supposed to be other record label people here or something?"

Country walked to the stage, gesturing toward it. There was a microphone, tape deck, and speakers set up on the floor. "Climb up on that stage, Destiny. Let's see what you can do."

He popped the tape into a cassette player and waited for her to settle herself in front of the microphone. "I'm the only one who needs to hear you. I told you I can make it happen for you."

He pushed Play and pulled a chair up to the center position. He sat back, smiling. "Show me what you got."

"This is weird, but, well, okay." Destiny launched into the first verse of "Desperado" timorously, her voice growing stronger as she saw Country's appreciative nods.

During the instrumental portion of the song, Country said, "Put more feeling into it. Use body language. Sell it to me."

Destiny nodded. She felt awkward as she began moving her body to the rhythm. Suddenly Country came up on the stage with her.

"Keep singing. I like it. You look real good." He put his hands on her waist and guided her hips to sway to the music, his hands reaching down around her buttocks.

Destiny dislodged herself. "That's not part of the audition, Mr. Davis."

Country locked eyes with her, a hurt expression in them. She noticed that his were as blue as hers, and his face was similar in shape. He grabbed her wrist before she could move away.

"You've got my eyes," he said, knowing she'd realized it. "Just like Sara. But your body is just like your mother's. Ain't that a nice combination?"

Destiny tried to free her wrist. "What are you talking about? Why are you acting so strange?"

Country's eyes didn't move from her face. He studied her lips. "I'm your father, Destiny. Your search has ended."

"That's ridiculous! My father is dead!"

"That's a lie. Ask your mother. She's been keeping you from me, Destiny. I'm not going to stand for that anymore. I came back to take charge of my family."

Destiny stopped. She examined Country's face more closely, suddenly seeing the uncanny resemblance for the first time. Unsure of what was happening, she shook her head vigorously.

"Let go of my hand, Country. I don't believe you. I want to leave."

"No way, girl. We're gonna have a little chat. Get to know each other. Bond. Know what I mean?"

Destiny finally broke out of his grip and backed off of the stage. "Look, Mr. Davis. This is too weird for me. I should've listened to my boyfriend. He told me this was bogus."

Country stamped his booted foot on the floor hard, making her jump. His angry blue eyes penetrated her.

"You won't be listening to him ever again, you got that? He's out of the picture."

Destiny glared at him, confused. "I don't know who you think you are, but you can't tell me what to do! Marco is my boyfriend!"

She grabbed her backpack. "I'm outta here." She flashed him a defiant look, missing the manic gloss in his eyes, and headed for the door. She almost made it before she heard a whooshing sound near her ear and felt a sharp blow to her head.

Through a fog she heard, "You're not going anywhere, little girl." Then she dropped to the floor, her head exploding in pain.

Country put the bottle down, grabbed hold of her arms, and dragged her semiconscious body from the stage. "I'm your father," he repeated. "It's time you accepted the truth."

She moaned as the light in the room closed in on her. Beads of sweat appeared on her forehead as the hot flash of unconsciousness took over. She fell limp, and blackness consumed her.

The first sensation Harvey noticed was the musty, damp odor. He was sprawled out on a cold cement floor at the bottom of a flight of wooden stairs. He couldn't see much, but concluded he was in an old cellar.

His hand moved to his head, groping it tenderly. There was a nasty cut and a huge bump on his balding scalp. Eventually, as his eyes focused in the dark, he discerned that his vision hadn't been impaired. He didn't think the damage to his head was too bad. Probably a concussion.

His face felt worse. His nose was swollen and sore. Broken, he was sure. After he carefully determined the severity of the large gash over his left eye, he found dried blood in his ear. *I must look a mess,* he thought. But at least he was alive.

Harvey heard a sound from above that he assumed was the front door slamming, then heavy footsteps on what must have been the front porch steps. He froze. But there were no footsteps heading his direction, and after a moment, he relaxed. He heard someone kick-start a motorcycle and listened as the bike spun off down the dirt road and out onto the highway beyond.

He didn't move until the sound of the motor had disappeared. Then, he slowly pushed himself up into a sitting position. He was trying to get his bearings when he heard a girl's voice.

Harvey tried to get up, but the world started to spin and he slid back down to the floor. Maybe he was hurt worse than he thought. He lay still for a moment to regain his equilibrium, then started to crawl along the cold floor. Harvey knew he had to stay conscious. He had to find a way out so he could call for help.

Chapter 18

MARCO KNEW HE WAS ONE LUCKY MAN. THE BLOWS HE'D BEEN dealt had broken his arm and a few ribs and crushed his jaw, but they had not been the fatal blows Country had meant to deliver.

After he regained consciousness, Marco found himself covered with blood and couldn't think straight for the pain. He had enough sense to realize he'd better get out of sight. Slowly, he crawled to a corner of the garage and curled up under a tarpaulin. He lay there, fading in and out of consciousness, until he was revived when the police and ambulance finally arrived.

Now, lying in a room in French Hospital with his mouth wired shut, foggy from pain medication and frantically worried, Marco tried desperately to get through to someone. The police officers handling the report had already left. He hadn't been in any shape to talk to them at the time.

Destiny was in danger. Marco knew she was at the bogus audition with that maniac. He had to tell someone. A nurse checking on him finally understood what he was trying to say through clenched teeth: "My father . . . retired police officer. McCauly. Lives in Pacifica. Please . . . call him."

As Collin's sports car hugged the curves of the northbound 101, he fought his encroaching panic. He thought about the violence of rape and the pain and trauma Alison endured. He thought about his daughter being stalked by a man capable of such horror. As he realized how much courage it would take for his wife to face her tormentor a second time, he pushed down on the accelerator.

Waking to a dull pain at the back of her head, Destiny breathed in sharply as she got her bearings. She was being carried in Country's beefy arms.

He placed her on a sofa in a small room behind the bar and turned away. A small lamp on a desk scattered the shadows around, and Destiny couldn't see much.

She reached up to touch her throbbing head and found it was wet and sticky. There was blood on her fingers. Country approached her and she gasped and recoiled, pressing her body back against the old cushions of the couch. She looked for a way to escape. But he didn't try to harm her. Instead, he dropped a bag of ice into her lap.

"Here. You know, it was for your own good I hit ya. Can't have you mouthin' off like that. It's no way to talk to your father."

"You're not my father," Destiny whispered.

Country regarded her, his expression fixed in a forced calm. He yanked her off the couch and walked her across the room to a wooden wall mirror hanging over the desk. Pressing his face close to hers, he said, "Check out those baby blues. Yours and mine. Exactly the same."

Reluctantly, she looked in the mirror at his face, then at hers, then at his again. She stared at his blue eyes.

The resemblance was uncanny. Destiny tried to wriggle free from his grip. "That doesn't mean anything," she said defiantly. "Lots of people have blue eyes. If you're my father, where've you been all my life?"

Country's arms moved swiftly to hers and forced her to sit in a chair.

"I've been illegally kept from you," he said, unruffled. He pulled a photo album from the desk drawer and opened it up in front of her. "Check this out. I've kept track of you all these years. Your mother tried to keep us apart. But I'm here now, and I've forgiven her. I'm taking you both back."

Destiny regarded him cautiously, afraid to argue, not wanting to encourage his anger. She turned her attention to the photo album.

Country pointed to the various articles and photos. "Turn the pages," he ordered gruffly. "Read it."

Destiny glanced at the photos of her and her mother and the newspaper articles. She was stunned.

"You're not in the record business, are you?" she said, already knowing the answer.

"I can make sure you're singin' to the right audience, little girl."

"Why'd my mother tell me my father was dead? She said he was a war hero. Why didn't she just tell me about you, if you're my real father?"

Country's eyes squinted into slits, his mouth curling into a frightening grin. "I'm a war hero, all right. Just not the war she was thinkin' of."

"I'd like to go home now, Mr. Davis. I'll think about everything you've said, and talk it over with my mother." Destiny started to rise from the chair, her eyes darting to the door, but Country's arm shot out and held her wrist in a viselike grip.

"You're not going anywhere, girl." Country reached into his pocket and took out a pair of Alison's pink lace panties—a trophy from his foray through Alison's townhouse—and dangled them in front of Destiny's face. She could see the monogrammed initials.

"See?" Country leered. "Your mother and I are real close."

Destiny sat back down, her stomach twisting with apprehension. "I should never have shared my dreams with you in the cafe. You're not who you said you were. I should have listened to Marco—"

Country slammed his fist on the desk. He released her wrist and quickly wrapped his hand around her hair and pulled it into a tight knot, making her shriek in pain. "Forget him!" he barked.

Tears welled up in her eyes as Country pulled the hair around the cut on her head. Her hands shot up, and she tried to pry him loose. "Okay, okay!"

He softened his hold and began to stroke her hair, the way someone would pet a dog.

"Thaaat's better." Country smoothed her hair to one side and kissed her neck. Destiny cringed.

Country chuckled, a frightening, throaty cackle. "You better hope all your lessons can be learned this easy," he said. "You got a lot to learn, too. I'm still not sure how I'm going to punish you for letting that boyfriend of yours touch you the way he did."

He leaned in close to her, smoothing her blouse with his hands, trying to close up the front where her young breasts were poking out seductively. His hands touched them briefly. "Is this what he did to you, baby?" he hissed.

Destiny shuddered. Country licked her cheek, and she recoiled in disgust.

"Is this how he turned you on?" he continued, his voice dripping with sarcasm.

Destiny pulled away from him. "Stop it!"

Country ignored her. He looked at a spot on the wall and started breathing hard. The muscles in his arms pumped up. His neck turned red. He cracked it and clenched his fists. Then suddenly he relaxed completely and turned an icy gaze on her.

"That boy'll never touch you again," he declared, reaching into a desk drawer to the left of Destiny and taking out the photo of her. "I took care of that."

Destiny recognized the photo and frame instantly. "How'd you get that? That's Marco's!"

"Not anymore it ain't."

Destiny's throat tightened. "What do you mean?" she croaked.

Country fished around in the same drawer for a bag of pot. He pulled out the papers and rolled a joint. He lit it and took a couple of deep drags on it, letting it burn down a quarter of an inch before he answered her.

"Let's just say he took the stairway to heaven." Country's face contorted into an evil laugh as he enjoyed his own private joke.

Destiny's mouth went dry and her hands became clammy. She stared at the man in front of her, a new sense of dread gripping her. "What have you done with him?"

Country's face was calm. "He's dead. What'd you think? That I'd let just anybody touch you? I'm here to protect you from that. Men want certain things from a beautiful girl like you. Just like Sara. Well, I won't let that happen. *I* decide what makes you happy, not you."

Destiny felt a tingling sensation. She sat immobilized, as if she'd sustained a crushing physical blow. Then, pulling her legs toward her body, knees bent, she held them in a near-fetal position and rocked softly from side to side. "Marco . . . oh my God . . . Marco."

Country took another deep drag and held the smoke in, savoring it before he coughed it out. He kept his gaze on Destiny. She looked away, tears streaming down her cheeks.

"Stop sniveling, girl. You should be glad. All those questions that have been rattling around in your head all these years have been answered. Now you know who you are. You know who your real family is. You belong to me."

Destiny's lips trembled. She wiped her nose on the back of her hand, hating herself for ever wanting to find out about her real father.

Suddenly she released her legs and sat bolt upright in the chair, staring at him. Country's expression was hideous. He devoured her when he stared at her, as though he were stripping her naked with his eyes. His lips curled into an icy smile, enjoying her misery.

Country dragged the phone on the desk closer to him and pulled the page from Alison's appointment book out of his pocket. "Time to bring your mama here," he drawled. "She oughtta be wondering where you are about now. Let's give her a call, shall we?"

Destiny's eyes went round, new alarms going off inside her. "Leave her alone!" she cried, leaping up.

Country cracked his neck again and flashed her a warning look. "Get back down there," he growled, eyes indicating the chair.

She froze. Country punched in the number, watching Destiny's reaction as he waited for Alison to answer it.

"Hello there, Ali," he purred into the phone. "I knew you'd be on your way. Better hurry. It's time for a little family gathering." He held up the phone toward Destiny. "Say hello to Mama, darlin'."

Destiny lurched for the phone. "Mom, no! Stay away!"

Country pulled the phone out of her reach and yanked the cord out of the wall, then grabbed her wrist with his other hand. He threw the phone across the room and slapped Destiny hard across the face. "Wrong answer, baby."

Five miles down the road, Alison cried in the dark, tears coursing down her cheeks in steady, salty rivers. She pushed down on the accelerator, speeding dangerously around the poorly lit curves on the Panoramic Highway as she approached the Stinson Beach turnoff. She was almost there.

Harvey heard a girl's muffled screams coming from the bar and knew instinctively that the voice was Destiny's.

Though he was still weak, the sound of Destiny's voice gave him a surge of strength. He had struggled to drag himself across the cellar floor to the only visible light in the room: a patch of moonlight that filtered in through what appeared to be an old wooden chute. The forgotten opening was overgrown with scrub and thorny bougainvillea, but Harvey thought it was big enough for him to crawl out. He fought back his pain and began tearing away the scrub desperately. It was difficult, but the sounds and scuffles from the room above spurred him on. He managed to clear away some of the brush. Through the opening, he saw his car not fifteen feet away.

He was nauseous and losing blood, but he had to get help. With a great deal of effort, he squeezed through the small opening and dragged himself, hand over hand, to his car. He opened the unlocked passenger door, cursing when the interior light went on, and grabbed the cell phone out of the glove box. Gingerly he shut the door and pushed the power button on the phone. As soon as the red button lit up, he dialed 911, thanking God he had listened to Bea's advice to buy the phone in the first place.

"Police emergency."

"This is Detective Harvey Anderson," he whispered hoarsely. "I'm calling in a code 30. Location, Stinson Beach Bar. Repeat. Code 30. Officer down, needs help!"

Harvey's voice gave out. He slid down beside the car, leaning against the door, faint from the exertion. He had lost a lot of blood. His head was throbbing. He focused his eyes on the front door of the bar. He had to get inside. Had to help Destiny.

Reaching down to touch his gun holster, he was grateful that the gun was still there. The fools hadn't bothered to take it. Thank God they thought he was dead.

Harvey crawled to the front steps, then felt himself pass out.

Alison parked her car on the highway and flung open the door. The moon was high in the sky now. She stood outside in the dark, listening to the sounds of the night. She heard crickets and a hoot owl, and somewhere far off in the distance, the sound of a siren, but that was all. She didn't hear Destiny's voice.

Walking silently up the dirt road, her eyes darted right and left at the bales of hay and old tables. Everything looked odd in the moonlight, as if the inanimate objects were alive and threatened to leap out at her as she passed. As she neared the perimeter of the bar, a raspy voice cut through the night. Alison gasped and jumped.

"Alison. It's Harvey Anderson."

"Oh, my God," she said softly, crouching down at his side. "What happened to you?"

"Country. He's got Destiny inside."

Alison's eyes darted to the door of the bar, the strain on her face visible even in the moonlight. "I've got to help her."

Harvey's face was pinched in pain, his breathing irregular. "Don't go in there alone. I've called the police. They'll be here soon, then we'll nail him."

"I've got to get her out of there now," Alison insisted.

"I'm not much help to you," he said, attempting to jockey himself into an upright position. The faint sound of a police siren could be heard through the night. "Please wait. You don't know what he's capable of."

"Yes I do, remember? God knows what he wants with Destiny. He might have convinced her that I'm the bad guy in this whole drama. But I'm not going to let him get away with it. I'll show proof of his crimes to Destiny, try to get her away from him before he goes berserk. I won't let him hurt her."

"Try to draw him outside," Harvey rasped. He made an effort to rise, but it was too much, and he fell back against the wall.

Alison spotted his gun and quickly pulled it out its holster.

Inside, Destiny made it as far as the end of the bar before Country grabbed her by the hair and pulled her down again.

"You stay put till your mother gets here, little girl. I told you I don't like to be messed with."

"You're crazy!" Destiny screamed. She struggled, but Country's hold on her was solid.

"I'm not gonna put up with your sassin' me. You'll do as you're told. I got it all planned, and you're not gonna fuck it up, Sara!"

"Who the hell is Sara?" Destiny cried. "Let me go!"

Alison pushed open the saloon doors so hard they flew back and smashed against the wall. Holding Harvey's gun straight out in front of her, she shouted, "Leave her alone, Country!"

Startled, Country whirled, and his lips curled into a cruel smile.

"Mom!" Destiny shouted, making eye contact with her mother.

Country tightened his grip on Destiny. "Welcome home, darlin'."

"This isn't our home, Country. Now let her go."

Country pushed Destiny into a nearby chair. "Stay put, girl. I mean it. You do as I say."

Destiny sat meekly in the chair, looking from Country to her mother. "Mom, is it true? Is he my real father?"

Alison held the gun in one hand and pulled a piece of paper from her pocket, waving it in front of her as she tried to put herself between Destiny and Country. "His sperm helped create you, but that's all. He raped me, Destiny."

Country walked toward Alison steadily, his eyes burning into her. "You're not tellin' it the way it was, Ali. You were with me. You wanted me. Everyone knew it. You were going to kill her, Ali. Tell her that! It's because of me she's alive today! Go ahead, tell her!"

Destiny's face was a mask of sadness and confusion as she stared at Alison, waiting for a response.

"Bullshit, Country!" Alison shot back angrily. "You were just one of the lowlifes on the beach. Don't delude yourself into thinking I wanted you! I should never have given you the time of day!"

She kept track of Country's slow approach while trying to maintain eye contact with Destiny. "Don't let him trick you into accepting him, honey," she appealed to her daughter. "He's a killer. He's killed more than once and gotten away with it. His sister, Sara, and her boyfriend among them."

Country's face twisted into a hateful snarl, the veins on his neck pulsing. "You wanted to kill *her*, Ali. Tell her."

She kept the gun pointed at him and moved to keep her distance. "When this is over, I'll explain everything, Destiny. But your safety and happiness have been my main concern since the moment you were born. Trust me!"

Realizing that Alison was trying to get closer to Destiny, Country turned, lunged, and grabbed Destiny in a bear hug. "You're gonna force me to do somethin' I shouldn't have to do, Ali."

As Destiny screamed, Alison pulled the trigger. The bullet struck the mirror behind the bar, sending shattered glass everywhere. Alison clasped the gun tighter and edged forward.

"I said, take your filthy hands off her! If you think you own anyone, take me!"

Alison continued moving steadily toward them.

"You're only half right, darlin'. I want you both, and I always get what I want. Destiny belongs to me, and I'm taking her. You'll just fuck her up."

Fierce and determined, Alison didn't waver. "The police are on their way, and you're going back to prison *forever*. Let go of my daughter, or I swear to God I'll kill you."

Country's eyes blazed. "You're the one who should rot in prison, bitch. What kinda mother are you? Lettin' some Mexican punk lay his hands all over her. You're just like all the rest!"

Alison aimed the gun at his belly, but he whipped Destiny around in front of him and pulled her arms back, exposing her bare midriff. "Go ahead. Squeeze the trigger. Kill us both. You were gonna get an abortion and throw her out with the bathwater anyway."

"Make him quit saying that!" Destiny cried, twisting and straining.

His arms moved to encircle her tightly, the venomous serpent tattoo sticking out on his muscular bicep like a sentinel.

"I told your mother I was willin' to let bygones be bygones, but if she wants to keep lyin' to you, I'll have to keep you here on my terms."

She stared at Alison in terror and confusion.

"Don't listen to him, Destiny," Alison said firmly. She moved closer, holding the gun steady in front of her.

Alison's voice was low but strong. "You're a nobody, Country. A filthy, demented nothing. You meant nothing to me. You raped me. You rape women because you want to control them. You're disgusting."

Country's face turned to stone. "You bitch! Nobody talks to me like that!" He threw Destiny aside and lunged for Alison.

"Run outside, Destiny!" Alison ordered.

"Mom!" her daughter screamed. "He'll kill you! He killed Marco!"

As Country leaped toward them, Alison squeezed the trigger again. The bullet hit him in the arm, stopping him cold. He stared at her, shocked, then tore off his jacket and inspected his bloody arm. He laughed menacingly. "You'll have to do better than that," he sneered, hurling himself toward Alison.

"Get out of here!" Alison screamed at Destiny. "Fast!"

He swung out at her, but Alison dodged the blow and threw a fist into his face, gouging him in the cheek with her ring.

"Bitch!" he yelled, clutching at his face. Flinging his good arm wildly, he knocked the gun out of her hand. It skittered across the floor beyond her reach. Alison backed away and rushed toward the rack of pool cues on the wall. Destiny scrambled for the gun.

Alison grabbed a pool cue, but Country was on her.
"Mom! Watch out!" Destiny shouted, snatching up the gun.

Alison was ready. With all her might, she smashed a cue down on Country's arm. The force of the blow broke the stick in half.

The blow only made Country grin. "Bitches don't get away with that shit where I come from." He grabbed another cue and turned on her.

Alison held on to the broken stick and moved toward the front door, pushing Destiny out before her. Country sprang across the room and hit her hard on the shoulder, sending her flying to the ground.

"Mom!" Destiny ran back inside, gun in hand. "Leave my mother alone! I don't care who you say you are!"

"Destiny! Don't!" Alison said, wincing in pain.

Country's blue eyes gleamed with pure malice. "Come over to me where you belong, girl. And drop that gun. Don't you know they're dangerous? What kinda upbringing did you have?"

Alison struggled to her feet and quickly went to the door. "Be a man, Country," she taunted. "You want a woman to control? I'm ready for you!" She backed out of the saloon and onto the porch.

Country followed. "Fine with me. I got all night and plenty of energy, bitch."

Behind him, Destiny stood paralyzed, her finger on the trigger.

Alison could hear the sirens growing louder. She faced Country, who was wielding the cue in his good arm, his other arm hanging limp and bleeding at his side. The ugly red scratch on his face had begun to swell, causing his grinning face to look even more hideous. Alison waited, her back against the porch railing. He approached her steadily.

"I shoulda killed you years ago. You're damaged goods now anyway."

Destiny came through the door as Harvey pulled himself to the bottom of the steps.

"Throw me the gun!" Harvey ordered, startling them all.

"Ain't you dead yet?" Country laughed. "Must be losin' my touch. Can't even kill a fuckin' cop."

Destiny tossed the gun, but it was too late. "I'm gonna put this pig out of his misery, then I'll take care of the two of you!" Country howled as he raised the pool cue high over his head. The arc of his swing was so wide that the stick smashed a window behind him, spewing shards of glass in every direction.

Alison lunged for the fallen gun. "Run, Destiny!"

But Destiny quickly leaped onto Country's back, stabbing him with a piece of broken glass.

Country shook her off, his voice a roar. "Bitch! You'll pay for that, girl!"

"Dammit, Destiny! Move!" Alison repeated.

Country whipped the pool cue through the air, missing Destiny by inches. Ignoring the lethal sliver slicing into his back and the rivulets of blood dripping from his arms, he took another step toward Alison.

She gripped the gun in both hands and fired.

This time the bullet hit Country squarely in the chest. He recoiled, his mouth curling into a pathetic growl. He started to make one last, defiant motion toward her, then fell backward onto the porch with a sickening thud.

Alison inched closer, still holding the gun. Country's eyes were wide and blank, but they seemed to be staring right into Alison's soul.

She kept the gun trained on him for several minutes, fearful that he might suddenly spring back to life. But he didn't move. Blood oozed onto the wood like ruby-black paint.

The police sirens were at their shrillest now, as a cavalry of black-and-whites poured into the dirt driveway. Harvey pulled himself to his feet and carefully took the gun from Alison.

Destiny, her hand covered with blood, huddled against the door-jamb, sobbing uncontrollably. Alison gathered her daughter in her arms as police officers surrounded them.

It was over.

Alison was aware of the commotion around her but felt strangely removed. Everything seemed to be happening in slow motion. Her body and mind were in such a state of shock that she'd been reduced to a bundle of raw nerve endings that recognized only the sensation of holding her daughter and the hardness of the wooden wall she was leaning against.

The bar was now overrun with police officers issuing clipped commands into walkie-talkies that beeped and crackled incessantly. A police photographer snapped pictures of everything in sight, the bright flashes illuminating the dingy shadow-filled bar like lightning.

Alison's senses were confused. One moment dull, seconds later acutely aware. Her ears picked up the rustle of heavy plastic sheeting as Country's lifeless body was covered. She saw white-garbed ambulance attendants hovering over Harvey Anderson, attaching IVs, and heard the rip of surgical tape as the tubing was attached to his arm.

She closed her eyes to block out the blur of activity but was suddenly overcome by the strong smell around her. Blood was everywhere. The reality of what had transpired moments earlier caused her to retch.

Destiny was still huddled against her, but neither of them attempted to speak. The depth of their despair was so vast that words could not begin to soothe their misery.

Gradually, a man's voice broke through the din, and Collin's strong, clear words pierced through to her consciousness. Alison looked up as gentle hands touched her. He knelt down, his arms enveloping them both, and the look that passed among the three of them was filled with such sadness that Alison could only collapse against his shoulder, her body racked by anguished sobs.

As they rode to the hospital, Alison watched the way Destiny clung to Collin's arm. Her daughter stared off into the distance, silent, brooding.

Chapter 19

THE FOLLOWING SIX WEEKS WERE STRESSFUL, EMOTIONAL JOUR-
neys for all of them, but for Alison they were especially cathar-
tic. As horrifying as that night had been, she now felt a profound
relief. Everything was out in the open. No more deception. No more
hiding.

Although Alison was free of the lies that had so entangled her life,
that freedom had not come without a price. And the price was much
higher than she and her family could ever have imagined. Alison
spent many late nights going through her photo albums, staring at
the happy faces, the loving poses, wishing she could go back in time
and change things—to find a cure for the pain.

But there was no cure. Her daughter and husband were struggling to find a way to come to terms with the truth Alison had finally
divulged, and their feelings of betrayal and anger were enormous.

How life goes on after such trauma is a miracle in itself, Alison
thought. Despite the chaos, people somehow persevere.

In some ways, a healing process of sorts had begun. Destiny's
hopelessness had been greatly diminished when she learned Marco
was alive and would recover from his wounds. As soon as she was
able, she returned to the apartment she shared with him, and they
clung to each other with a new sense of devotion and commitment.

Alison knew, however, that Destiny and Marco were staying vir-
tually silent about what had happened. Outside of the family, only

Destiny's closest girlfriend, Caroline, was made privy to the terror they had all been through.

Graduation and Destiny's birthday had come and gone with no fanfare. Her choice. Now that school was finally over, Destiny spent many hours with Anna, who remained her most steadfast confidante. To Alison's relief, Destiny opened up more to Collin as well. At long last, her daughter and her husband were trying to tune in to each other, searching for answers, attempting to share private parts of themselves. A father longed for, a daughter acknowledged.

For Alison, watching them reach out for each other was bittersweet. The closeness she had built with Destiny over the years had been wrenched from her. Now, mother and daughter were almost like strangers, stepping gingerly around the new facts of their lives.

Alison looked up from her morning coffee as Collin entered the kitchen, attaché case in hand.

"Hi," he said, touching her shoulder. He sat down across from her.

Alison reached for the coffeepot. "Can I get you some coffee? Something to eat?"

He took the pot from her and helped himself. "Just coffee. I'll get something on the plane."

Collin was leaving for Seattle this morning, and Alison felt a pang of sadness. Searching his face for compassion, she saw a man who was reluctant and pensive.

"I'm sorry, Collin," she said softly. "I wish there was something I could do . . ."

Collin gazed at her, his eyes showing signs of the strain they'd both been under for the past several weeks. Alison noticed new strands of gray hair at his temples and was acutely aware of her husband's vulnerability as well as her own. He sipped his coffee thoughtfully.

"I know you're sorry, Alison. And logically, I understand that you had your reasons for doing what you did. But emotionally, it's still a very hard pill to swallow. We've all changed, and I'm sorry, too."

Alison's eyes filled with tears. "If you want a divorce, I'll understand."

Collin put his hand on hers. "Putting our lives back together is going to be hard, Ali, but I'm not saying it'll be impossible. I just need time, I guess."

Alison nodded, returning his gaze hollow-eyed, then stared down at her cold coffee. Her hair fell from her shoulder and hung in front of her face, the new length of her unshaped curls harder to control. Going to a hairstylist had been the farthest thing from her mind.

Collin reached out and cradled her chin. She looked up. "I'll be back in a couple of days. If you need me, I'll be at the Four Seasons." Offering her a half smile, he got up and headed for the door.

Alison rose from the table and rushed to his side. Standing near him, feeling his strength, his underlying anger and disappointment, and the slightest bit of compassion, her hands quivered as she touched his arm. This was the man she loved with all her heart. The man with whom she'd hoped to spend the rest of her life. The distance between them was unbearable.

She wanted so badly to say something that would bridge the gap, but she couldn't find the words. Instead, she kissed him softly on the lips. "I love you, Collin. Please believe that."

Collin touched her cheek, a glimmer of understanding in his eyes, then turned and walked silently out the door.

Alison waited until her tears were dry before driving to the office. Immersing herself in work had been her best medicine. Though most of her colleagues had heard differing versions of what had happened, they had the grace to refrain from discussing it in her presence, allowing her to regain some sense of order in her daily life.

Marlene Burkette had proven to be a staunch ally. Alison had conducted the interview with her as planned, but rather than focus entirely on Marlene's career and her endeavors as an activist, their conversation also included discussions of the painful issues Alison had been grappling with for two decades. Marlene had helped her put into words her most private thoughts, her most buried hurts—feelings she had locked away for half her lifetime.

For the first time in years, Alison allowed herself to speak openly about domestic violence, rape, abuse, and finally abortion. Their discussion of abortion was especially powerful and poignant. Though she herself had chosen not to have an abortion, Alison felt strongly that all women should have the right to make that choice. As she knew only too well, the issue was intensely personal and emotionally charged with pros and cons. There were no easy solutions.

The Burkette article was the perfect forum in which to expose the inadequacies of the legal system that had dealt with rape and abuse in the past, while acknowledging the supportive agencies that had evolved to address the problem in the present. Writing the piece in broad strokes, backed by appropriate data, facts, and figures, Alison thoroughly and intelligently explored the overall issue of violence against women.

But the personal consequences of her own experience were harder to face. In that arena, facts and figures didn't help. She had a daughter, husband, and mother-in-law whose lives would never be the same.

Sitting at her computer, Alison thought about Destiny and sighed. Collin was right. It would take time to rebuild the deep bond they once shared.

The hole in her heart was deepest where Destiny was concerned. Her daughter was a complicated, volatile, headstrong young woman, and at the same time, she was still her precious little girl. Despite all that had happened, Destiny hadn't abandoned her passion for music. Alison's stomach tightened at the thought, still uneasy with her daughter's career choice.

She visualized her own youth, when her father had discounted every idea and dream she'd ever had. He never trusted her to make decisions for herself, never gave her the joy of feeling capable of it. He had always been so quick to be cynical. Alison realized she had behaved nearly the same way with Destiny. Now she would have to learn to trust her daughter before she could expect trust in return.

Alison glanced at her watch, logged off, and gathered her jacket and purse. Destiny had agreed to meet her at a coffeehouse on Union, and she didn't want to be late.

When Marco dropped Destiny off on the corner, Alison was already sitting at a window table inside the Java Bar. She watched the two young people hug each other protectively. Even from that distance, she felt the tenderness between them. Alison silently acknowledged that her daughter was indeed capable of choosing the right guy.

She rose when Destiny entered the coffeehouse, breathing in the fresh scent of gardenia perfume that hung in the air when her daughter approached. Alison wanted to grab her and hold her tightly in her arms, laughing and kissing her and openly, unabashedly loving her. But the tension between them didn't allow for that. There was no obvious invitation for physical displays of affection. Though they had clung to each other the night of Country's death, Destiny had since then retreated to an arm's-length distance from her mother, and communication between them had been hesitant and measured until now.

"Hi, Mom," Destiny said, her voice barely above a whisper. She made eye contact briefly, then turned away. She took off her leather jacket, revealing a silver chain necklace with a small guitar charm dangling from it. A birthday gift from Collin.

Destiny sat down and ordered a caffe latte. As she silently stirred the milky concoction, Alison saw that Destiny was also wearing the diamond stud earrings Alison had given her, and she felt inwardly triumphant. There was so much Alison wanted to tell her, so much Destiny was not grasping. But she couldn't force Destiny to see things her way. Her daughter was a teenager, a woman-child. It was difficult to tell an eighteen-year-old anything she didn't want to hear.

Alison regarded her daughter, taking note of yet another piece of jewelry. "You got your nose pierced," she said.

"Yeah, three days ago."

Alison guessed that Destiny was waiting for a sign of disapproval, but this time Alison wasn't going to offer one. "I can't say I love it," she said, "but if you like it, that's what matters, isn't it?"

Destiny gazed at Alison. "Yes. That's what matters, when it comes to things that involve me. I'm glad you realize it."

Alison felt the sharp bite of Destiny's words more than she heard them, and her shoulders slumped down a little further. Destiny had put up an emotional wall ten feet tall. Alison sipped her coffee, staring at her child, the distant, indignant person sitting across from her. "How are you doing, honey?"

"Oh, I'm just great, thanks." Destiny tossed her long curls behind her shoulders. "Marco and I have been getting along really well. We're busy with our music, you know."

"Good. I'm glad for you," Alison said wholeheartedly.

Destiny eyed her suspiciously, then shrugged. She fiddled with her cuticles, then took another look at Alison. "You look kind of out of it, Mom. Did you lose weight or something?"

Alison's eyes wrinkled into a half smile. At least Destiny was still perceptive. "I've been sick, Des." She hesitated for a moment before adding, "I had a miscarriage several days ago."

Destiny's eyes went round, then narrowed angrily. "You're kidding. Boy, it sure didn't take you long—"

"It wasn't like that, Destiny," Alison interrupted. "I wasn't trying. With everything that's been going on, I didn't realize I was pregnant—and I wasn't that far along."

Alison gazed at the floor, another reason for her sadness surfacing. "There were complications. Getting pregnant again might not be possible."

Silence. Finally Destiny said, "That must be hard on you and Collin. I know you wanted to have a child."

Alison gazed into her daughter's stormy, youthful face. "I have a child, Destiny, and I thank God every day that I do. I love you. Don't forget that."

Destiny's body tensed, and her eyes bore into Alison's. "Are you sure about that?"

The way Destiny looked at her with such doubt and bitterness made Alison realize it was time to lay some of her daughter's fears to rest.

"Destiny, we haven't spoken about this since you learned the truth, but I guess if there is ever to be a true, unconditional closeness between us again, I have to be completely straight with you."

"It'd be about time, I think," Destiny said curtly.

Alison didn't balk at the remark. She would have to let her daughter vent as often as she needed to.

"Nineteen years ago, I was no different from any other scared, inexperienced eighteen-year-old girl, except I had been beaten and raped. I was frightened and reluctant to tell anyone about it. When I discovered I was pregnant, I thought my life was over. I *did* want an abortion at first."

Alison watched Destiny's reaction, proud that her daughter was at least holding her gaze, listening intently.

"But thank God, circumstances prevented me from getting one. Believe me, I've been forever grateful for that. A day doesn't go by that I don't say a silent prayer.

"When I felt you growing inside me, Destiny, I *did* worry about how I'd react to you, and what you'd look like. I wondered if I'd see visions of what happened that night when I saw your face. But when you were born, and I held you for the first time, all those fears melted away. You were beautiful, pure, and priceless, and you were mine. All the rest didn't matter anymore."

Destiny nodded solemnly, accepting the information. Alison watched a shadow of sadness cloud her daughter's face, but this time Destiny didn't look at her with blame in her eyes. Confusion perhaps, but not blame, and for this Alison was grateful.

Destiny reached into her backpack, pulled out a cassette tape, and placed it on the table. As she rose to leave, she smiled cautiously at her mother. A genuine yet fragile smile, one that Alison hadn't seen for quite some time. Sadness and love gripped Alison's heart.

"I made this for you," Destiny explained as she pulled on her jacket. "It's a song Marco and I have been working on together. We're performing it next week at the Limelight Club. Maybe you and Collin can come see us."

Destiny flicked her long curls behind her ears and grabbed her backpack. "I better get going."

She granted her mother another long glance and a fragment of a smile before she ducked out of the coffeehouse.

Alison held on to that glance for dear life, taking it as a genuine step toward reconciliation. It was a gift—one that she would not take lightly.

With a deep sense of longing, she watched Destiny jump onto the trolley. Her daughter was forging ahead with her own goals, her own dreams, her own life. Destiny was growing up and was her own person now. Alison had learned the hard way that children aren't possessions, and she hoped Destiny would someday realize that parenthood was more than a biological connection.

As she walked to her car, Alison felt as if she'd taken the first steps toward a new beginning. She had found that place inside herself where she was willing to take the risk of trust. And something in her daughter's parting glance gave her hope that Destiny would find it, too. Perhaps someday, Destiny would come to understand the motivations behind the choices Alison had made so long ago, and in time, forgive her for them.

Author's Note

RAPE IS A VIOLENT CRIME. IT AFFECTS NOT ONLY THE PERSON violated, but also that person's family, friends, and community. The road to recovery after a rape is not an easy one, and many victims have had to tread that path alone.

Rape is usually defined as the act of forcing sexual intercourse on an unwilling victim. Legally, there are two kinds of rape: forcible and statutory. *Forcible rape* is defined as sexual intercourse with a non-consenting victim through the use or threat of force. *Statutory rape* is defined as sexual intercourse with a person under a specified age. This age varies from state to state and from country to country but is usually between twelve and eighteen years. (Sexual intercourse with a person who is mentally deficient or unconscious and therefore incapable of giving consent is also sometimes considered statutory rape.)

The origin of rape laws can be traced to the once-widespread belief that women were the property of men. A female was considered first the property of her father. Once a woman was married, that ownership was transferred to her husband. Because her virginity was considered her principal asset, rape was considered theft. Rape was treated as a crime against a husband's exclusive sexual rights to his wife. Legally, it was not possible for him to rape his own wife. This obvious error in the law made it difficult, if not impossible, for women to bring charges against husbands who violated their bodies by force.

Because penalties for rape were severe, rape laws came to include elements that protected men against false accusations. The consent of the victim was often an issue, and the defense frequently argued that the woman had not resisted her alleged attacker, implying consent. By the twentieth century, it had become increasingly difficult in U.S. courts for the victim to legally prove that she had been raped. The victim had to establish, often with a corroborating eyewitness, that intercourse had taken place, that it had not been provoked (a highly subjective point), and that violence had been threatened.

Thanks to the efforts of women's rights activists, we have come a long way since. Beginning in the 1970s, rape was redefined as a crime of violence. In many Western countries, legal definitions were expanded and penalties adjusted according to the degree of aggressive force that was used. Measures were adopted to protect the identity of rape victims, and the phenomenon of "acquaintance rape," or "date rape," was broadly publicized, all part of the ongoing effort to encourage and allow more active prosecution.

Police departments and the medical and legal systems have been urged by women's groups to practice greater sensitivity in handling rape victims, and counseling and crisis centers have been established nationwide to offer support and assistance to victims in dealing with the judicial process.

Heightened awareness of women's rights and preventive measures such as self-defense training, and improved lighting in parking lots, shopping malls, and the workplace are considered to have great potential in deterring rape, especially on college campuses, where rape continues to be a growing problem.

Rape awareness has thankfully engendered many support groups. The D.C. Rape Crisis Center (DCRCC) was legally incorporated as one of the first two rape crisis centers in the nation. This organization maintains a deep commitment to the empowerment of women. The DCRCC provides a twenty-four-hour hotline, low-cost self-defense classes, and group and individual counseling services for rape and incest survivors and their families and friends. There is also a companion program in which representatives accompany women to hospitals, courts, and police proceedings. But sadly, despite the amount of work accomplished, the problem persists.

Rape is considered the most underreported of violent crimes. Convictions are difficult to obtain, and even when convicted, the average rapist spends less than four years in prison. Fortunately, there has been a growing willingness to report the crime. Between 1979 and 1988, the number of reported rapes increased by 65 percent. *However, it has been variously estimated that 50 to 90 percent of rapes occurring in the United States are not reported, because of shame, threat of retribution, or the victim's fear that she will not be believed.*

AUTHOR'S NOTE: If you or someone you know has been raped, seek help. Don't lock it up inside. Crisis centers staffed with compassionate, gentle, and understanding people are ready to guide you toward resolution and recovery. You need not bear the burden of your pain and humiliation alone. Call the Rape/Sexual Abuse Hotline at 1-800-638-0008.